綠野仙蹤
The Wonderful Wizard of Oz

中英雙語典藏版

李曼·法蘭克·包姆——著

李毓昭——譯 威廉·丹斯洛——圖

晨星出版

導讀

又遠又近的追尋之路

靜宜大學台灣文學系講師 林美蘭

　　好久好久以前，有個名叫桃樂絲的女孩跟一隻叫托托的小狗，連著房子被一陣胡亂吹的龍捲風吹到了陌生的神奇國度——奧茲王國，為了找尋回家的路，她一路冒險也接連解救了想要有腦袋的稻草人、渴望有顆心的錫樵夫與尋找勇氣的膽小獅子，成為她旅途的夥伴。

單純之心的冒險故事

　　這故事正是大家耳熟能詳的《綠野仙蹤》，即使你不知道故事的名字，也會記得那隻叫托托的約克夏狗、稻草人、錫樵夫與膽小的獅子，以及那位叫桃樂絲的女孩，還有美麗奇幻的奧茲王國。

　　桃樂絲的經歷或許會讓人想起格林童話韓森與葛蕾特的故事，不論媽媽如何想要遺棄他們，他們仍想辦法記住回家的路，雖然森林盡頭的糖果屋魅惑了兄妹，但是他們仍沒忘吃飽了要回家的。回家，是小孩很單純的想法，不論大人如何對不起他們，玩過後，小孩終究還是想要回家的。作者法蘭克·包姆緊抓住這樣單純的念頭創作了小孩尋找回家的路的冒險故事。作者企圖給桃樂絲的誘惑，除了讓她來到有別於堪薩斯老家的荒涼沙漠的美麗奇幻奧茲王國，還有意外獲得讓她足以成為偉大女巫的魔鞋與魔法帽，大家都要她留下來將來再回去荒涼的沙漠，當奧茲國偉大又好心的女巫。但是桃樂絲很堅持要找到翡翠城裡的偉大巫師——奧茲，幫助她找到回家的路，雖然終究是一場大騙局，偉大的巫師只不過是一個不會魔法的大騙子，桃樂絲仍然不放棄回家。最後大家才驚訝的發現，原來桃樂絲要回家其實是很容易的，那個因為意外壓死女巫而獲得的魔法鞋其實是可以帶她到任何地方的，她如果知道魔法鞋的偉大魔法，她在到奧茲王國的第一天就可以回家了。桃樂絲最後靠著那雙魔法鞋終於回到了堪薩斯老家。

故事的結局真是讓人大嘆一口氣，原來要回家是那麼容易，但是桃樂絲卻繞了那麼一大圈。正如想要腦袋的稻草人、渴望一顆心的錫樵夫與尋找勇氣的膽小獅子，其實他們早已具備了腦袋、一顆心和勇氣。

　　其實，事情一直都很簡單，如果沒有親身尋找體驗，就不覺得彌足珍貴，或許也不會發現自己本來就具備的東西。西方有漂鳥精神，藉由浪遊在自然中找尋生活真理、歷練生活能力。這樣的漂鳥浪遊，似乎也展示在桃樂絲尋找回家的經歷中。《綠野仙蹤》除了展現作者的奇幻想像力，故事裡的桃樂絲、稻草人、錫樵夫、膽小獅子單純的尋找信念，也跳出文字框架，向每一位讀者投射出令人堅強的漂鳥精神。

意外的「桃樂絲情結」

　　1900 年出版的《綠野仙蹤》，1939 年拍成了電影，成了家喻戶曉的故事，意外的成為了美國二次大戰時期的憂慮與想望。即使來到了二十一世紀，桃樂絲找尋回家的路的故事仍然是美國觀眾最重要的共同記憶。這或許真的只是一個意外，但這的確真實的反映出人類最單純的願望：家。自從美國加入二次大戰戰局後，這個「尋找回家的路」的「桃樂絲情結」，蔓延在美國人的心裡，當時的美國人無不希望自己或是在戰場的親人能像桃樂絲一樣找到回家的路；故事裡的好女巫、壞巫婆，似乎也在無形中成了當時侵略者或參與戰爭的領袖們的象徵。大家想要結束戰爭的焦慮，讓「桃樂絲的追尋」成了美國人的夢想和希望寄託。或許大家都期望著，看來遠在天邊的回家的路，應該跟桃樂絲回堪薩斯的路一樣，近在眼前：魔鞋就穿在自己的腳上。

　　激起美國人的「桃樂絲情結」，想當然爾一定不會是作者掌握中的結果，但是他希望創作一個真正屬於美國的童話，就像丹麥有安徒生、德國有格林兄弟，或是英國有彼得兔、愛麗絲。除卻「桃樂絲情結」投射，美國人對《綠野仙蹤》喜愛，世界各國對《綠野仙蹤》的熟悉也不下於美國，這情況，該是作者夢想的成真吧！美國國家圖書館將這書列為經典保藏，不就說明了這現象：丹麥的安徒生童話、德國的格林童話、英國的彼得兔、美國的綠野仙蹤？

目錄

CONTENTS

作者序

　　不論是在什麼時代，民間傳說、鄉野傳奇、神話和童話故事始終與童年密不可分，因為每個健康的小孩天生都熱愛奇幻、驚豔的，以及顯然不真實的故事。格林與安徒生童話中有翅膀的仙女們，為孩童心靈帶來的樂趣，比其他人類的創作還更多。

　　然而，舊有的童話故事歷經許多世代的傳遞，可能在兒童圖書館已被歸類為「歷史」。該是推出一系列新「神奇故事」的時候了，沒有刻板的精靈、侏儒和仙女，作家為了警世道德觀所設計的，每個驚懼膽寒的恐怖情節也都必須摒除。現代的教育已將道德包含在內，現代的小孩只想在神奇的故事中尋求娛樂，也樂於擺脫所有不愉快的情節。

　　抱著這樣的想法，我寫下《綠野仙蹤》，純粹只是為了讓孩子從中得到快樂。這是一篇現代的童話故事，驚奇和喜悅依舊，但是刪去了教人心碎與噩夢般的內容。

李曼・法蘭克・包姆

芝加哥，一九〇〇年四月

第 1 章

龍捲風

　　桃樂絲與當農夫的亨利叔叔、艾姆嬸嬸住在堪薩斯的大草原上。他們的房子很小，因為木材必須用馬車從好幾公里外運過來。四面牆壁和地板、天花板圍成的一個房間裡，有看起來很破舊的爐子、裝碗盤的櫥櫃、桌子和三、四把椅子，還有兩張床。亨利叔叔和艾姆嬸嬸的大床在一個角落，桃樂絲的小床則在另一頭。屋子沒有閣樓，只有一個在地上挖出的小洞，稱為「龍捲風地窖」。萬一刮起大旋風，強烈得足以摧毀沿路的房屋時，就可以躲到裡面去。從地板中間的活門沿著梯子走下去，就可以進入那幽黑的小洞。

　　桃樂絲站在門口張望時，一眼望去只有灰色的大草原。不論是哪個方向，都沒有樹或房屋阻擋遼闊平原一覽無遺的天際線。太陽把田地曬成灰暗土塊，布滿裂痕。連草都不是青色的，因為太陽把長葉片頂端也烤成了灰色，和舉目所見的顏色沒有兩樣。這棟房子曾經油漆過，可是被太陽曬得起泡，雨水又將漆料沖刷掉，變得和其他東西一樣灰暗無光。

　　艾姆嬸嬸剛來這裡生活時，還是個年輕貌美的妻子。太陽跟風帶走了她眼中的光芒，使她的臉頰和嘴脣失去紅潤，留下清冷的灰暗。她現在枯瘦憔悴，不再有笑容。孤兒桃樂絲剛來時，艾姆嬸嬸時常被這孩子的笑聲嚇到，每次聽到桃樂絲快樂的聲音，她就會尖叫，把手按在胸前。她仍然會驚訝地看著這個任何事都覺得好玩的小女孩。

　　亨利叔叔從來都不笑。他從早到晚賣力地工作，不曉得快樂是什麼。他的人也是黯淡無光，從長鬍鬚到粗糙的靴子都是，而且他看起來很嚴肅冷酷，很少開口說話。

　　是托托逗笑桃樂絲的，讓她不會變得和四周一樣灰暗。但托托一點也不灰暗，牠是一隻黑色小狗，有柔軟的長毛，在牠滑稽的小鼻子兩旁，小小的黑眼睛閃閃發亮。托托整天玩，桃樂絲也整天陪牠玩，桃樂絲非常疼愛牠。

　　然而，今天他們並沒有一起玩耍。亨利叔叔坐在門階上，憂慮地望著比平常更灰暗的天空。桃樂絲抱著托托站在門口，同樣仰望著天空。艾姆嬸嬸正在洗碗盤。

　　遙遠的北方傳來低沉的風聲，亨利叔叔和桃樂絲看見長草在暴風雨來臨前，如波浪般下彎。這時尖銳的呼嘯聲從南方傳來，草上的漣漪也是來自那個方向。

　　亨利叔叔突然站起身。「艾姆，龍捲風要來了，我去照顧牲畜。」他對妻子喊完後跑到畜養牛馬的棚子。

　　艾姆嬸嬸放下手邊的工作，走到門口瞥一眼就知道危險迫在眉睫。「快，桃樂絲！快點躲進地窖！」她大叫。

　　托托從桃樂絲的懷裡跳開躲到床底下，桃樂絲過去抓牠。艾姆嬸嬸嚇壞了，趕緊打開地板的活門，沿著梯子爬下陰暗的小洞。桃樂絲終於抓到托托了，準備跟在嬸嬸後面。

她正要穿過屋子時，聽見一道尖銳的風聲，屋子搖晃得很厲害，她一時站不穩，突然跌坐在地上。

奇怪的事情發生了。

屋子旋轉了兩、三圈後慢慢升到空中。桃樂絲覺得好像坐著氣球往上升。

北風和南風在屋子座落的地方會合，成了龍捲風的中心。在龍捲風中心，空氣通常是靜止的，四面八方的風產生巨大的壓力，把屋子抬得越來越高，直到抵達龍捲風頂端，然後被帶到好幾公里以外的地方，跟移動羽毛一樣容易。

雖然陰暗無光，又有可怕的風聲在四周咆哮，桃樂絲發現她飛得很自在。屋子經過幾次旋轉，還有一次嚴重傾斜，她覺得自己好像搖籃裡的嬰兒，被人輕柔地搖著。

托托並不喜歡這樣。牠在房間裡跑來跑去，大聲吠叫。可是桃樂絲安靜地坐在地上看會發生什麼事。

有一次托托太靠近打開的活門而掉出去，起初小女孩以為她失去托托了。可是不久之後，她看到托托的耳朵從洞口冒出來，因為強大的氣壓使托托往上升，而沒有掉下去。她爬到洞口，抓住托托的耳朵，把牠拉到房間裡，然後關上活門，以免再發生意外。

一個小時又一個小時過去了，桃樂絲慢慢克服了恐懼，可是她覺得很孤單，風在四周呼嘯得那麼大聲，她幾乎要聾了。起初她猜想自己會在房子掉下來時摔得粉身碎骨，可是隨著時間一點一滴地過去，都沒有發生慘事，她就不再憂慮了，決定要冷靜地等待。最後她爬過不斷晃動的地板，在床上躺下來，托托也跟過來躺在她身邊。

　　雖然屋子還在搖晃，風聲呼呼直叫，桃樂絲卻閉上眼睛，很快就睡著了。

第 2 章
曼其金人

　　一陣既突然又猛烈的震動吵醒桃樂絲，要不是她躺在柔軟的床上，可能就受傷了。這樣的震動使桃樂絲屏息以待。托托冰冷的鼻子湊到她臉上，哀傷地嗚咽。桃樂絲坐起來，發現屋子已經不動了，有明亮的陽光從窗戶射進來，照亮了小房間。她從床上跳起來打開門，托托跟在她的腳邊。

　　看著四周奇妙的景象，她眼睛睜得越來越大。

　　龍捲風已經非常輕柔地把房子放在優美的田野上。四處都是青翠的草地，結滿美味果實高大樹木。兩邊是一叢叢繽紛的花朵，鳥兒身穿燦爛奪目的羽衣，在樹叢中飛舞。再過去是一條小溪，在綠色的堤岸間奔流、閃亮，淙淙的水聲聽起來是多麼輕快悅耳。

　　桃樂絲站在那裡，熱切地欣賞奇特而美麗的景象時，發現有三個男人和一個女人正朝她走來。他們穿著古怪，戴著三十公分高的圓帽，頂端有個小球，邊緣掛著小鈴鐺，會在他們走動時發出清脆甜美的聲音。男人戴著藍帽，矮女人戴著白帽，她穿著白色的長袍，肩領打褶垂下，上面滿布發亮

的小星星，在陽光下如鑽石一般閃爍。男人們都穿著藍衣、藍帽，腳上套著磨亮高筒靴，露出一大截藍襪子。矮小的婦人明顯老多了，她的臉上都是皺紋，頭髮幾乎都白了。

那矮小的老婦人走向桃樂絲，深深一鞠躬，溫柔地說：「最高貴的女魔法師，歡迎妳來到曼其金。我們很感謝妳殺死了東方的壞女巫，讓我們的人民從奴役中恢復自由。」

桃樂絲驚訝地聽著這番話。這個矮小的女人稱她是女魔法師是什麼意思？桃樂絲只是個天真無邪的小女孩，被龍捲風遠從家鄉帶來這裡，這輩子也不曾殺過任何人。

可是婦人顯然在等她回答，所以桃樂絲遲疑地說：「妳很好心，可是你們一定弄錯了，我沒有殺死任何人。」

「是妳的房子殺的，」矮小的老婦人笑著繼續說：「所以等於是妳殺的。妳看！」她指著房子的角落。「從一大塊木頭底下伸出來的是她的兩隻鞋尖。」

角落的屋柱下，有兩隻穿著尖頭銀鞋的腳伸出來。

「哎呀，我的天！」桃樂絲驚愕地握緊雙手。「這房子一定是掉在她身上了。我們該怎麼辦呢？」

「什麼都不用做。」矮小的婦人平靜地說。「她是東方的壞女巫，許多年來，她把所有曼其金人都當成奴隸，讓他們日夜做工。現在他們都自由了，並且很感謝妳的幫忙。」

「誰是曼其金人？」桃樂絲問。

「他們是住在東方，被壞女巫統治的人民。」

「妳是曼其金人嗎？」桃樂絲問。

「不是，可是我是他們的朋友，只是住在北方。一看到東方女巫死了，曼其金人就迅速派信差來通知，我就立刻趕來了。我是北方的女巫。」

「天啊，妳真的是女巫嗎？」桃樂絲叫著。

「我真的是，」矮小的婦人回答。「可是我是好女巫，人民都喜歡我。我的法力沒有統治這裡的壞女巫那麼強，不然我早就去解救他們了。」

「可是我以為女巫都很壞。」小女孩說。面對真的女巫讓她有點害怕。

「噢，不是的，這是天大的錯誤。奧茲國只有四個女巫，住在北方和南方的是好女巫。我知道這是真的，因為我就是其中的一個，不可能弄錯。住在東方和西方的，確實是壞女巫，不過現在其中一個已經被妳殺死了，奧茲國只剩下一個壞女巫，就住在西方。」

桃樂絲想了一會兒才繼續說：「可是艾姆嬸嬸跟我說過，女巫在很久很久以前就都死光光了。」

「誰是艾姆嬸嬸？」矮小的老婦人問。

「她是我住在堪薩斯的嬸嬸，我就是從那裡來的。」

北方的女巫想了一會兒，她低下頭，眼睛盯著地上。然後抬起頭說：「我不知道堪薩斯在哪裡，因為我從沒有聽說過那個地方。但是妳可以告訴我，那是個文明的國家嗎？」

「噢，是的。」桃樂絲回答。

「那就對了。我相信在文明的國家已經沒有女巫，也沒有男巫、魔法師或魔術師。可是，奧茲國不曾開化過，因為我們和其他的世界隔開來，所以還有女巫和男巫。」

「誰是男巫？」桃樂絲問。

「奧茲本身就是個偉大的男巫。」女巫低語回答。「他的力量比我們加起來的還要大，他就住在翡翠城裡。」

桃樂絲正想要問另一個問題，默默站在旁邊的一名曼其金人這時卻大叫一聲，指著壞女巫躺著的角落。

「怎麼了？」矮小的老婦人問著，一看此景就笑了出來。死女巫的腳已經完全消失，只剩下銀鞋子在那裡。

「她年紀太大了，」北方的女巫解釋說，「太陽一曬，很快就蒸發掉了。這雙銀鞋是妳的了，妳可以穿上去。」她過去撿起鞋子，抖掉上面的灰塵，遞給桃樂絲。

「東方的女巫很得意能擁有這雙銀鞋，它一定有什麼魔法，可是我們從來都不知道。」一名曼其金人說。

桃樂絲把鞋子拿進屋裡，放在桌上，然後出來對曼其金人說：「我急著想回去叔叔和嬸嬸那裡，我相信他們一定在擔心我。你可以幫我找路回家嗎？」

曼其金人和女巫先看看彼此，才對桃樂絲搖搖頭。

「離這裡不遠的東邊有一片大沙漠，沒有一個人能夠活著穿過那裡。」一名曼其金人說。

「南方也是一樣。」另一個人說：「因為我去過那裡，親眼看過。南方是夸德林。」

「我聽說西方也是一樣。」第三個人說：「那裡是溫基人居住的地方，由西方的壞女巫統治，如果妳經過那裡，她會把妳抓去當奴隸。」

「北方是我的家鄉，」老婦人說，「北方邊境同樣有大沙漠圍繞著奧茲國。我想妳不得不和我們一起生活了。」

桃樂絲開始啜泣，在這裡她覺得很孤單。矮小的老婦人摘下帽子，用鼻尖平衡帽子的頂端，同時嚴肅地數著「一、二、三」。帽子立刻變成石板，上面用白色的大粉筆寫著：

讓桃樂絲去翡翠城。

老婦人拿起石板，讀完後問：「妳名字叫桃樂絲？」

「是的。」小女孩回答，抬起頭來，擦乾眼淚。

「那麼妳一定要去翡翠城，也許奧茲會幫助妳。」

「那座城在哪裡？」桃樂絲問。

「就在這個國家的中間，由奧茲統治，也就是我跟妳說過的那個偉大男巫。」

「他是個好人嗎？」女孩焦急地問著。

「他是個好男巫。至於他是不是一個人，我就無從分辨，因為我沒有見過他。」

「要怎麼去那裡？」桃樂絲問。

「妳得用走的。這段路很長，穿越這個有時很歡樂，有時陰森恐怖的國家。不過我會用我的所有魔法來保護妳。」

「妳可不可以跟我去？」女孩要求。

「不，我不能跟妳去。」女巫回答說：「可是我會親妳一下，沒有人敢傷害北方女巫親過的人。」

女巫溫柔地在桃樂絲額頭上親了一下。她的吻在女孩額頭上留下一個閃亮的圓形印記，桃樂絲不久之後才會發現。

「到翡翠城的路是用黃磚塊鋪成的，所以妳不會走錯路。」女巫說：「見到奧茲時，千萬不要害怕，只要說出妳的事情，請他幫助妳。再見了，親愛的。」

三名曼其金人對桃樂絲深深一鞠躬，祝她旅程愉快，然後就走進了林子。女巫對桃樂絲友善地點點頭，用左腳跟旋轉了三次，就直接消失了。這讓小托托嚇了一大跳，在她消失時，牠在後面狂吠一番，因為女巫還在旁邊時，托托可是怕得叫不出來。

第 3 章

桃樂絲解救稻草人

　　桃樂絲單獨一人時覺得肚子餓了。於是走到櫥櫃切了些麵包，塗上奶油，又拿一些給托托吃，然後從架子上拿起桶子，走到小溪那裝滿清澈閃亮的水。托托跑到樹林裡對著枝頭的鳥兒吠叫。桃樂絲看到樹枝上懸掛著美味的水果，就採了一些，發現那正是她想要吃的早餐。

　　她回到屋子裡，和托托喝了許多清涼、乾淨的水，就開始為翡翠城的旅程做準備。

　　桃樂絲另外只有一件衣服，剛洗好掛在床邊。是件藍白格紋的棉布衣，雖然經過多次洗滌，藍色已經有點褪了，但還是一件漂亮的衣裳。桃樂絲小心梳洗後穿上乾淨的棉布衣，把粉紅色的遮陽帽戴在頭上，拿起一個小籃子，裝滿櫥櫃裡的麵包，上面用一塊白布蓋著。然後她看看雙腳，發覺自己的鞋子好破舊。

　　「穿這雙鞋一定沒辦法走長路，托托。」她說。托托黑色的小眼睛仰望著桃樂絲，同時搖搖尾巴。

　　這時桃樂絲看到桌子上那雙東方女巫的銀鞋。

「不知道那雙鞋合不合我的腳。」她對托托說:「這雙鞋一定可以用來走長路,因為絕對穿不破。」

她脫掉舊皮鞋,試穿那雙鞋,結果就像是為她訂做的一樣合腳。

最後她拿起籃子。「走吧,托托。」她說:「我們要去翡翠城,請教偉大的奧茲要怎麼回堪薩斯。」

然後她步上旅程,托托認真地在後面快步跟隨。

不一會兒她就找到了黃磚路。她精神飽滿地走向翡翠城,銀鞋在堅硬的黃色路面上發出輕快的聲音。陽光普照,鳥兒田唱。一個小女孩突然被風捲離家園,來到陌生的地方應當感到悲傷,可是桃樂絲一點也不。

一路上,她驚訝於四周的景色是如此美麗。道路兩旁的欄杆整潔乾淨,漆上了優雅的藍色,欄杆之外是種著豐盛穀物和蔬菜的片片田地。曼其金人的房子都是形狀怪異的住宅,每一間都是圓形的,還有個巨大的圓屋頂。全部都漆成了藍色,因為在東方,那是最討人喜歡的顏色。

到了傍晚,桃樂絲已經走了很長的路,覺得很疲倦,正想著不知道要在哪裡過夜時,看到一間比別家大很多的房子。屋前的綠色草坪上,男男女女正在跳舞。五名矮小的提琴手大聲地盡情演奏,人們歡唱高歌,旁邊的大桌子擺滿了可口的水果、堅果、餡餅和蛋糕,還有許多美味的食物。

大家都親切地歡迎桃樂絲,邀請她一起用餐過夜,因為屋主是當地一個富有的曼其金人,他和朋友在這裡齊聚慶祝脫離壞女巫的統治。

　　桃樂絲吃了一頓豐盛的晚餐，由屋主波克親自伺候。波克看到她的銀鞋子，就說：「妳一定是個偉大的魔法師。」

　　「為什麼？」女孩問。

　　「因為妳穿著銀鞋，而且殺死了壞女巫。何況妳的衣服有白顏色，只有女巫和魔法師才會穿白色的衣服。」

　　「我的衣服是藍色和白色的格子花紋。」桃樂絲說著，拉平衣服上的皺紋。

　　「妳真好心。」波克說：「藍色是曼其金人的顏色，而白色是女巫的顏色，所以我們知道妳是友善的女巫。」

　　桃樂絲不知道該說什麼，所有人都以為她是女巫，而她很清楚自己只是個平凡的女孩，碰巧被龍捲風帶來這個奇怪的地方。

　　波克帶桃樂絲進屋，她在鋪著漂亮藍色床單的床上，熟睡到清晨，托托則靠在她旁邊的藍色地毯上。

＊　＊　＊

　　「這裡離翡翠城有多遠？」女孩問。

　　「我不知道，因為我從來沒有去過那裡。」波克嚴肅地回答：「人們離奧茲遠一點比較好，除非和他有生意往來。到翡翠城要走很多天。這裡是個富裕、愉快的國家，可是在抵達旅途的終點之前，一定會經過許多艱困危險的地方。」

　　這讓桃樂絲有點擔心，可是只有偉大的奧茲能幫助她回

到堪薩斯，所以她勇敢地下定決心，絕對不回頭。

　　她道別後再度走到黃磚路上，來到好幾公里外，她想停下來休息，就爬到路邊的欄杆上坐下。欄杆外是一大片玉米田，她看到不遠的地方有一個稻草人，用一根竹竿高高插著，防止鳥兒來吃成熟的玉米。

　　桃樂絲用手撐著下巴，若有所思地盯著稻草人。它的頭是塞著稻草的小袋子，上面畫著眼睛、鼻子和嘴巴。還有一頂曼其金人的尖頂藍帽放在它頭上，身體同樣塞著稻草，穿著一套已經破舊褪色的藍衣。腳上一雙舊靴子，藍襪反摺下來，模樣就像這裡的每一個男人。

　　桃樂絲專注地看著稻草人那畫上去的怪臉時，很驚訝地看到有一隻眼睛正在慢慢對她眨眼。她起先以為

自己的眼睛花了，可是眼前的稻草人又友善地對她點點頭。她於是從籬笆上爬下來，走向稻草人，托托則繞著竹竿邊跑邊叫。

「午安。」稻草人說，聲音相當沙啞。

「你會說話？」女孩驚奇地問。

「當然，妳好嗎？」稻草人回答。

「我很好，謝謝。」桃樂絲禮貌地回話：「你好嗎？」

「我覺得不大好，因為日夜都被插在這裡趕烏鴉，覺得很厭煩。」稻草人微笑著說。

「你不能下來嗎？」桃樂絲問。

「不行，因為有竹竿插在我的背上。如果妳能幫我拿下來，我會非常感謝。」

桃樂絲舉起兩隻手臂，把稻草人從竿子上拿下來。因為它裡面只塞著稻草，身體很輕。

「非常謝謝妳。」稻草人被放到地上時說：「我覺得好像重生了。」

「妳是誰？」稻草人邊問邊伸懶腰、打呵欠。「妳要去哪裡？」

「我叫桃樂絲。」女孩回答：「我要去翡翠城，請偉大的奧茲把我送回堪薩斯。」

「翡翠城在哪裡？」他繼續問：「奧茲是誰？」

「怎麼你不知道？」她驚訝地反問。

「不，真的，我什麼都不知道。妳看，我是填充的人，所以沒有腦子。」他悲哀地回答。

「噢,我真為你難過。」桃樂絲說。

「妳想,如果我跟妳去翡翠城,那偉大的奧茲會不會給我一點腦子?」他問。

「我不知道。」她回答說:「如果你願意,可以跟我去。就算奧茲不肯給你腦子,你也不會比現在糟。」

「妳說的沒錯。」稻草人繼續熱絡地說:「我不介意手腳和身體都是填充的,因為這樣子我就不會受傷。如果有人要踩我的腳趾或是用針刺我,我都不介意,因為沒有感覺。可是我不希望有人說我是傻瓜,如果我的頭繼續塞著稻草,而不是像妳一樣有腦子,我怎麼會明白任何事情呢?」

「我了解你的心情。」桃樂絲說,真的很為他難過。「如果你跟我去,我會請奧茲盡量幫助你。」

「謝謝妳。」他回答,充滿感激。

桃樂絲幫他越過籬笆,開始沿著黃磚路走向翡翠城。

托托一直嗅著這個填充的人,好像在懷疑稻草裡面有個老鼠窩,也經常不友善地對稻草人吠叫。

「請不要在意托托。」桃樂絲說:「牠不會咬人的。」

「噢,我不怕。」稻草人回答,邊走邊說:「牠傷不了稻草。讓我來幫妳提籃子吧。我不介意,因為我不會累。告訴妳一個秘密,這個世界我只害怕一件事。」

「什麼事?把你做出來的曼其金人嗎?」桃樂絲問。

「不,是燃燒的火柴。」稻草人回答。

第 4 章
穿越森林之路

　　路面越來越崎嶇，也越來越難走，稻草人常常被凹凸不平的黃磚絆倒。有時候磚塊根本就裂開或消失不見，留下坑洞。沒有腦子的稻草人會直接跌進洞裡面，全身撲倒在堅硬的磚塊上。可是他不會受傷，桃樂絲把他扶起來時，他還跟著桃樂絲一起為自己的災難放聲大笑。

　　到了中午，他們在路邊靠近一條小溪的地方坐下，桃樂絲打開籃子拿了一片給稻草人，可是他推辭說：「幸好我從來不會餓，因為我的嘴巴是畫上去的，要吃東西就要挖洞，塞在裡面的稻草掉出來，我的頭就會變形。」

　　桃樂絲吃完晚餐時，說了堪薩斯的一切，包括那裡所有的東西有多灰暗，龍捲風如何把她帶到這奇怪的奧茲國來。

　　稻草人聽得很專心。「我想不通為什麼妳要離開這美麗的國家，回到那麼乾燥、灰暗，叫做堪薩斯的地方。」

　　「那是因為你沒有腦子思考。」女孩說。「不論家鄉是多麼的荒涼、灰暗，我們有血有肉的人都寧可在那裡生活，也不願離開，無論是多麼美麗的地方。都比不上家。」

稻草人歎了一口氣。「我當然不懂。如果妳們像我這樣都塞滿稻草，可能會住在像這樣美麗的地方，那堪薩斯就沒有人了。堪薩斯很幸運，因為妳們都有腦子。」

「你要不要說說你的故事呢？」桃樂絲問。

稻草人責難地看著她說：「我是前天才誕生的，在那之前的世界我都不認識。我的腳碰不到地上，不得不留在那根竿子上。我過得很寂寞，因為才剛誕生，沒有事情好思考。

「起初有許多烏鴉和鳥兒飛到田裡，一看到我就飛走了，以為我是曼其金人。這讓覺得自己很重要。可是不久有一隻老烏鴉靠近我，仔細看了一下，就停在我的肩膀上說：『真是奇怪，那農夫竟然用這種笨方法來愚弄我。任何有腦的烏鴉都看得出來，你只是用稻草做的。』然後牠跳到我的腳邊吃玉米，想吃多少就吃多少。其他鳥兒看見我沒有傷害牠，就跟著飛下來吃，很快地我就被一大群鳥包圍了。

「我覺得很難過，因為那表示我終究不是個稱職的稻草人，可是那隻老烏鴉安慰我說：『如果你有腦子，就會和任何人一樣好，而且會比一部分人還要好。不管是對烏鴉還是人來說，腦子都是世界上唯一值得擁有的東西。』

「那群烏鴉離開後，我想了想，決定要努力得到腦子。很幸運的，妳來了，把我從竿子上放下來，而且聽了妳的話，我相信一到翡翠城，偉大的奧茲就會給我腦子。」

「但願如此，因為你是那麼渴望有腦子。」桃樂絲說。

「是的，我很渴望。」稻草人回答：「知道自己是傻瓜真的很不舒服。」

「那我們走吧。」女孩說著，把籃子交給稻草人。

現在路邊都沒有欄杆了，路面都是坑洞。快傍晚時，他們來到一座大森林，樹木長得很高大且密集，樹枝在黃磚路上方交錯。樹底下幾乎沒有亮光，因為樹枝擋住了光線。

「既然有路進入，那就有路出去。既然翡翠城在路的另一頭，那我們一定要跟著路走。」稻草人說。

「這誰都知道。」桃樂絲說。

「當然，這就是為什麼我會知道。」稻草人回答：「如果要有腦子才會知道，我就不會說出這句話了。」

光線逐漸消失，他們必須在黑暗中蹣跚行走。桃樂絲什麼也看不見，但是托托可以，因為有些狗在黑暗中也可以看得很清楚，而稻草人聲稱他看得和白天一樣清楚。所以桃樂絲抓著他的手臂，勉強可以繼續往前走。

「如果你看到任何屋子或可以過夜的地方，一定要告訴我，因為在黑暗中走路很不舒服。」她說。

不久，稻草人就停下了腳步。「我看到右邊有一間小屋子，用木頭和樹枝蓋的。我們要進去嗎？」

「當然要，我累死了。」小女孩回答。

稻草人領著她穿過樹林，來到小屋。桃樂絲看到角落有張用乾樹葉鋪成的床，就立刻躺下來進入夢鄉，托托也躺在她旁邊。從來不疲倦的稻草人就站在另一個角落，耐心等到天亮。

第 5 章

解救錫樵夫

　　桃樂絲醒來時，陽光已照耀著樹林，托托已追逐著小鳥和松鼠。她起身看看四周。稻草人還在角落耐心地等著她。

　　「我們要出去找水。」她對稻草人說。

　　「妳為什麼需要水？」稻草人問。

　　「因為路上有灰塵，我需要把臉洗乾淨，也要喝點水，免得乾麵包哽在我的喉嚨。」

　　「有血有肉的人一定很不方便，因為必須睡覺、吃東西，還要喝水。不過妳有腦子，為了正確思考，再麻煩也值得。」稻草人邊說邊想。

　　他們離開小屋，穿過樹林後看見一窪淨澈的泉水，桃樂絲喝完水、洗完澡後吃早餐。籃子裡剩下的麵包不多了，慶幸稻草人不需要吃東西，勉強還夠她和托托吃午餐、晚餐。

　　準備回到黃磚路上時，附近傳來低沉的呻吟聲，似乎是來自他們後方。他們轉身往樹林裡走了幾步，桃樂絲就看到有東西在樹林間的陽光下發亮。她跑過去看後發出驚叫聲。

　　有一棵大樹被砍了一些，旁邊站著一個全身用錫鑄成的人，高舉著斧頭。他的頭和四肢都好好地連接在身體上，可是靜止著，好像完全不能活動。

桃樂絲驚訝地看著他，稻草人也是，托托則凶猛地吠叫，張口咬錫人的腳，卻傷了自己的牙齒。

「是你在呻吟嗎？」桃樂絲問。

「對，是我。我已經呻吟了一年多，沒有人聽到我的聲音，或是來幫助我。」

「我可以幫你什麼忙？」她溫柔地問。

「拿油罐來，潤滑我的關節。」他回答：「我的關節生鏽得太嚴重，害我完全不能動。如果我上了油，很快就會沒事。妳可以在我小屋的架子上找到油罐。」

桃樂絲立刻跑回屋子，找到油罐，再跑回來，焦急地問：「你的關節在哪裡？」

「先塗一塗我的脖子。」錫樵夫回答。桃樂絲為他塗上去。由於生鏽得很嚴重，稻草人輕輕扶著錫頭左右轉動，直到那人可以自己靈活擺動為止。

「現在把油塗在我的手臂關節上。」他說，桃樂絲就在上面塗油，稻草人小心地幫忙彎曲手肘。

錫樵夫大呼了一口氣，放下斧頭，把它靠在樹幹上。

「這真是太舒服了，自從我生了鏽，我就一直把斧頭高舉在空中，很高興終於可以放下來了。現在，如果你們能在我的腿關節上塗油，我就會恢復原樣了。」

他的腿也上了油，直到能活動自如，他不斷感謝他們解

救了自己，他似乎很有禮貌，也懂得感謝別人。

「如果你們沒有出現，我可能會一直站在這裡，所以你們真的救了我一命。你們怎麼會來到這裡？」他問。

「我們要去翡翠城見偉大的奧茲，途中在你的小屋過夜。」她回答。

「你們為什麼要去見奧茲？」他問。

「我希望他把我送回堪薩斯，稻草人希望奧茲給他一點腦子。」她回答說。

錫樵夫似乎沉思了一會兒，然後說：「妳想奧茲會不會給我一顆心？」

「當然，我想他會的。」桃樂絲回答：「那跟給稻草人腦子一樣簡單。」

「沒錯。」錫樵夫回答：「所以，如果讓我加入你們，我也可以去翡翠城請奧茲幫助我。」

「那就一起去吧。」稻草人熱情地說。

錫樵夫請桃樂絲把潤滑油放在籃子裡。他說：「我淋到雨就會再生鏽，那時會非常需要油罐。」

幸好有新的同伴加入，因為上路後不久，樹木和樹枝濃密到無法通過。錫樵夫熟練地用斧頭開路，很快就為所有人清出一條小徑。

桃樂絲走得太專注了，沒有注意到稻草人被坑洞絆倒，翻滾到路邊。其實，他不得不出聲叫桃樂絲扶他起來。

「你為什麼不繞過坑洞呢？」錫樵夫問。

「我沒辦法思考啊。」稻草人愉快地回答：「這就是為什麼我要去請奧茲給我一點腦子。」

　　「噢，原來如此，」錫樵夫說：「可是頭腦並不是世界上最好的東西。」

　　「你有頭腦嗎？」稻草人問。

　　「沒有，我的頭是空的，可是我曾經有，也有一顆心，所以兩種東西都曾擁有過，我比較喜歡有一顆心。」

　　「為什麼呢？」稻草人問。

　　他們穿過樹林時，錫樵夫說了他的故事。

　　「我父親是樵夫，在森林砍樹，靠著賣木材過活。我長大以後也成了樵夫。父親死後，我照顧老母親直到她過世。後來我想要結婚，這樣才不會孤單寂寞。」

　　「我很快就全心全意地愛上了一個非常漂亮的曼其金女孩。她答應我，只要我賺到足夠的錢蓋一間更好的房子，她就會嫁給我。可是這女孩和一個老婦人住在一起，她希望女孩留在身邊煮飯做家事。所以她和東方壞女巫交換條件，給她兩隻羊和一頭牛，只要能阻擋這樁婚事。壞女巫就對我的斧頭施法，有一天斧頭突然滑下來，切斷了我的左腿。

　　「起初我感到很不幸，因為只有一條腿的人沒辦法好好砍材。我就去找錫匠，請他幫我做一條錫腿。可是我又開始砍樹時，斧頭滑下來切斷了我的右腿。我再度去找錫匠，他又給我做了條錫腿。後來斧頭又接連切斷了我的兩隻手臂，可是都沒有嚇倒我，我還是裝上了錫手。可是斧頭又切斷了我的頭，我以為這輩子完了，正好錫匠經過幫我做了個頭。

　　「我以為打敗壞女巫了，工作得更認真，可是敵人多麼的殘酷。她想到方法來毀滅我對美麗曼其金女孩的愛。斧頭再度滑落，將我的身體切成了兩半。錫匠再一次幫助我，為我用錫做身體，再用關節連接我的錫手臂、錫腿和錫頭，讓我可以和以前一樣活動。可是，天啊！我從此沒有心了，也失去了對曼其金女孩的愛，不再介意是否可以娶她。我想她仍然和老婦人住在一起，等著我去找她。

　　「現在就算斧頭再滑下來也沒有關係了，因為傷不了我。唯一的危險是我的關節會生鏽，所以在屋子裡存放油罐，需要時可以為自己上油。可是，有一天我忘了上油，又遇到暴風雨，還來不及察覺，關節就生鏽了，只能獨自站在樹林中，直到你們出現。這一年我思考著，我最大的損失是沒有了心。戀愛的時候，我是世界上最快樂的人，可是沒有心的人沒辦法愛人，所以我決定要請奧茲給我一顆心。」

　　「我還是希望有頭腦，而不是心，因為傻瓜就算有了心，也不知道要用它來做什麼。」稻草人說。

　　「我會選擇心，因為頭腦不能讓人快樂，而快樂是世界上最好的東西。」錫樵夫回答。

　　桃樂絲很困惑，不知道哪個是對的。不過她最擔心的是麵包快要吃完了，她和托托只要再吃一頓飯，籃子就空了。她不是錫或稻草做的，沒有東西吃，她就活不下去了。

第 6 章

膽小的獅子

掉落的乾樹枝和枯葉覆蓋黃磚路上，並不是很好走。

偶爾會聽到藏在林子裡的野生動物發出低吼。讓小女孩的心跳加速，因為她不知道那是什麼動物，可是托托知道，牠走到桃樂絲的旁邊，而且沒有回應那個動物。

「還要多久才能離開樹林？」小女孩問錫樵夫。

「我不知道。」錫樵夫回答：「我沒有去過，不過我父親去過一次，那時我還小，他說那是段漫長的旅程。」

這時森林裡傳來怒吼聲，緊接著一隻大獅子跳出來。牠一掌就使稻草人旋轉飛到路邊，再用利爪攻擊錫樵夫，但沒辦法在錫皮上抓出傷痕，儘管樵夫被打倒在地一動也不動。

小托托跑過去對獅子吠叫，那巨獸張嘴想要咬托托，桃樂絲怕托托被殺死，不顧危險地衝向前，奮力一巴掌打了獅子的鼻頭，然後大叫：「你休想咬托托！你應該覺得羞恥，這麼大的野獸竟然要咬一隻可憐的小狗！」

「我沒有咬牠。」獅子用腳掌搓揉桃樂絲打過的地方。

「可是你有這個念頭。」她反駁說：「你是膽小鬼。」

「我知道。」獅子說，慚愧地低下頭。「我一直都知道，可是我能怎麼辦？」

「你為什麼這麼膽小？」桃樂絲好奇地看著那隻巨獸，因為牠和一般小馬一樣高大。

「這是個謎。」獅子回答：「我想是天生的。其他森林裡的動物都很自然地以為我很勇敢，因為獅子被視為獸王。如果我大吼，每個動物都會嚇得逃開。如果大象、老虎或是熊想要攻擊我，我應該也會逃跑，因為我是如此懦弱，可是一聽到我的吼聲，牠們就會離我遠遠的。」

「可是那是不對的，獸王不應該是懦夫。」稻草人說。

「我知道。」獅子回答，用尾巴擦掉眼裡的淚水。「這是我最悲哀的傷心事，也讓我很不快樂。可是每次遇到危險，我的心就會跳得很快。」

「也許你有心臟病。」錫樵夫說。

「如果你有心臟病，你應該高興，因為那表示你有一顆心。至於我，我沒有心，所以不可能有心臟病。」

「或許真是這樣。」獅子邊想邊說：「如果我沒有心，應該就不會是膽小鬼了。」

「你有腦子嗎？」稻草人問。

「應該有吧。我從沒留意過頭裡面。」獅子回答。

「我要去找偉大的奧茲，請他給我一些，因為我的頭裡面塞的是稻草。」稻草人說。

「我要去請他給我一顆心。」錫樵夫說。

「我要去請他送我和托托回堪薩斯。」桃樂絲接著說。

「你想奧茲會給我勇氣嗎？」膽小獅子問。

「那應該和給我腦子一樣簡單。」稻草人說。

「也和給我心一樣。」錫樵夫說。

「也和送我回堪薩斯一樣。」桃樂絲說。

「那麼如果你們不介意的話，我要跟你們一起去。因為沒有一點勇氣，我的生活實在過不下去了。」獅子說。

「歡迎你，因為你可以幫我們趕走其他野獸。我想牠們那麼容易就被你嚇跑，一定比你還膽小。」桃樂絲說。

　　「真的是這樣，可是那不會讓我變得比較勇敢，只要我知道自己是個膽小鬼，我就不會快樂。」

　　獅子邁著威武的步伐，走在桃樂絲的旁邊。托托起初並不接受這個新夥伴，因為牠忘不了差點被獅子大嘴咬碎的事，可是過了一會兒，牠就放下心來，很快地和膽小獅子成了好朋友。

　　有一次錫樵夫踩到一隻在路上爬的甲蟲，殺死了那個可憐的小東西。這讓錫樵夫很難過，因為他一直很小心不去傷害任何生物，所以沿路掉了好幾滴眼淚。眼淚滑落臉龐，流到下巴上的鉸鏈，使那裡生鏽。他沒辦法張開嘴巴說話，因為鏽把下巴黏緊了。他恐慌起來，做很多手勢要桃樂絲救他，可是她不明白怎麼一回事。獅子也看不出哪裡出錯了。但是稻草人從桃樂絲的籃子裡拿出油罐，為錫樵夫的下巴上油。過了幾分鐘，錫樵夫就可以和之前一樣說話了。

　　「這給我上了一課，要留意腳步。如果我又殺死一隻蟲子，我一定又會哭，倘若使下巴生鏽，就不能說話了。」

　　從此錫樵夫眼睛盯著路面，看到小螞蟻就會跨過去，以免傷害牠。他很努力留意不要對任何生物殘酷或不友善。

　　「你們人都有心，有東西引導你們，就不會出錯。可是我沒有心，所以必須很小心。等到奧茲給了我一顆心，我當然就不需要顧慮這麼多了。」他說。

第 7 章
拜訪偉大的巫師奧茲

當晚他們不得不在森林的一棵大樹下過夜,因為附近沒有房舍。濃密的樹蔭可以遮擋露水,錫樵夫用斧頭砍了一大堆木柴,讓桃樂絲用來生火,不僅保暖,也讓她比較不孤單。她和托托吃完了最後一塊麵包,現在她不知道隔天的早餐該怎麼辦。

「我可以去森林獵一隻鹿給妳,這樣妳就可以用火烤,明天就有美味的早餐了。不過你們口味真是奇怪,喜歡煮過的食物。」獅子說。

「不要!請不要麼做!」錫樵夫說:「如果你殺死可憐的鹿,我一定會哭,下巴就會再生鏽。」

但獅子還是進入森林,去找牠自己的晚餐。稻草人找到一棵結了很多堅果的樹,裝滿桃樂絲的籃子,讓她很長一段時間都不會飢餓。桃樂絲覺得稻草人很好心也很為人著想,稻草人不介意要花多少時間裝滿籃子,只要不靠近火堆就行,免得火星跑進他的稻草裡,把他燒掉。所以他離火焰遠遠的,只有在桃樂絲躺下來睡覺時,過來為她蓋上枯葉。這樣讓桃樂絲暖和地熟睡，直到天亮。

　　天亮時，桃樂絲在一條潺潺的小河流中洗好了臉，很快就啓程前往翡翠城。

　　這一天發生了很多事。他們走了不到一個小時，就看到前面有一條很大的渠溝切斷了路，把森林一分為二，隔得遠遠的。他們小心地走到旁邊，發現水很深，底下堆著許多大而尖的石頭。岸邊陡峭得沒有人可以爬下去，一時之間，他們的旅程似乎要畫下句點了。

　　稻草人說：「可以確定我們不會飛，也不能爬到這個大水溝裡。所以，如果不能跳過去，就只能停在這裡了。」

　　「我想我跳得過去。」膽小獅子說，牠已經在腦海裡仔細量過距離。

　　「那我們都可以過去，因為你可以把我們馱在背上，一次一個。」稻草人說。

　　「我來試試看，誰要先過去？」獅子說。

　　「我，因為如果你跳不過去這個深坑，桃樂絲會摔死，錫樵夫會被底下的岩石撞壞，可是我摔下來也不會受傷。」

　　「我自己倒是非常怕摔下來。」膽小獅子說：「可是非這麼做不可。騎到我的背上，我們來試試看。」

　　稻草人騎到獅子的背上，然後獅子走到渠溝邊蹲伏。

　　「你怎麼不先助跑再跳？」稻草人問。

　　「那不是我們獅子跳躍的方法。」牠說著，用力跳起來，越過空中，在另一邊安全落地。大家都很高興地輕鬆地做到了。等稻草人從背上下來，獅子就又跳過渠溝。

　　桃樂絲一手抱起托托，騎到獅子的背上，另一手抓緊獅子的鬃毛。接下來她覺得自己好像在空中飛，還來不及反應，就在另一邊安全落下了。獅子跳回去，第三次將錫樵夫接過來，然後他們都坐下來，讓獅子休息一會兒，因為用力跳躍使牠呼吸急促，像奔跑很久的大狗一樣不斷喘氣。

　　他們發現這一邊的森林很茂密，看起來很陰暗。獅子休息夠了以後，開始順著黃磚路走。不久就有奇怪的聲音從森林的深處傳來，獅子對他們低聲說，這裡就是「卡厲達」住的地方。

　　「什麼是『卡厲達』？」桃樂絲問。

　　「牠們是熊身虎頭的怪獸，有長長的利爪，可以把我撕成兩半，就像我對付托托一樣輕鬆。我怕死了卡厲達。」獅子回答道。

　　「你會害怕並不意外，牠們一定是很可怕的野獸。」桃樂絲說。

　　獅子正要回答時，突然看到另一條切斷路面的深溝。可是這一條更寬更深，獅子一看就知道，牠跳不過去。

　　他們坐下來思考該怎麼辦，稻草人努力想了一會兒說：「這裡有一棵大樹，離岸邊很近。如果錫樵夫把它砍下來，它就會倒向另一邊，我們就可以輕鬆走過去了。」

　　「這真是個好主意，不禁懷疑你的頭裡面裝的就是腦子，而不是稻草。」獅子說。

錫樵夫的斧頭很銳利，很快就要把樹砍倒了。這時獅子強壯的前腳搭在樹幹上，奮力一推，大樹就慢慢地傾倒，橫過渠溝，發出碰的一聲，頂端樹枝就躺在另一邊了。

　　他們正要走上這座奇異的橋時，一道尖銳的咆哮聲使他們把頭抬了起來，看到兩隻熊身虎頭的卡厲達往這裡衝過來，他們都嚇壞了。

　　「那就是卡厲達！」膽小獅子說著，開始發抖。

　　「快點！我們快過去！」稻草人大叫。

　　桃樂絲先過去，懷裡抱著托托，接著是錫樵夫，然後是稻草人。獅子當然很害怕，可是牠轉過身面對卡厲達，發出又大又嚇人的吼聲，嚇得桃樂絲發出尖叫聲，稻草人也往後倒，連那二隻凶猛的野獸都突然停住，驚訝地看著獅子。

　　可是，卡厲達發覺自己的個子比獅子大，而且牠們有兩隻，獅子只有一隻，就繼續往前衝。獅子過完橋後轉身看牠們，猛獸一刻也沒停，也跟著要想通過樹幹，獅子說：「我們輸了，因為牠們一定會用利爪把我們撕成碎片。妳要緊靠在我後面，我會和牠們奮戰到最後一刻。」

　　「等一下！」稻草人大叫。他一直在想怎麼做比較好，現在他要樵夫把倒在他們這邊的樹幹砍斷。錫樵夫立刻揮動斧頭，就在兩隻卡厲達快要通過時，樹幹斷了，摔到深淵裡，卡厲達也跟著跌了下去，牠們大聲咆哮著，撞上坑底尖銳的岩石，粉身碎骨。

　　「呼～」膽小獅子放鬆地呼了一口氣。「我們可以再活

久一點了。無法活著一定很不舒服。那兩隻野獸真把我嚇壞了，我的心還在怦怦跳呢！」

「唉，真希望我有顆跳動的心。」錫樵夫難過地說。

這件驚險的事讓他們更急著想離開森林，他們走得很快，以至於桃樂絲很疲倦，必須騎在獅子的背上。慶幸的是越往前走，樹木就越稀疏，到了下午，一條寬闊的河流在他們面前湍流。他們可以看到對岸的黃磚路，穿越美麗的田野間，翠綠的草地上點綴著鮮艷的花朵，而且整條路兩邊都有結著美味果子的樹。

「我們要怎麼過河呢？」桃樂絲問。

「很簡單，只要錫樵夫造一個木筏，我們就可以划到對岸。」稻草人回答。

錫樵夫舉起斧頭，開始砍下小樹做木筏。錫樵夫工作時，稻草人發現河邊有一棵樹，長了許多漂亮的果實。這讓桃樂絲很高興，因為整天只有堅果可以吃，成熟的水果正好可以讓她飽餐一頓。

可是，雖然錫樵夫工作得很勤奮，而且永遠不會疲倦，但是做木筏需要時間，到了晚上還沒有做好，他們就在樹下找舒適的地方熟睡到天亮。桃樂絲夢見翡翠城，也夢到了心腸好的巫師奧茲很快就會把她送回家鄉。

第 8 章

致命的罌粟田

　　這一群小夥伴隔天早上精神奕奕地醒來，充滿希望。木筏已經快要做好了。錫樵夫再多砍了幾根木頭，用木釘固定在一起後就可以準備出發了。桃樂絲坐在木筏中間，懷裡抱著托托。膽小獅子跨上來時，木筏嚴重傾斜，可是有稻草人和錫樵夫站在另一邊來平衡。他們手上拿著長竿渡河。

　　起初相當順利，可是來到河中央時，湍急的水流把木筏沖向下游，離黃磚路越來越遠。而且水深越來越深，連長竿都碰不到底了。

　　「糟了，如果不能靠岸，我們會被帶到西方的壞女巫那裡，她會對我們施法變成她的奴隸。」錫樵夫說。

　　「那我就得不到腦子了。」稻草人說。

　　「那我就得不到勇氣了。」膽小獅子說。

　　「我也得不到心了。」錫樵夫說。

　　「我就永遠回不去堪薩斯了。」桃樂絲說。

　　這時稻草人用力划動長竿，結果竿子快速地牢牢卡在河底的爛泥裡，他還來不及拔出來或放手，木筏就被沖走了，留下可憐的稻草人在河中央攀著竿子。

「再見！」他在後面大叫，其他人都很難過。

木筏已經漂到下游，可憐的稻草人被遠遠留在後面。獅子說：「一定有辦法可以救我們。我想我可以拖著木筏游到岸邊，只要你們抓緊我的尾巴。」

牠跳進水中，錫樵夫快速抓住牠的尾巴，獅子開始用盡全力游向岸邊。雖然牠很巨大，但這麼做仍然很費力，可是他們逐漸掙脫了水流。桃樂絲拿起錫樵夫的長竿，把木筏划到岸邊。

終於抵達河岸時，他們都累慘了。

「我們該怎麼辦呢？」錫樵夫問。這時獅子正趴在草地上讓太陽曬乾身子。

「我們一定要想辦法回到那條路。」桃樂絲說。

「最好的辦法是沿著河岸走到黃磚路。」獅子說。

於是休息過後，他們開始沿著青翠的河岸往回走。眼前是一片可愛的田野，有許多花朵、果樹和陽光鼓舞著他們，要不是為可憐的稻草人難過，他們應該會很快樂。

他們加快腳步往前走，過了一會兒，錫樵夫就大叫：「你們看！」

他們看到稻草人在河中央攀著竿子，看起來好孤單，也好悲傷。

「我們要怎麼救他呢？」桃樂絲說。

獅子和樵夫都搖搖頭，想不出辦法。他們在岸邊坐下，憂愁地望著稻草人，直到有一隻鸛鳥飛到河邊停下歇息。

　　「你們是誰？要去哪裡？」鸛鳥說。

　　「我是桃樂絲，這兩個是我的朋友，錫樵夫和膽小獅子。我們要去翡翠城。」桃樂絲說。

　　「不是這條路啊。」鸛鳥說著，扭了扭牠的長脖子，眼神銳利地看著這支奇怪的隊伍。

　　「我知道，可是我們失去了稻草人，正在想辦法救他回來。」桃樂絲回答。「他在哪裡？」鸛鳥問。

　　「就在河中央。」桃樂絲回答。

　　「只要他不大，也不很重，我就可以幫你們帶他回來。」鸛鳥表示。

　　「他一點都不重，因為他全身都是稻草，如果你幫我們，我們會非常非常地感謝你。」桃樂絲急切地說。

　　「好，我來試試看，可是如果我發現他太重，就得把他丟在河裡面。」鸛鳥說。

　　這隻大鳥飛到稻草人攀著竿子的地方，用大爪抓住稻草人的手臂，把他帶到空中，然後回到岸邊。

稻草人重回朋友身邊，高興得擁抱每一個人，包括獅子和托托在內。

　　「謝謝你。」桃樂絲說著，好心的鸛鳥隨後飛到空中，很快就消失不見了。

　　他們繼續走著，羽毛光鮮亮麗的鳥兒鳴唱著，可愛的花朵繁盛得遍布滿地。有黃有白，也有藍色和紫色的，旁邊還有一大叢鮮紅色的罌粟花，鮮艷得讓桃樂絲眼花撩亂。

　　「真是漂亮，不是嗎？」小女孩問，同時聞著花香。

　　「我一直都很喜歡花，花如此柔弱無助，但森林裡沒有如此耀眼的花。」獅子說。

　　他們很快就身處在一大片的罌粟花海裡。當這種花的數量很多時，香味會強烈得讓人一聞就睡著，如果睡著的人沒有遠離花香，就會一直沉睡不醒。

　　可是桃樂絲不知道，她的眼皮馬上就變得沉重，很想坐下來休息，好好睡上一覺。

　　可是錫樵夫不讓她睡覺。

　　「我們一定要趕快在天黑前走回黃磚路。」他說，稻草人也表示贊同。直到桃樂絲再也無法忍受。她禁不住閉上了眼睛，忘了身在哪裡，倒在罌粟田裡很快便睡著了。

　　「我們該怎麼辦？」錫樵夫說。

　　「把她丟在這裡，她一定會死。」獅子說：「這種花的氣味會害死我們所有人。連我要睜著眼睛都很勉強了，而那隻狗早就睡著了。」

果然沒錯，托托已經倒在小女主人的身邊。可是稻草人和錫樵夫都不是血肉之軀，不會受到花香影響。

　　「你跑快一點，」稻草人對獅子說，「儘快離開這片會致命的花田。我們可以帶小女孩走。」

　　於是獅子打起精神盡全力往前奔跑，一溜煙就不見了。

　　「我們用手搭個椅子載她吧。」稻草人說。他們撿起托托，把牠放在桃樂絲的腿上，然後帶著沉睡女孩穿過花田。

　　致命的花海似乎沒有盡頭。他們跟著河岸蜿蜒前進，看到獅子躺在罌粟花海中睡著了，倒在離罌粟田邊界很近的地方，前方就是布滿青草的美麗原野了。

　　「我們幫不了牠的忙，因為牠太重了。」錫樵夫傷感地說：「也許牠會夢見自己終於找到勇氣了。」

　　「真令人難過。」稻草人說：「對一隻膽小的獅子來說，牠真是個好夥伴。我們還是走吧。」

　　他們抬著沉睡的女孩來到河邊一處美麗的地方，離罌粟田夠遠，她不會再聞到有毒的花香。他們輕輕將她放在柔軟的草地上，等清新的風把她吹醒。

第 9 章

田鼠皇后

　　錫樵夫聽到一聲低吼，他轉過頭來，看到一隻奇怪的野獸跳過草地直衝過來，那是一隻巨大的黃色野貓。錫樵夫心想，牠一定是在追趕著什麼。因為牠的耳朵緊貼在頭上，嘴巴張得很大，露出兩排醜陋的牙齒，眼睛如火球般發亮。牠靠近時，錫樵夫看到一隻灰色的小田鼠跑在前面，雖然他沒有心，但知道野貓要殺死這隻美麗而無害的動物是不對的。

　　於是樵夫舉起斧頭，在野貓跑過來時用力一砍。

　　那隻田鼠從天敵的追逐中獲救，頓時停下，慢慢走到樵夫前面，聲音小而尖銳，「謝謝你！非常感謝你救了我！」

　　「請不要這麼說。」樵夫回答：「我沒有心，所以小心幫助所有需要朋友的人，即使只是個小老鼠。」

　　「只是個小老鼠！」小動物氣憤地叫著，「我可是個女皇，是田鼠國的女皇！」

　　「噢，當然。」樵夫彎腰行禮。

　　「你英勇地救了我！你立下了大功！」皇后接著說。

　　這時有幾隻老鼠奮力快跑過來，看到皇后時驚喜地大叫：「陛下，我們以為您被殺了！您是怎麼擺脫那隻大野貓的？」牠們全都對皇后深深一鞠躬，頭幾乎都要著地了。

「多虧這個好笑的錫人殺死野貓，我才能夠得救。你們以後得要好好服侍他，幫他達成任何願望。」她回答著。

「遵命。」所有老鼠都以尖聲回應。

有隻最大的老鼠出聲說：「為了報答你解救我們的女皇，有什麼事可以讓我們為你效勞的嗎？」

「我想不到。」錫樵夫說，可是稻草人很快地開口說：「有的，你們可以去救我們的朋友，那隻膽小獅子，牠正在罌粟花田裡睡覺。」

「獅子！」小女皇大叫，「牠會把我們吃光光！」

「不會的，這隻獅子是膽小鬼。」稻草人說。

「真的嗎？」田鼠女皇說。

「牠自己說的，而且牠不會傷害我們的朋友。如果你們幫忙救牠，我保證牠一定會對你們很和氣。」稻草人回答。

「好吧，我們相信你。可是要怎麼做呢？」女皇說。

「奉妳為女皇的老鼠很多嗎？牠們都願意聽從妳嗎？」

「沒錯，總共有數千隻。」她回答。

「那叫牠們盡快趕來這裡，每一隻都要帶一條長繩。」

女皇轉身要老鼠隨從立刻去通知所有子民集合。一聽到命令，牠們就快速地跑向四面八方。

「現在你要去河邊砍樹，做一個可以載運獅子的推車。」稻草人對錫樵夫說。

錫樵夫馬上進到林子裡，開始工作，很快就用幾條大樹枝做成一個推車，枝葉也都被切除了。他用木釘固定好，再用截短的大樹幹做成四個輪子。他做得又快又好，當老鼠開始一一抵達集合時，推車已經準備好了。

　　老鼠從各個方向湧來，數量多達數千隻：大老鼠、小老鼠，還有體型中等的，每一隻嘴上都啣著一條繩子。這時桃樂絲從長眠中醒過來，睜開眼睛。發現身旁有好幾千隻老鼠害怕地盯著她，她嚇了一大跳。稻草人把事情來龍去脈都告訴她。

稻草人和錫樵夫開始把老鼠帶來的繩子繫在推車上。繩子的一端圍在每一隻老鼠的脖子上，另一端和推車連接。推車比老鼠大一千倍，可是所有老鼠一起使力時，就可以輕易拉動它。連稻草人和錫樵夫都可以坐在上面，這群奇特的小馬快速地將他們拉到獅子睡覺的地方。

　　經過一番折騰，他們才把很重的獅子抬上推車。女皇趕忙命令子民開始拉車，因為牠擔心在罌粟田裡待太久，牠們也會睡著。

　　起初這群小動物根本拉不動沉重的推車，雖然數量眾多，錫樵夫和稻草人在後面幫忙推，才終於可以拉動車子。很快就把獅子從罌粟花田拉到綠地，讓獅子再度呼吸到清新甜美的空氣。

　　桃樂絲熱情地感謝小老鼠救了她同伴的性命。然後老鼠們解下繩子，穿過草地跑回自己的家。田鼠女皇是最後一個離開的。

　　「如果你們還需要我，就來這片田野呼叫，我聽到你們的聲音，就會過來幫忙。再見了！」

　　「再見！」他們齊聲回答。女皇跑開了。

　　接著他們都坐在獅子旁邊，等牠醒過來。稻草人從附近的果樹摘來一些水果，給桃樂絲當午餐。

第10章
守門人

　　膽小獅子終於睜開眼睛。「我已經盡可能跑得很快了。可是花的香味實在太強了。你們是怎麼把我弄出來的？」

　　他們把田鼠好心解救牠的事情告訴牠，膽小獅子聽了笑著說：「我一直都覺得自己很龐大，也很可怕，可是連那麼小的花都能夠差點要了我的命，而那麼小的老鼠都能夠解救我。好奇怪啊！可是，各位同伴，我們現在要怎麼辦？」

　　「我們一定要繼續走，走到黃磚路。」桃樂絲說：「再一直走到翡翠城。」

　　等獅子恢復精神他們就愉快地穿過柔軟、青翠的草地。不久就看到黃磚路了，於是他們繼續朝翡翠城走去。

　　路變得平整，四周的田野也很美，他們很高興已將森林遠遠拋之在後，忘卻在樹蔭下多次遇到的危險。路邊的欄杆又出現了，可是這裡漆的是綠色。那天下午，他們經過好幾間同樣漆成綠色的房子，有時候會有人走到門口盯著他們想要發問，但大獅子讓他們害怕地不敢靠近或攀談。

　　「這裡一定是奧茲的領土，我們快要走到翡翠城了。」

桃樂絲說。

「沒錯,這裡什麼東西都是綠色的,而曼其金人就比較喜歡藍色。可是這裡的人不像曼其金人那麼友善,我們恐怕找不到地方過夜。」稻草人回答。

他們走到一間很大的農舍前,桃樂絲大膽地向前敲門。一個女人打開一條足以窺看的門縫說:「孩子,妳要什麼?為什麼妳會和大獅子在一起?」

「我們想借住一晚。獅子是我們的朋友和同伴,絕對不會傷害妳。」桃樂絲說。

「牠是溫馴的嗎?」女人問,把門再打開一點。

「當然。」女孩說:「牠也非常膽小,所以妳怕牠的程度還比不上牠怕妳呢。」

「好吧。」女人想了一會兒,然後說:「如果真是這樣,你們可以進來,我可以提供晚餐和睡覺的地方。」

他們進屋後發現除了那個女人,還有兩個小孩和一個男人。那男人問:「你們要去哪裡?」

「去翡翠城找偉大的奧茲。」桃樂絲說。

「噢!」男人大叫。「你們確定奧茲會見你們?」

「為什麼不會?」她回答。

「因為據說他從來不見人。我去過翡翠城很多次,那是個無比美麗的地方,可是我從來沒有機會晉見偉大的奧茲,我認識的人裡也沒有人見過他。」

「他從來不出門嗎?」稻草人說。

「從來沒有。他每天都待在宮殿裡的寶座宮，連服侍他的人也不能當面見到他。」

「他長什麼樣子？」女孩問。

「很難說。」男人邊想邊說：「奧茲是個偉大的巫師，想變成什麼就變成什麼。有的人說他看起來像隻鳥，有人說像大象，有人說像貓。有時以美麗的仙女、小精靈和其他模樣出現。可是哪一個才是奧茲的真實樣貌，沒有人知道。」

「那好奇怪，可是我們一定要想辦法見到他，不然我們的旅程就沒有意義了。」桃樂絲說。

「你們為什麼想要見可怕的奧茲？」男人問。

「我希望他給我一點腦子。」稻草人熱切地說。

「噢，奧茲可以輕易做到。」那人說：「他有很多腦子用不到。」

「我希望他給我一顆心。」錫樵夫說。

「那不難，因為奧茲收集了很多心，有各種尺寸和形狀。」那人繼續說。

「我希望他給我勇氣。」膽小獅說。

「奧茲在他寶座宮裡收藏了一大桶勇氣，上面用金板蓋著，以免它跑掉。他會很樂意給你一些。」

「我希望他能夠送我回堪薩斯。」桃樂絲說。

「堪薩斯在哪裡？」那人驚訝地問。

「我不知道。」桃樂絲回答，一臉悲傷。「可是我的家在那裡，我相信一定在某個地方。」

「很有可能。奧茲沒有做不到的事情,所以我想他會幫你找到堪薩斯。可是你們得先見到他,那是很困難的事,因為他不喜歡見人。你呢,希望什麼?」他接著問托托。托托只是搖搖尾巴,說來奇怪,因為他不會說話。

*　*　*

第二天早上,他們天一亮就上路了,很快就看到空中有一團美麗的綠光。

「那一定就是翡翠城了。」桃樂絲說。

越往前走,綠光就越亮,好像終於要接近旅程的終點了。然而,到了下午,他們才靠近城市的大圍牆。城牆又高又厚,塗著鮮綠色。

他們走到黃磚路的盡頭,面前是一道大門,上面點綴著翡翠,在陽光下閃耀,連稻草人畫上去的眼睛也看花了。

桃樂絲按了門旁邊鈴,聽到裡面傳來清脆的鈴噹聲。接著門慢慢地打開,有個矮小的人站在前面,個子和曼其金人差不多。他從頭到腳穿戴的衣物都是綠色的,連皮膚都泛著綠色。他旁邊有個綠色的大盒子。

這個人看到桃樂絲和她的同伴時,就問:「你們來翡翠城做什麼?」

「我們來這裡是要見偉大的奧茲。」桃樂絲說。

這個人聽到這個回答時驚訝得坐下來思考。

「已經很多年沒有人說要見奧茲了。」他說著,疑惑地

綠野仙蹤

搖搖頭。「如果你們拿愚蠢或無聊的事去打擾奧茲沉思，他可能會很生氣，一下子就把你們都消滅掉。」

「可是我們的事情不愚蠢也不無聊。」稻草人回答說：「我們的事情很重要，而且我們聽說奧茲是個好巫師。」

「他的確是。」綠人說：「他把翡翠城治理得很好。可是對那些不誠實或懷著好奇心接近他的人，他是很可怕的。既然你們要求晉見偉大的奧茲，我就要帶你們去他的宮殿。可是你們要先戴上眼鏡。」

「為什麼？」桃樂絲說。

「因為不戴眼鏡的話，翡翠城閃耀的光線會使你們瞎掉。即使是翡翠城的居民也要日夜戴著眼鏡。這是奧茲在這座城剛蓋好時下的命令，只有我才有鑰匙打開。」

他打開大盒子，桃樂絲看到裡面裝滿各種大小和形狀的眼鏡，鏡片都是綠色的。守門人找到一副剛好適合桃樂絲的幫她戴上。上面有兩條金帶子繞到腦後，守門人用一把小鑰匙將金帶子鎖在一起。戴上眼鏡之後，桃樂絲就不能隨便把它取下，可是當然她也不希望被翡翠城的光芒刺瞎。

綠人接著為稻草人和錫樵夫、獅子，甚至小托托找到合適的眼鏡，全部都用鑰匙鎖緊了。

然後守門人戴上自己的眼鏡說，他準備好帶他們去宮殿了。他從牆上的釘子上取下一把金色的大鑰匙，打開另一扇門，所有人就跟著他穿過入口，踏上翡翠城的街道。

第11章

奧茲翡翠城

　　即使有綠色的眼鏡保護，桃樂絲和同伴剛開始仍然被這美妙城市的炫光刺得睜不開眼睛。街道兩旁都是一排排美麗的房屋，全部是用綠色的大理石建造，而且到處點綴著亮晶晶的翡翠。他們走過同樣是綠色大理石的步道，而街區交會的地方是用成排的翡翠鋪著，在陽光下閃閃發亮。連城市的上空都泛著綠色，而太陽光線也是綠色。

　　路上有男有女，也有小孩，全都穿著綠色的衣服，有泛綠色的皮膚。街上有許多商店，綠色的糖果和綠色的玉米花正以特價出售，還有綠色的鞋子、帽子和各種綠色的衣物。小孩子正在買綠色的檸檬汽水，付的錢也是綠色的硬幣。

　　每個人好像都很快樂、滿足，也很富有。

　　守門人帶領他們來到偉大巫師奧茲的宮殿。門前有一個士兵，穿著綠色制服，留著長長的綠鬍鬚。

　　「這些陌生人要晉見偉大的奧茲。」守門人說。

　　「進來吧，我會替你們通報。」士兵回答。

他們進入宮殿，被帶到一個大房間。士兵要他們在綠踏墊上擦擦腳底再走進房間，他們坐下來時，士兵很有禮貌地說：「請不要拘束，我這就去寶座宮告訴奧茲你們來了。」

　　他們等了好久，士兵還不回來。等到他終於回來了，桃樂絲就問他：「你見到奧茲了嗎？」

　　「噢，沒有。」士兵回答：「我從來沒有見過他。我向他報告你們的事情，他坐在屏風後面。他說如果你們這麼想見他，可以見你們一面。可是你們必須單獨進去，他每天只見一個人。所以你們要在宮殿裡住幾天，我會帶你們去房間，讓你們在旅行過後好好休息。」

　　「謝謝你，奧茲真好心。」桃樂絲回答。

　　士兵吹了一聲綠哨子，立刻進來一個身穿美麗綠絲袍的女孩，有著漂亮的綠頭髮和綠眼睛。她對桃樂絲深深一鞠躬，然後說：「請跟我去妳的房間。」

　　桃樂絲她把小狗抱在懷裡，跟著綠女孩來到世界上最美好的小房間，有柔軟、舒適的床，舖著綠色絲質床單和綠色天鵝絨床罩。房間中央有個小噴泉，把綠色的香水噴到空中，再落到美麗的綠色大理石雕盆上。

　　衣櫥裡有許多綠色的衣服，都是用絲、綢緞和天鵝絨做的，對桃樂絲來說都很合身。

　　「請不要拘束，需要什麼東西就搖搖鈴。奧茲明天早上會召見妳。」綠女孩說。

　　每個人都被帶到自己的房間。稻草人一直呆站在門邊等到天亮，整晚都盯著一隻在房間角落織網的小蜘蛛。錫樵夫睡不著，整夜上上下下地移動關節，確定身體運作良好。獅子寧可睡躺在森林裡的乾樹葉上，但牠夠理智，沒為此困擾，牠跳到床上像隻貓蜷曲身體，很快就呼嚕嚕地睡著了。

　　隔天早上，吃過早餐，綠女孩幫桃樂絲穿上最漂亮的長袍——用綠錦緞做成的。桃樂絲幫托托綁上綠色的緞帶。

　　他們先是來到一個大廳，裡面有很多朝廷的紳士淑女，全都穿著華麗的服裝。這些人每天早上都會在外面等，儘管一直得不到奧茲的召見。桃樂絲進來時，他們都好奇地看著她，其中一人低聲說：「妳真的要去見那可怕的奧茲嗎？」

　　「當然，如果他要見我的話。」桃樂絲回答。

　　「噢，他會見妳的。」之前向奧茲報信的士兵說：「事實上，起先他很生氣，他說我應該把你們送回去。後來他問我妳長什麼樣子，我提到妳那雙銀色鞋子時，他很有興趣。最後我告訴他妳額頭上的印記，他就決定要見妳了。」

　　這時傳來一聲鈴響，綠女孩就對桃樂絲說：「信號來了，妳必須單獨進入寶座宮。」

　　她打開一道小門，桃樂絲就大膽地走過去，發現裡面是個很大的圓形房間，有高高的圓頂，牆壁、天花板和地板都緊密貼著大塊翡翠。天花板中間有個大燈，和太陽一樣明亮，使翡翠發出璀璨的光芒。

　　房間中央有綠色大理石做的大王座。它的形狀像椅子，發出寶石的亮光。椅子中間有個無比巨大的頭，沒有身體支

撐，也沒有手臂或雙腳。頭上沒有毛髮，可是有眼睛、鼻子和嘴巴，比最大的巨人的頭還要大。

不久那張嘴巴動了起來，桃樂絲聽到聲音說：「我是偉大、可怕的奧茲。妳是誰，為什麼要找我？」

聲音並沒有預料中的恐怖，所以她鼓起勇氣回答：「我是渺小、溫順的桃樂絲，我是來請你幫忙的。」

那對眼睛盯著她足足有一分鐘，似乎在思考。然後那聲音又說：「妳是怎麼得到那雙銀鞋子的？」

「從東方的壞女巫那裡得到的，我的房子掉在她身上，把她殺死了。」她回答。

「妳額頭上的印記是怎麼來的？」那道聲音繼續問。

「那是北方的好女巫叫我來找你，跟我道別時，在我額頭上親吻所留下的記號。」桃樂絲說。

那對眼睛銳利地望著她，發現她說的是真話。奧茲又問她：「妳要我為妳做什麼？」

「送我回堪薩斯，也就是艾姆嬸嬸和亨利叔叔住的地方。」她認真地說：「我不喜歡你的國家，雖然這裡很美。

第11章

但我離開那麼久，艾姆嬸嬸一定擔心得要命。」

那對眼睛眨了眨，然後仰望天花板，俯視地板，像要看遍房間的每個角落。最後奧茲問：「我為什麼要幫助妳？」

「因為你很強大，而我很脆弱。因為你是偉大的巫師，而我只是個無助的小女孩。」她回答。

「可是妳強大得足以殺死東方的壞女巫。」奧茲說。

「那只是碰巧而已，不是我能控制的。」桃樂絲說。

「那麼，」那顆大頭說：「我的回答是這樣，妳沒有權利要我把妳送回堪薩斯，除非妳回報我。每個人要得到什麼東西都必須先付出。如果妳希望我用魔法把妳送回家，妳就必須先為我做事。幫助我，我就會幫助妳。」

「我應該做什麼？」桃樂絲說。

「殺死西方的壞女巫。」奧茲說。

「可是我沒有這個能力！」桃樂絲非常驚訝地大喊訝。

「妳殺死了東方的女巫，而且穿著法力強大的銀鞋。現在這個國家只剩下一個壞女巫了，等到妳告訴我她死了，我就會把妳送回堪薩斯，在那之前是不可能的。」

桃樂絲開始哭泣，她好失望，而那對眼睛眨了眨，焦急地望著她，好像偉大的奧茲覺得，只要她願意就幫得上忙。

「我從來沒有想要殺人，就算我想，又該怎麼殺掉壞女巫呢？連偉大、可怕的你都不能殺死她了，怎麼能指望我去殺她呢？」她嗚咽說著。

「我不知道。」奧茲說：「可是那是我的回答，除非壞女巫死了，否則妳沒辦法再見到嬸嬸和叔叔。一定要殺死那個壞透的女巫才可以。走吧，任務完成前不要再來見我。」

　　桃樂絲悲傷地離開寶座宮，回到獅子、稻草人和錫樵夫等待的地方，他們想知道奧茲說了什麼。

　　「我沒有希望了，因為奧茲不肯送我回家，除非我去殺死西方的壞女巫，但我永遠做不到。」女孩說得好悲傷。

　　朋友們都為她難過，卻幫不了什麼忙，於是她回到自己的房間，躺在床上哭到睡著。

　　隔天早上，有綠鬍鬚的士兵去跟稻草人說：「跟我來，奧茲要召見你。」

　　稻草人就跟著他去，獲准進入大寶座宮，看到一個無比美麗的女人坐在翡翠寶座上。她的肩膀長著翅膀，色彩艷麗，看起來好輕，好像連最輕微的氣息都會搧動它們。

　　稻草人在那美麗的人物面前優雅地行禮。她甜美地說：「我是偉大、可怕的奧茲。你是誰，為什麼要見我？」

　　稻草人非常吃驚，原本以為會見到桃樂絲跟他說過的大頭，但他還是勇敢地回答：「我只是個塞著稻草的稻草人，沒有腦子，所以來這裡請求妳讓我的頭有腦子而不是稻草，我就能夠變得和妳的子民一樣。」

　　「為什麼我要為你做這件事？」女人說。

　　「因為妳很聰明，而且能力高強，沒有其他人可以幫我。」稻草人說。

　　「我從來不做沒有回報的事。」奧茲說：「我頂多只能答應你,如果你殺死西方的壞女巫,我就賜給你很多腦子,有了那麼多好腦子,你會變成整個奧茲國中最聰明的人。」

「我以為妳是要桃樂絲去殺女巫?」稻草人驚訝地說。

「是的。我不介意由誰去殺她。可是除非她死了,不然我不會成全你的願望。現在你走吧,等到你有資格得到你那麼渴望的腦子時,再來見我。」

稻草人很難過地回去見朋友,告訴他們奧茲說的話。桃樂絲很訝異,偉大的巫師竟然不是如她所見的一顆大頭,而是個美女。

「但她和錫樵夫一樣都需要一顆心。」稻草人說。

隔天早上,換錫樵夫跟著士兵,進入大寶座宮。他看到的既不是大頭,也不是美女,因為奧茲這次變成了最可怕的大野獸。野獸的頭就像犀牛,只是臉上有五個眼睛。身體長出五條長手臂,同樣有五條長長的瘦腿。每個部分都覆蓋著濃密的毛髮,沒有人想像得出比牠更恐怖的怪物。幸好錫樵夫在那時沒有心,不然那顆心會因為恐懼而跳得又快又響。

「我是偉大、可怕的奧茲。」那隻野獸以嘶吼的聲音說:「你是誰,為什麼想要見我?」

「我是錫做的樵夫,所以我沒有心,不能去愛。我請求你賜給我一顆心,我就能夠和其他人一樣。」

「我為什麼要為你做這件事?」野獸質問他。

「因為我有需要,而只有你能成全我。」錫樵夫回答。

奧茲聽了就低吼一聲,粗魯地說:「如果你確實想要有一顆心，就要努力去得到。」

「怎麼努力？」樵夫問。

「幫桃樂絲殺死西方的壞女巫。」野獸回答：「女巫死了，我就會給你奧茲國中最大、最善良，也最有愛的心。」

錫樵夫不得不難過地回到朋友身邊，告訴他們他所看到的恐怖野獸。他們都對偉大的奧茲的多種樣貌感到驚奇。獅子就說：「如果我去見他時，他是隻野獸，我就會全力大聲地吼，讓牠嚇得答應我所有的要求。而如果是個美女，我會假裝要撲到她身上，強迫她成全我。而如果他是顆大頭，它會被我滾來滾去，直到它答應我們的所有請求。」

隔天早上，有綠鬍鬚的士兵就帶獅子到寶座宮來，請牠進去見奧茲。

獅子立刻進門，四處張望，卻很驚訝地發現，寶座前面有一顆火球，那光芒是那麼的猛烈，使牠很難直視。牠的第一個念頭是，奧茲可能意外著火而燒了起來。牠想靠近時，熱氣強烈得把牠的鬍鬚燒焦了，使牠顫抖著爬回門邊。

一道低沉、平和的聲音從火球傳出，它說：「我是偉大、可怕的奧茲。你是誰，為什麼要見我？」

獅子就回答：「我是什麼都怕的膽小獅子。我想要請你賜給我勇氣，我就可以真的成為野獸之王。」

「我為什麼要給你勇氣？」奧茲質問牠。

「因為你是最偉大的巫師，只有你能成全我的願望。」獅子回答。

火球猛烈地燃燒了一會兒，發出聲音說：「把壞女巫死掉的證據帶來給我，我就會馬上給你勇氣。可是只要那女巫還活著，你仍然是個膽小鬼。」

　　獅子聽到後感到很生氣，可是牠說不出話來，眼看那火球燒得越來越熱，牠就轉過身，從房間竄出。

　　「我們現在要怎麼辦呢？」桃樂絲難過地說。

　　「我們只能去把西方的壞女巫給消滅。」獅子回答。

　　桃樂絲很想哭，但她說：「我想我們一定要去試試。可是就算再也見不到艾姆嬸嬸，我也不想殺死任何人。」

　　「我會去，可是我太膽小了，不敢殺女巫。」獅子說。

　　「我也會去。」稻草人表示：「可是我可能幫不上什麼忙，我太笨了。」

　　「我連傷害女巫的心都沒有，可是你們要去的話，我當然也要跟去。」錫樵夫說。

　　大家因此決定隔天早上出發。樵夫用綠色的磨刀石把斧頭磨利，並且把所有關節都塗上油。稻草人用新鮮的稻草塞滿身體，桃樂絲為他用新漆重描眼睛，讓他看得更清楚。綠女孩對他們很好，幫桃樂絲把籃子裝滿好吃的東西，還用綠絲帶在托托的脖子綁上一個小鈴鐺。

　　他們早早上床，熟睡到天亮，直到被宮殿後院綠公雞的啼叫聲，還有母雞下綠蛋時的咯咯聲給吵醒。

第 12 章
尋找壞女巫

　　守門人解下他們的眼鏡，放回大盒子裡，然後禮貌地為四個人打開城門。

　　「哪一條路可以通到西方的壞女巫那裡？」桃樂絲問。

　　「沒有路可以去，沒有人想去那裡。」守門人回答。

　　「那我們要怎麼找她呀？」女孩問。

　　「很容易。」那人回答：「她一知道你們在溫基國，就會去找你們，把你們變成她的奴隸。」

　　「也許不會，因為我們是去消滅她。」稻草人說。

　　「噢，那就不一樣了。」守門人說：「你們只要一直沿著太陽下山的方向走去，就一定可以找到她。」

　　他們向他致上謝意並道別，然後就朝著西邊，通過柔美的草地，開著零星雛菊和毛茛的田野。桃樂絲仍然穿著宮殿的美麗絲袍，可是現在她驚訝地發現，那不再是綠色的了，而是純白色的。托托脖子上的綠絲帶也褪了色，和桃樂絲的衣服一樣白。

西方沒有農莊或房舍，土地也沒有任何開墾。地面越走越崎嶇，也越來越陡。到了下午，太陽把他們的臉曬得熱烘烘。天還沒黑，桃樂絲和托托、獅子都累癱了，一躺在草地上就睡著了，樵夫和稻草人則在一旁看守。

他們還離得很遠，可是獨眼的西方壞女巫視力很好，一眼就看到他們。她吹響了掛在脖子上的銀哨子。

一大群狼立刻從四面八方湧來。牠們有長長的腿、凶猛的眼睛和銳利的牙齒。

「去找那些人，把他們撕成碎片。」女巫說。

「妳不想把他們抓來當奴隸嗎？」狼群的頭子說。

「不了。」她回答：「一個是錫做的，一個是稻草做的，有一個是女孩，另一個是獅子，沒有一個適合做工。」

於是那隻狼隨後就全速跑開，後面跟著其他的狼。

幸好稻草人和樵夫清醒著，聽到狼群的聲音。

「我來應戰。」錫樵夫說：「躲到我後面，牠們過來時，由我來對付牠們。」

他拿起磨得鋒利的斧頭，當狼群的首領跑來時，錫樵夫舉起手臂，砍下那隻狼的頭，使牠立刻斃命。他又舉起斧頭時，來了另一隻狼，同樣倒在錫樵夫的利刃下。總共有四十隻狼，被殺死的也有四十隻，所以到了最後，他們的屍體在錫樵夫的面前堆成小山。

他放下斧頭，在稻草人旁邊坐下。稻草人對他說：「幹得好，朋友。」

隔天早上桃樂絲醒來，看到一大堆毛茸茸的狼屍時，相當害怕。錫樵夫將事情的經過告訴她，她感謝錫樵夫救了他們的命。她坐下來吃完早餐後繼續上路。

　　這天早上，壞女巫來到城堡門口，發現她所有的狼都死了。她更生氣了，就吹了兩聲銀哨子。

　　一大群野烏鴉馬上遮蔽了整個天空，飛了過來。壞女巫對烏鴉王說：「去啄出他們的眼睛，把他們撕成碎片。」

　　野烏鴉就成群飛向桃樂絲和她的同伴。稻草人說：「我來應戰。在我旁邊躺下，你們就不會受傷。」

　　所以他們全部躺在地上，只有稻草人站著舉起手臂。烏鴉看到他時都很害怕，不敢再靠近。可是烏鴉王說：「那只是個填充的人，我這就去啄掉他的眼珠子。」

　　烏鴉王撲向稻草人，稻草人一把抓住牠的頭，脖子一扭，牠就斷氣了。又一隻飛向他，稻草人同樣扭斷牠的脖子。總共有四十隻烏鴉，稻草人總共扭斷四十次脖子，最後所有死屍都堆在他身邊

　　壞女巫又往外張望時，看到烏鴉的屍體聚集成堆時火冒三丈，就吹了三次銀哨子。

　　空中馬上傳來響亮的嗡嗡聲，一大群黑蜜蜂飛了過來。

　　「去把他們螫死！」女巫下令，蜜蜂就轉過身，快速飛到桃樂絲和同伴行走的地方。可是樵夫看到牠們過來了，稻草人也決定好要怎麼應付牠們。

　　「拿出我的稻草，撒在小女孩和狗、獅子身上。」他對

樵夫說：「蜜蜂就螫不到他們了。」錫樵夫趕緊照辦，桃樂絲摟著托托，緊靠著獅子，稻草把他們都蓋起來。

蜜蜂飛過來，發現只有錫樵夫可以螫，就都撲向他，用刺攻擊他，卻一點都傷不了他。蜜蜂的刺受損就活不了，黑蜜蜂的生命就這樣結束，疊成一堆，好像一堆黑木炭。

桃樂絲和獅子站起來，女孩幫錫樵夫把稻草塞回稻草人身上，讓他恢復原狀。然後他們再度上路。

壞女巫氣得咬牙切齒。於是她召來十二名溫基人奴隸，給他們尖銳的矛，要他們去刺殺那群陌生人。

溫基人並不勇敢，可是他們必須聽話，就邁開大步走向桃樂絲他們。獅子發出一聲怒吼，就撲向他們，可憐的溫基人嚇得拔腿就逃。

壞女巫不明白為什麼詭計都失敗了。

她的櫥櫃裡有一頂金色的帽子，上面鑲著一圈鑽石和紅寶石。這頂帽子擁有魔法，擁有它的人可以召喚三次有翅膀的猴子，牠們會遵從任何指令，但是沒有人可以命令這種奇怪的生物超過三次。壞女巫已經使用過兩次帽子，一次是讓溫基人變成她的奴隸。第二次是把偉大的奧茲趕出西方的領土。她只能再用一次這頂金帽，現在她凶猛的狼群、野烏鴉和螫人的蜜蜂都死了，而她的奴隸又被膽小獅子嚇跑，她想這是唯一可以消滅桃樂絲他們的方法。

所以壞女巫從櫥櫃拿出金帽，放在頭上。然後她用左腳站立，慢慢唸著：「伊－貝，貝－貝，卡－開！」

接著用右腳站立,「希－洛,霍－洛,哈—囉!」

然後雙腳站立,「吉－吉,主－吉,吉克!」

魔法生效了。天空變暗,空中傳來低沉的隆隆聲。先是許多翅膀的窸窣聲、吵雜的喧嘩和笑聲,然後太陽從黑暗的天空露出,看得出壞女巫已經被一群猴子包圍,牠們的肩膀上都有一對巨大有力的翅膀。

有一隻個子比其他還大,似乎就是牠們的首領。牠飛向女巫說:「這是妳第三次,也是最後一次召喚我們。妳有什麼吩咐?」

「去把他們全部消滅,除了那隻獅子。」壞女巫說:「把那隻野獸帶來給我,我要把牠當馬騎,叫牠做工。」

「遵命。」領袖說。又是一陣喧嘩和噪音,有翅膀的猴子飛到桃樂絲和朋友行走的地方。

有些猴子抓住錫樵夫,帶著他飛到布滿尖石的地方。可憐的錫樵夫就這樣被丟下來,從高處墜落到岩石上,因此嚴重毀損,既不能動,也叫不出聲來。

有些猴子抓住稻草人,用長指頭把他的稻草都掏出來,再把他的帽子、靴子和衣服丟到一棵大樹上的樹梢。

其他的猴子則是朝獅子扔下結實的繩子,把牠的身體和頭腳纏繞好幾圈,直到牠不能咬、抓或掙扎為止。然後帶牠飛到女巫城堡的一個小院子裡,四周圍著高高的鐵欄杆。

可是牠們並沒有傷害桃樂絲。她抱著托托站著,看著同伴悲慘的遭遇。有翅膀的猴子首領飛向她,伸出長毛手臂,

醜陋的臉在
獰笑，但一
看到好女巫
在她額頭上
親吻的印記，
就突然停下，
指示其他猴子不
要碰她。

　　牠對手下說：「她受到
善良的力量保護，那比邪惡的力量
還大。不能傷害她，我們只能把她帶到
壞女巫的城堡。」

　　牠們小心溫柔地用手臂舉起桃樂絲，帶著她快速飛過天空，來到城堡，把她放在前門的臺階上。然後猴子首領對女巫說：「我們已經盡所能遵從妳的命令。錫樵夫和稻草人都被消滅了，而獅子也被綁起來放在妳的後院。我們不敢傷害小女孩和她懷裡的狗。妳對我們的控制力已經結束，妳再也見不到我們了。」

　　隨著許多笑聲、喧嘩和噪音，有翅膀的猴子全部都飛到空中，很快就不見蹤影了。

　　壞女巫看到桃樂絲額頭上的印記時又驚訝又擔心，因為她很清楚，不僅是有翅膀的猴子，連她也不敢傷害這個女孩。然後她看到銀色的鞋子，嚇得發抖，因為她知道這鞋子具有多麼強大的魔力。起初女巫很想逃走，可是她無意中發現小女孩並不知道銀鞋賦予她的強大威力。壞女巫兀自大笑，然後兇巴巴地對桃樂絲說：「跟我來，我說什麼，妳都要記住，不然的話，我就要結束妳的生命。」

桃樂絲跟著她來到廚房。女巫命令她把鍋盆、水壺洗乾淨，還要掃地板，不斷把柴薪丟進火裡。

桃樂絲溫順地照做。

然後女巫跑去院子想給膽小獅子套上馬具當馬騎。可是她一開門，獅子就大聲吼叫，凶猛地撲向她，女巫害怕地跑出去把門關上。

「就算不能騎你，我也可以餓死你。」女巫透過門上的欄杆對獅子說：「除非你聽話，不然就沒得吃。」

後來壞女巫很想得到女孩穿在腳上的銀鞋。只要取得銀鞋，她能夠擁有的力量比她失去的加起來還要多。

她大可以把鞋子偷走。可是這孩子很喜歡那雙漂亮的鞋子，從來不會脫掉鞋子，除了晚上洗澡的時候。可是女巫怕水，所以不敢在桃樂絲洗澡時接近她。事實上，這個老女巫從來不碰水，也不讓一滴水沾到她。

可是這個壞傢伙很狡猾，她終於想到一個詭計，可以達成目的。她在廚房的地板中央裝上一條鐵棍，用魔法把鐵棍變成隱形的。所以桃樂絲經過時，因為看不到鐵棍而被絆倒，整個人趴到地上。她沒有受傷，可是跌倒時掉了一隻銀鞋，來不及撿起來，就被女巫搶走，套在她瘦巴巴的腳上。

壞女巫很得意，因為只要有一隻鞋子，她就有了一半魔力，就算桃樂絲懂得使用，也無法用來對付她。

　　小女孩氣極了，就對女巫說：「把鞋子還我！」

　　「不要，現在這是我的鞋子了。」女巫反駁她。

　　「壞東西！妳沒有權利拿走我的鞋子。」桃樂絲大叫。

　　「不管怎樣，我都不會還妳。」女巫對她大笑，「而且我總有一天會拿到妳那一隻。」

　　桃樂絲聽了更生氣，拿起旁邊的一桶水，就往女巫身上潑去，把她從頭到腳都弄濕了。

　　壞女巫嚇得大叫，桃樂絲則驚訝地看著女巫縮小消失。

　　「看妳做的好事！我快要融化了。」她尖叫著，「妳不知道水會殺死我嗎？」女巫邊哀嚎邊絕望地問。

　　「當然不知道。」桃樂絲回答：「我怎麼會知道？」

　　「再過幾分鐘，我就會融化了，這個城堡就會是妳的了。我在世的時候很壞，可是從沒有想到像妳這樣的小女孩就能夠讓我融化，結束我的惡行。小心，我要走了！」

　　說完這些話，女巫就倒下來，融成一灘看不出形狀的褐色東西，還漫延到廚房乾淨的地板上。看到女巫真的融掉了，桃樂絲就又打了一桶水，把地板沖洗乾淨，然後撿起女巫唯一留下的銀鞋，用布擦乾淨，再把它穿回腳上。

　　終於忙完時，她跑到後院告訴獅子西方壞女巫已死的消息。他們不用再被關在異地了。

第 13 章

解救同伴

膽小獅很高興壞女巫被一桶水融化了，桃樂絲立刻打開牠的門，放牠出來。他們一起進入城堡，桃樂絲做的第一件事就是召集所有溫基人，跟他們說，他們不是奴隸了。

黃色的溫基人大聲歡呼，因為他們已經為壞女巫辛苦工作許多年，那女人對他們非常殘酷。他們把這一天訂為假日，當天和往後的這一天都要設宴跳舞。

「如果我們的朋友，也就是稻草人和錫樵夫和我們在一起，我一定會很高興。」獅子說。

「我們不能去救他們嗎？」桃樂絲焦慮地說。

「我們試試看。」獅子回答。

他們找來黃色的溫基人，詢問他們是否能幫忙搭救他們的朋友，溫基人說，他們很願意盡全力幫忙桃樂絲，因為是她帶給他們自由。所以她選了一些看起來懂很多事的溫基人，然後一道出發。他們花了一天多的時間，才來到錫樵夫跌落的岩石曠野。他全身到處凹陷及彎曲變形，他的斧頭就在旁邊，可是刀刃已經生鏽，刀柄也折斷了。

溫基人小心地把他抬起來，帶回黃色的城堡，桃樂絲看到老朋友的慘況不禁掉了些眼淚，獅子則板著臉，顯得很難過。到達城堡時，桃樂絲對溫基人說：「你們有錫匠嗎？」

　「有的，我們有技術高超的錫匠。」他們說。

　「那就帶他們來。」她說。錫匠都來了，帶著裝有全部工具的籃子，她跟他們要求：「你們可以把錫樵夫身上的凹陷弄平，讓他恢復原來的模樣，再銲接他斷裂的地方嗎？」

那些錫匠仔細檢查樵夫，回答說，他們可以把他修得和以前一樣好，於是開始在城堡最大的黃色房間，整整工作了三天四夜。經過敲打、扭彎、銲接、磨亮、用力撞擊樵夫的兩腿、身體和頭部，終於把他調整成老樣子，他的關節也和以前一樣靈活。當然他的身上還是多了幾塊補釘，可是錫匠的手藝很好，何況樵夫並不是個虛榮的人，一點都不在乎那些補釘。

　　桃樂絲又找來了一些溫基人幫忙，一起走了一天多的路，才來到一棵大樹下，有翅膀的猴子就是把稻草人的衣服扔在那一棵樹的上方。

　　那棵樹很高大，而且樹幹平滑，沒有人爬得上去，可是樵夫立刻說：「我把它砍下，就能拿到稻草人的衣服了。」

　　錫匠們在修補樵夫的身體時，有一名職業是金匠的溫基人，用純金做了個斧頭柄，接在樵夫的斧頭上，代替原先斷裂的柄。另一些人則把刀刃磨利，去除上面的鏽，使它閃亮得像是光潔的銀。

　　樵夫一說完話，就開始砍樹，那顆樹很快就轟地一聲倒下，稻草人的衣服從樹梢掉落，滾到地上。

　　桃樂絲把衣服撿起，讓溫基人帶回城堡，重新塞進乾淨的稻草。瞧！稻草人就回來了，和以前一模一樣。他不斷感謝救了他們的人。

　　現在他們團圓了，桃樂絲和朋友們在黃色的城堡過了幾天快樂的日子，所有令生活舒適的東西城堡裡都有。可是有一天，女孩想起了艾姆嬸嬸，就說：「我們一定要回去找奧茲，要他實現諾言。」

「對，我終於可以得到我的心了。」錫樵夫說。

「我可以得到腦子了。」稻草人歡喜地說。

「我可以得到勇氣了。」獅子邊想邊說。

「我可以回堪薩斯了。」桃樂絲拍手大叫：「我們明天就出發去翡翠城！」

他們一致同意。第二天，他們召集溫基人，跟他們告別。溫基人很難過他們要離開，而且他們越來越喜歡錫樵夫，希望他留下來治理這個黃色的西方。發現他們執意要離開時，溫基人給托托和獅子各一條金項圈，送給桃樂絲鑲有鑽石的漂亮手鐲，給稻草人一把金柄手杖，讓他免於跌跤，而錫樵夫則收到銀油罐，上面鑲著金子和珍貴的寶石。

桃樂絲走到女巫的櫥櫃，在籃子裡裝滿路上吃的食物，看到一頂金帽，就試試戴在頭上，發現尺寸正合適。她不知道這頂金帽帶有魔力，只覺得它很漂亮，就決定戴著它，而把自己的遮陽帽放進籃子。

準備好以後，他們就出發去翡翠城，溫基人為他們歡呼了三次，並給予很多祝福。

第 14 章
有翅膀的猴子

　　他們知道，一定要往東走，面向升起的太陽，朝著正確的方向出發。可是到了中午，太陽高掛在頭上時，他們不知道哪裡是東，哪裡是西，這就是他們在大原野迷路的原因。然而，他們仍然繼續走，直到晚上月亮出來，投下亮光。他們在充滿甜香的黃花叢中躺下，一覺到天亮，但是稻草人和錫樵夫除外。

　　隔日早上，太陽被一片烏雲遮住，但他們還是出發了，好像很確定要往哪裡走。

　　「如果走得夠遠，我相信一定會去到某個地方。」桃樂絲說道。

　　可是過了一天又一天，他們眼前只有紅色的花田，看不到其他東西。稻草人開始有點抱怨。

　　「我們一定迷路了。」他說：「除非趕快找到路抵達翡翠城，不然我永遠都得不到腦子。」

　　「我也得不到心。」錫樵夫宣稱：「我已經等不及要見到奧茲了，你必須承認，這段旅程夠漫長的。」

「知道嗎，哪裡都到不了的話，我就沒有勇氣再走下去了。」膽小獅哭著說。

「如果我們呼喚田鼠，牠們也許會告訴我們去翡翠城的路。」桃樂絲提議。

「牠們一定可以，我們怎麼沒想到呢？」稻草人叫著。

桃樂絲吹響一直掛在脖子上的小哨子，是田鼠皇后給她的。隔了幾分鐘，他們聽到小腳啪嗒走動的聲音，許多小灰鼠跑向她。其中有一隻是田鼠皇后，以她細細的吱吱聲問道：「有什麼事要我效勞嗎？朋友們。」

「我們迷路了，可以告訴我們翡翠城在哪裡嗎？」桃樂絲說。

「當然可以。」皇后回答：「可是那是在很遠的地方，因為你們一直在往反方向走。」她注意到桃樂絲的金帽，就說：「妳怎麼不利用那頂帽子的魔法，召來有翅膀的猴子？不用一個小時，牠們就能把你們送到奧茲的城市。」

「我不知道它有魔法。」桃樂絲驚奇地說。

「就寫在金帽裡面。」田鼠皇后說：「不過如果妳要召來有翅膀的猴子，我們就要先跑開，因為牠們喜歡惡作劇，覺得欺負我們很好玩。」

「牠們會傷害我嗎？」女孩焦慮地問。

「不會的，牠們一定要聽從帽主的吩咐。再見！」田鼠皇后一下子就溜走了，所有田鼠都緊跟在後。

桃樂絲看了看金帽內側，裡面寫著一行字，她想那一定是咒語，就小心地閱讀上面的指示，然後把帽子戴回頭上。

「伊－貝，貝－貝，卡－開！」她說，用左腳站立。

稻草人不知道她在做什麼，就問她：「妳說什麼？」

桃樂絲再唸：「希－洛，霍－洛，哈—囉！」這回是用右腳站立。

「哈囉！」錫樵夫平靜地回答。

「吉－吉，主－吉，吉克！」桃樂絲說，現在是用雙腳站立。咒語說完了，他們就聽到喧嘩與拍翅的聲響，一群有翅膀的猴子飛向他們。

猴王對桃樂絲深深一鞠躬，問她：「妳有什麼吩咐？」

「我們想要去翡翠城，卻迷路了。」桃樂絲說。

「我們會帶你們去。」猴王說，話一說完，就有兩隻猴子用手臂托著桃樂絲飛走。其他猴子也托起稻草人、錫樵夫和獅子，有一隻小猴子則抓著托托，跟在大家後面，雖然那隻狗努力想要咬牠。

稻草人和錫樵夫起初好害怕，因為他們還記得有翅膀的猴子們之前是怎麼殘酷地對待他們，可是這回他們看得出這群猴子沒有惡意，就相當愉快地飛過空中，慢慢欣賞遠在底下的美麗花園和森林。

桃樂絲覺得自己騎在兩隻大猴子之間非常輕鬆，其中一隻就是猴王。牠們用手搭成一把椅子，小心避免傷到她。

「你們為什麼要聽從金帽的咒語呢？」

「說來話長。」猴王笑著說：「既然我們有一大段路要飛，妳想聽的話，我就告訴妳。」

「我很想聽。」她回答。

猴王開始說：「我們以前是在大森林快樂地自由生活著，在樹上飛來飛去，吃堅果和水果，隨心所欲，根本不需要稱呼別人主人。有些猴子太調皮，會飛下去扯沒有翅膀的動物尾巴、追逐鳥兒，還會對穿過森林的人丟堅果。可是我們無憂無慮，充滿樂趣，享受每一天每一刻。那是許多年以前的事，那時候奧茲還沒有從雲裡面冒出來統治這塊土地。

「遙遠的北方住著一個美麗的公主，她也是個法力強大的魔法師，會用所有法力來幫助人，而且絕不會傷害善良的人。她的名字是『葛葉蕾』，住在一棟用大塊紅寶石建造的漂亮宮殿裡。每個人都愛她，可是她最大的缺憾是找不到可以愛的對象，因為所有男人都太笨也太醜了，配不上她的美麗和聰明。可是最後她還是找到了一個英俊、有男子氣概，而且智慧超齡的男孩。葛葉蕾決定等他長大成人就要嫁給他，就把他迎進紅寶石宮殿，用所有的魔法使他變得強壯、善良和可愛,任何女人都會欣賞。他長大後,這個名叫『克拉拉』的的青年據說是全國最好、最有智慧的男人,而他的模樣是那麼的俊俏,使葛葉蕾非常愛他,趕著準備婚禮。

「我的祖父那時是有翅膀的猴子王,住在靠近葛葉蕾宮殿的森林裡,那老傢伙愛開玩笑的程度比飽吃一頓還要大。有一天,就在婚禮前,我祖父和一些夥伴飛出去,看到克拉拉走在河邊。他穿著粉紅色絲綢和紫絨布做的盛裝,我祖父想要測試他的能耐,就發令和夥伴飛下去抓克拉拉,帶著他飛到河中央,把他丟進水裡。

「『游上岸吧,好傢伙!』我祖父叫著,『看看河水會不會弄髒你的衣服。』克拉拉很聰明,他當然會游泳,而且沒有被他的好運氣給寵壞。他笑了笑,浮上水面,游到岸邊。可是葛葉蕾跑出來看到他的絲絨衣都被河水泡壞了。

「公主非常生氣,當然知道是誰幹的好事。她要全部有翅膀的猴子來到她面前,起先說要把牠們的翅膀都綁起來,像牠們對克拉拉那樣,把牠們丟進河裡。可是我祖父拼命懇求,這群猴子在水裡時翅膀被綁著一定會淹死,克拉拉也為牠們求情,葛葉蕾才饒了牠們,但是有個條件,就是有翅膀的猴子要聽從三次金帽主人的要求。這頂帽子是送給克拉拉的結婚禮物,據說讓公主耗掉整個王國的一半資產。當然我祖父和其他猴子立刻答應這個條件,這就是為什麼我們要為金帽主人當三次奴隸,不論他是誰。」

「他們後來呢？」桃樂絲問，對這個故事很有興趣。

「克拉拉是金帽的第一個主人。」猴子回答：「他第一個對我們許願。由於他的新娘不想再看到我們，他在婚後在森林召喚我們，命令我們永遠都不能再讓葛葉蕾看到一隻有翅膀的猴子，我們很樂意遵從，因為我們都很怕她。

「我們一直很遵守這件事，直到金帽落入西方的壞女巫手中，她叫我們把溫基人變成奴隸，後來又把奧茲趕出西方的領土。現在金帽是妳的了，妳可以對我們許三次願望。」

猴王說完故事時，桃樂絲往下看，發現眼前就是閃著綠光的翡翠城牆。猴子飛行的速度令她十分驚訝，可是她很高興旅程結束了。這群奇怪的傢伙把旅行者小心地放在城門前，猴王對桃樂絲深深一鞠躬，然後就迅速飛走了，後面跟著牠的夥伴。

「這趟旅程好愉快啊。」桃樂絲說。

「對，也是儘快解困的方式。」獅子說：「幸好妳把那頂帽子帶來了。」

第 15 章
奧茲的真面目

　　四名旅行者走到翡翠城的大門按鈴。鈴聲響了好幾次，來開門的是他們見過的那個守門人。

　　「咦！你們又回來了？」他驚訝地問。「我以為你們去找西方的壞女巫了。」

　　「我們是去找她了。」稻草人說。

　　「她讓你們回來？」守門人驚奇地說。

　　「她不得不，因為她被融化了。」稻草人解釋。

　　「融化！真是好消息。」那人說：「是誰融化她的？」

　　「桃樂絲。」獅子嚴肅地說。

　　「太好了！」守門人叫著，在她面前深深一鞠躬。

　　然後他帶領他們進入自己的小房間，和上一次一樣，為他們鎖上從大盒子拿出來的眼鏡。然後他們穿過翡翠城門，人們聽守門人說他們把西方的壞女巫融化了，就都聚在這群人的旁邊，他們就在一大群人的簇擁下來到奧茲的宮殿。

　　有綠鬍鬚的士兵仍在門口看守，可是他立刻就讓他們進去，他們再度遇到美麗的綠女孩，也立刻被一一帶到房間，在那裡休息，直到偉大的奧茲準備好接見他們。

士兵已直接向奧茲報告說，桃樂絲和其他旅行者消滅了壞女巫，已經回來了，可是奧茲沒有回應。他們以為偉大的奧茲會立刻召見他們，他卻沒有。第二天、第三天、在那之後，還是沒有他的消息。等待的時日又煩又悶，他們終於生氣了，奧茲怎麼可以在派他們去受苦受難之後，以這麼差的態度對待他們。稻草人最後要綠女孩帶另一個口信給奧茲說，如果他不馬上讓他們進去見他，就要請有翅膀的猴子來幫忙，看他要不要守信用。巫師收到這份訊息時非常惶恐，就傳話說，請他們在隔天早上九點四分到寶座宮來。他在西方見過一次有翅膀的猴子，可不想再看到牠們。

四名旅行者過了一個無眠的夜晚，每個人都在想著奧茲答應賞賜的禮物。桃樂絲只睡了一會兒，夢到她在堪薩斯，艾姆嬸嬸告訴她，多麼高興她的小女孩回來了。

隔日早上九點一到，綠鬍鬚的士兵就來接他們，過了四分鐘，他們就都走進了偉大奧茲的寶座宮。

當然每個人都以為巫師會顯出之前的模樣，沒想到環顧四周卻發現房間裡一個人也沒有，令他們非常驚訝。他們站在靠門的地方，彼此靠得很近，因為安靜的空房間比他們看過的奧茲模樣更嚇人。

沒過多久，他們聽到聲音，似乎是從圓頂上方傳過來的。那聲音莊嚴地說：「我是偉大、可怕的奧茲，你們為什麼要見我？」

綠野仙蹤

　　他們又看遍了整個房間，沒有看到人。桃樂絲就問：「你在哪裡？」

　　「我無所不在。」那聲音說：「但是凡人的眼睛是看不見我的。我現在坐在寶座上，妳可以和我講話。」事實上那聲音似乎就直接來自那張寶座，他們就向前排成一列，由桃樂絲開口說：「我們來要求你實現諾言，奧茲。」

　　「什麼諾言？」奧茲問。

　　「你答應我，等消滅了壞女巫，就要送我回堪薩斯。」女孩說。

　　「你答應說要給我腦子。」稻草人說。

　　「你答應說要給我一顆心。」錫樵夫說。

　　「你答應說要給我勇氣。」膽小獅說。

　　「壞女巫真的被消滅了嗎？」那聲音問，桃樂絲覺得聽起來有點顫抖。

　　「是的。」她回答：「我用一桶水讓她融化了。」

　　「天哪！」那聲音說：「真是意外！好吧，明天來見我，給我時間想一想。」

　　「你已經有太多時間想了。」錫樵夫火大地說。

　　「我們一天也不要多等。」稻草人說。

　　「你一定要實現給我們的諾言！」桃樂絲說。

　　獅子心想可以嚇嚇那個巫師，就大吼一聲，又凶猛又可怕，讓托托驚慌地從牠旁邊跳開，把擺在角落的屏風打翻。聽到碰撞聲，他們都往那裡看過去，下一秒大吃一驚。因為

他們看到屏風裡面站著
一個矮小、禿頭、滿
臉皺紋的老人，
他似乎和他們
一樣驚訝。錫
樵夫舉起斧
頭，衝向小矮
人大叫說：
「你是誰？」

「我是偉
大、可怕的奧
茲。」小矮人以
顫抖的聲音說：
「可是別打人，請不要打！
你們要我做什麼都可以。」

他們驚訝地看著他，有點灰心。

「我以為奧茲是個大頭。」桃樂絲說。

「我以為奧茲是個美女。」稻草人說。

「我以為奧茲是隻可怕的野獸。」錫樵夫說。

「我以為奧茲是個火球。」獅子叫著。

「不，你們都錯了。」小矮人柔順地說：「那都是我假
裝的。」

「假裝！」桃樂絲大叫：「你不是偉大的巫師？」

綠野仙蹤

　　「噓，親愛的。」他說：「不要說得那麼大聲，別人會聽到，那我就完蛋了。大家都以為我是偉大的巫師。」

　　「你不是嗎？」她問。

　　「一點也不是，親愛的，我只是個普通人。」

　　「你不只是普通人，你是個騙子。」稻草人悲地說。

　　「沒錯！」小矮人邊說邊搓手，好像聽到那句話很高興。「我是個騙子。」

　　「可是那太糟糕了，這下子我要怎麼得到心呢？」錫樵夫說。

　　「我的勇氣呢？」獅子說。

　　「我的頭腦呢？」稻草人邊哭邊用衣袖擦眼淚。

　　「我親愛的朋友。」奧茲說：「不要提這些小事了。想一想我被拆穿時會有什麼下場。」

　　「沒有人知道你是個騙子嗎？」桃樂絲說。

　　「沒有人知道，除了你們四個，還有我自己。」奧茲回答：「我騙了每個人這麼久，以為永遠都沒有人知道。讓你們進來寶座宮是天大的錯誤，通常我連臣民都不見的，這樣子他們才會以為我是個可怕的人物。」

　　「可是，我不明白。」桃樂絲很疑惑。「你要怎麼在我面前顯出大頭的模樣呢？」

　　「那是我使的把戲。」奧茲回答：「請過來這裡，我來告訴你們那是怎麼做的。」

　　他帶領他們走到寶座後面的小房間，指著一個角落，那

090

裡放著那個大頭，是用許多厚紙板做成的，上面仔細描出了人臉。

「我用鐵絲吊在天花板上。」奧茲說：「然後站在屏風後面拉著線，使眼睛活動，嘴巴也可以張開。」

「那聲音怎麼辦？」她問。

「噢，我會說腹語。」小矮人說：「我可以把聲音帶到任何地方，讓人以為就是來自這顆頭。這裡還有其他用來欺騙你們的東西。」他給稻草人看他裝成美女時穿的衣服和面具，錫樵夫也看到那可怕的野獸不過是用許多皮革縫起來的，裡面用木條撐開。至於那顆火球，假巫師也是把它吊在天花板上，那其實是個棉球，倒些油就會燒得猛烈。

「真是的。」稻草人說：「你應該為自己感到羞恥，因為你是個大騙子。」

「我當然覺得很慚愧。」小矮人悲傷地說：「可是那是我唯一能做的事情。請坐下來，這裡有很多椅子，我要告訴你們我的經歷。」

他們就坐下來聽他講了以下的故事。

「我是在奧瑪哈出生的……」

「咦，那裡離堪薩斯不很遠！」桃樂絲大叫。

「不遠，可是離這裡可遠得很。」他說，難過地對桃樂絲搖頭。「我長大以後，接受一個大師的訓練，成為很厲害的腹語藝人。我可以模仿任何鳥兒或野獸的叫聲。」他像小貓一樣喵喵叫著，使得托托豎起耳朵，四處張望，想知道那小傢伙在哪裡。奧茲繼續說：「過了一段時間，我厭倦了說腹語，就當起了飛氣球的人。」

「那是在做什麼？」桃樂絲問。

「馬戲團來的時候，需要有個人乘著氣球上升，吸引群眾花錢來看馬戲團。」他解釋說。

「噢，我知道。」她說。

「有一天，我乘著氣球要飛上去時，繩子纏住了，使得我下不來，氣球一直飄到雲上面，高得被一陣氣流捲走，把我帶到許多公里外的地方。我在空中飛了整整一天一夜，第二天早上醒來時，發現氣球飄在一個奇怪又美麗的地方。

「氣球慢慢地飄下來，我一點也沒有受傷，接著就發現自己被一群奇怪的人包圍，他們看到我從雲端走下來，以為我是個偉大的巫師。當然我也讓他們這麼想，因為他們很怕我，什麼事都願意為我做。

「為了消遣，也為了讓這些好人有事做，我命令他們建造這座城市和我的宮殿，他們都很心甘情願，也做得很好。然後我認為，既然這個地方是這麼翠綠美麗，我就叫它『翡翠城』，而且為了讓這個名字更加貼切，我要每個人都戴上綠色的眼鏡，使他們看到的一切都是綠色的。」

「可是這裡的東西不都是綠色的嗎？」桃樂絲問。

「綠色的東西不會比其他的城市多。」奧茲說：「可是你戴上了綠色的眼鏡，當然看到的東西就全是綠色的了。翡翠城是在很久以前建造的，我被氣球帶來這裡時還很年輕，現在已經很老了。可是我的人民在眼睛上戴著綠鏡片已經很久了，大部分人都真的以為這裡是翡翠城，當然這個地方真的很美，充滿寶石和貴金屬，還有一切讓人快樂的好東西。我對人民很好，他們喜歡我，可是自從宮殿建好以後，我就把自己關起來，不想見任何人。

「我害怕很多事情，女巫是其中之一。雖然我沒有一點法力，卻很快就發現，女巫真的能夠做很多神奇的事。這個國家總共有四個女巫，統治著住在東、西、南、北方的人民。幸好南北兩方的女巫有善心，我知道她們不會傷害我，可是東西兩方的女巫非常惡毒，要不是她們以為我的法力比她們還大，一定會來消滅我。這也就是說，我多年來都活在對她們的恐懼中，所以妳可以想像，聽到妳的房子壓死了東方的女巫時，我有多麼的高興。妳來找我時，我真的很願意答應妳任何事情，只要妳能把另一個女巫收拾掉。可是現在妳把她融化了，我只能慚愧地說，我沒有辦法實現諾言。」

「我認為你是很壞的人。」桃樂絲說。

「噢，不是的，親愛的，我其實是非常好的人。不過我要承認，我是個很壞的巫師。」

「你不能給我腦子嗎？」稻草人問。

「你不需要腦子。你每天都在學習新的東西。嬰兒雖然有頭腦，知道的事情卻很少。唯有經驗才能帶給你知識，而你活得越久，就能夠得到越多經驗。」

「你說得可能都對。」稻草人說：「可是除非你給我頭腦,不然我不會快樂。」

　　假巫師仔細地看看他。

　　「好吧。」他說著,嘆了一口氣。「我說過,我不是什麼魔術師,可是如果你明天早上再來找我,我可以把腦子塞進你的頭,只不過我沒辦法告訴你要怎麼使用,你必須自己去想辦法。」

　　「噢,謝謝,謝謝你!」稻草人大叫:「我會想辦法去使用,絕不害怕!」

　　「那我的勇氣呢?」獅子著急地問。

　　「你的勇氣夠多了,這我很確定。」奧茲回答:「你只需要對自己有信心。每個人在面對危險時都會害怕。真正的勇氣是在害怕時仍然能面對危險,而在這方面你已經有很多勇氣了。」

　　「也許我有,可是我還是很害怕。」獅子說:「除非你給我那種可以使人忘記害怕的勇氣,不然我不會快樂。」

　　「好吧,明天我會給你那種勇氣。」奧茲回答。

　　「我的心呢?」錫樵夫問。

　　「哎,說到那個。」奧茲回答:「我覺得你想要一顆心是不對的。心使大部分的人不快樂。但願你能夠明白,你沒有心是很幸運的事。」

　　「那要看你是怎麼想的。」錫樵夫說:「對我來說,如果你給我一顆心,我就會忍受所有的不愉快,一點都不抱怨。」

「好吧。」奧茲溫順地說：「明天來找我，你就會得到一顆心。我已經扮演巫師很多年，大可以再多演一會兒。」

　　「該我了。」桃樂絲說：「我要怎麼回堪薩斯？」

　　「這我們必須想一想。」小矮人說：「給我兩、三天來思考這個問題，我會想個法子帶妳越過沙漠。在這同時，我會把你們當成貴賓一般看待，你們住在宮殿裡時，我的人民會侍候你們，再小的事情也會為你們做。我只希望你們用一件事來回報我的幫助，雖然這個幫助並不大。你們必須保守秘密，不告訴任何人我是個騙子。」

　　他們同意不透露知道的事情，然後興高采烈地回到自己的房間。連桃樂絲都希望她所稱呼的「那偉大、可怕的騙子」想得出送她回堪薩斯的方法，如果真是這樣，所有的一切她都可以原諒。

第 16 章

大騙子的神奇技倆

　　隔天早上，稻草人對朋友說：「恭喜我吧，我要去找奧茲，終於可以得到腦子了。等我回來時，就會和其他人一樣聰明。」

　　「我一直都喜歡你現在的樣子。」桃樂絲只是這麼說。

　　「妳真好心，會去喜歡一個稻草人。」他回答：「可是等妳見到我的新頭腦產生了不起的思想時，妳對我的評價會更高。」他以愉快的聲音對所有人說了再見，就走到寶座宮敲門。

　　「進來。」奧茲說。

　　稻草人走進去，看到小矮人坐在窗邊，正在沉思。

　　「我來拿我的腦子。」稻草人說著，有點不自在。

　　「噢，對，請坐在那張椅子上。」奧茲回答：「我得先拿下你的頭，才能將你的腦子塞在適合的地方。這你可要體諒一下。」

　　「沒關係。」稻草人說：「你可以把我的頭拿下來，只要你放回去的是更好的頭。」

巫師取下他的頭，掏空裡面的稻草，然後進入後面的房間，拿來一些麥麩，裡面混有大頭針和縫衣針。他把東西搖勻，塞進稻草人的腦裡，剩下的空隙就用稻草塞滿，以便固定。接著他把那顆頭接回稻草人的身體，跟他說：「從此以後，你就是偉大的人了，因為我給了你很多新麥麩腦子。」

　　稻草人最大的願望實現了，他覺得好高興，也很驕傲，他熱情地謝了謝奧茲，回到朋友那裡。

　　桃樂絲好奇地看了看他。他的頭頂因為腦子而脹大。

　　「你覺得怎樣？」她問。

　　「覺得自己好聰明。」他認真地回答：「等我習慣了這個腦子，就可以什麼都知道了。」

　　「為什麼那些針從你的頭突出來呢？」錫樵夫問。

　　「那表示他的腦子夠敏銳。」獅子說。

　　「我要去找奧茲拿我的心了。」錫樵夫說。他來到寶座宮敲門。

　　「進來。」奧茲大喊。錫樵夫走進去說：「我來拿我的心了。」

　　「好。」小矮人說：「可是我要先在你的胸膛挖一個洞，才能把心放在正確的地方。希望這不會傷害你。」

　　「噢，不會的。」錫樵夫說：「我一點感覺也沒有。」

　　奧茲就拿出一個錫剪，在錫樵夫的左胸剪出一個小方洞，然後從抽屜櫃拿出一個漂亮的心，那是用絲布塞進木屑做成的。

「這是不是很漂亮？」他問。

「確實很漂亮！」錫樵夫回答，非常高興。「可是這是一顆善心嗎？」

「是的，非常和善！」奧茲回答，把心放進樵夫的胸膛，再把方形的錫片放回去，仔細焊接剪除的部分。

「好了。」他說：「現在你有了能令任何人感到驕傲的心了。很抱歉讓你的胸膛出現修補的痕跡。」

「不用介意這個痕跡。」快樂的樵夫大聲說：「我很感謝你，永遠不會忘記你的恩德。」

「別提了。」奧茲回答。

錫樵夫回到朋友那裡，朋友都祝他這份幸運能為他帶來快樂。

現在換獅子走到寶座宮敲門了。

「進來。」奧茲說。

「我是為我的勇氣來的。」獅子走進來說。

「好，我會給你的。」奧茲回答。

他走到一個櫥櫃，從高高的架子上取下一個綠色的方瓶，把裡面的東西倒進雕得很漂亮的金綠色盤子裡，擺在膽小獅的前面。獅子嗅一嗅，好像不怎麼喜歡，巫師就開口說：「喝下去。」

「這是什麼？」獅子問。

「如果進到你的體內，它就是勇氣。當然，你知道勇氣總是在人的體內，所以要等到你吞下去，才可以真的把它叫做勇氣。建議你儘快喝下它。」

　　獅子不再遲疑，把盤子裡的東西喝光。

　　「你現在覺得怎樣？」奧茲問。

　　「充滿了勇氣。」獅子回答，然後快樂地回到朋友那裡，告訴他們自己的好運。

　　奧茲單獨一個人帶著微笑想著，他順利帶給稻草人、錫樵夫和獅子自以為需要的東西。「當所有人都要我做到誰都知道不可能做到的事情時，我要如何不當騙子呢？要讓稻草人、獅子和樵夫快樂很容易，因為他們想像我無所不能。可是要帶桃樂絲回堪薩斯可不能只有想像力，我確定自己不知道該怎麼做。」他說。

第 17 章

氣球升起

　　整整三天，桃樂絲都沒有聽到奧茲的消息。她的朋友都好快樂，也很滿足。稻草人跟他們說，他的頭腦裡有一些美妙的思想，可是他不肯說出來，因為他知道只有他自己能夠了解。錫樵夫走路時感覺得到心在胸膛裡撲撲跳動，他跟桃樂絲說，他發現這顆心比還是肉身時擁有的那一顆還要溫柔善良。獅子也宣稱在這世界上他什麼也不怕，很樂意面對大批人或十多隻凶狠的卡厲達。

　　因此這個小團體的每個成員都很滿意，除了桃樂絲，她比以前更想回到堪薩斯了。

　　到了第四天，奧茲召見她了，讓她好興奮。進入寶座宮時，奧茲愉快地說：「坐下，親愛的，我想我有辦法讓妳離開這個國家了。」

　　「也能回到堪薩斯嗎？」她急切地問。

　　「嗯，我不確定是不是可以回堪薩斯。」奧茲說：「因為我一點都不知道那地方在哪裡。可是先穿過沙漠，然後要找到妳回家的路就簡單了。」

「我要怎麼穿過沙漠呢？」她問。

「我來告訴妳我的想法。」奧茲說：「妳知道的，我是坐著氣球來到這個國家，而妳是被龍捲風帶著穿過空中，所以我相信飛行是穿過沙漠最好的辦法。不過我沒有能力製造龍捲風，可是我仔細想過，我相信我可以做個氣球。」

「怎麼做？」桃樂絲問。

「氣球是用絲綢做成的，外面塗上膠，把氣體封在裡頭。這座宮殿有許多絲綢，所以要做一個氣球並不困難。可是整個國家都沒有可以讓氣球浮起來的煤氣。」

「如果不能浮起來，對我們就沒有用了。」桃樂絲說。

「沒錯，可是有另一個方法可以讓它浮起來，那就是讓它充滿熱空氣。熱空氣不比煤體好，因為如果空氣變冷了，氣球就會掉進沙漠，我們也會迷失方向。」

「我們！」女孩大叫：「你要跟我去？」

「是的，當然。」奧茲回答：「我厭倦當騙子了。如果我走出宮殿，我的人民馬上會發現我不是巫師，一定會怪我欺騙他們，所以我必須整天都關在房間裡，這樣子實在很悶。我寧可和妳回到堪薩斯，再去找個馬戲團待著。」

「我很高興有你做伴。」桃樂絲說。

「謝謝妳。現在，如果妳幫我把絲綢縫起來，我們就可以開始做氣球了。」他回答。

桃樂絲就拿起針線，一等到奧茲把絲綢剪成適當的形狀，就靈巧地把布塊縫起來。先是一塊淡綠色的絲綢，接著是一塊深綠色的，再來就是翡翠綠，因為奧茲喜歡讓氣球有不同的色調。他們花了三天時間把所有絲綢縫起來，完成一個大袋子，長度超過六公尺。

奧茲在內側塗上一層薄膠，使袋子不會漏氣，然後宣布氣球做好了。

「不過我們還需要一個可以乘坐的籃子。」他說。於是他叫有綠鬍鬚的士兵拿來一個大洗衣籃，用許多繩子綁在氣球底下。

一切都準備好時，奧茲傳話給人民說，他要去拜訪住在雲裡面的巫師大哥。這個消息很快就傳遍了整個城市，每個人都跑過來看這個壯觀的場面。

奧茲下令把氣球帶到宮殿前面，人民都很好奇地盯著它。錫樵夫已經砍了一大堆木頭，現在就用木頭生起了火。奧茲將氣球底部放在火堆上面，讓絲質袋子包住升起的熱空氣。氣球漸漸膨脹，升到空中，最後只有籃子還能接觸地面。

奧茲爬進籃子裡，以響亮的聲音告訴所有人民：「我現在就要出發去訪問了。我不在時，由稻草人來領導你們。我命令你們要像服從我一樣服從他。」

氣球這時正在和綁在地上的繩子拔河，因為裡面的空氣是熱的，重量比空氣輕很多。如果沒有繩子用力拉著，氣球就會浮上天空。

「過來，桃樂絲！」巫師大叫：「快一點，不然氣球要飛走了。」

「我到處都找不到托托。」桃樂絲回答，她可不想把小狗留下來。托托跑到群眾裡，對著一隻小貓吠叫，桃樂絲好不容易才找到牠。她抱起托托，跑向氣球。

她只剩幾步路，奧茲也伸出雙手，想要把她迎進籃子，卻聽到啪的一聲，繩子斷了，氣球沒有載到她就升到空中。

「回來！」她尖叫著：「我也要去！」

「我沒辦法，親愛的。」奧茲大喊：「再見！」

「再——見！」每個人都叫出聲，所有眼睛都往上盯著巫師搭乘的籃子，看著它越升越高，進入空中。

那是他們最後一次看到那神奇的奧茲巫師，雖然我們知道，他現在很可能已經安全抵達奧瑪哈。可是人民都很懷念他，對彼此說著：「奧茲永遠是我們的朋友。他在這裡時，為我們建造美麗的翡翠城，現在他離開了，卻留下聰明的稻草人來統治我們。」

許多日子過去，他們仍然在為神奇巫師的離開悲嘆，那種失落感是無法彌補的。

第 18 章

前往南方

　　回去堪薩斯的希望破滅時，桃樂絲哭得很傷心，可是她重新把整件事想了一次，又很高興沒有隨著汽球升空，也為失去奧茲覺得難過，她的朋友也跟她一樣。

　　稻草人現在是翡翠城的統治者，雖然他不是巫師，人民還是以他為榮。他們說：「這是因為世界上其他城市的統治者沒有一個是填充的人。」就他們目前所知，他們說得對極了。

　　汽球帶著奧茲升空後，當天早上，四名旅行者在寶座宮會商。稻草人坐在大寶座上，其他人尊敬地站在他面前。

　　「我們的運氣不錯。」新統治者說：「因為這座宮殿和翡翠城屬於我們，我們可以想做什麼就做什麼。記得不久以前，我還在農田的竿子上，現在卻是這座美麗城市的統治者，我對自己的運氣很滿意。」

　　「我也很高興有了新的心，那真的是這世界上我唯一想要的東西。」錫樵夫說。

　　「至於我，我和任何野獸一樣勇敢，即使沒有比較勇

第18章

敢，我還是很滿足。」獅子說得很謙虛。

「如果桃樂絲能甘於住在翡翠城，我們就能快樂地在一起了。」稻草人繼續說。

「可是我不想住這裡，我想去堪薩斯，和艾姆嬸嬸和亨利叔叔住在一起。」桃樂絲叫道。

「那該怎麼辦呢？」樵夫問。

稻草人開始動腦筋，努力到針都從腦子裡突出來了。最後他說：「怎麼不召喚有翅膀的猴子，請牠們帶妳穿過沙漠？」

「我怎麼沒有想到呢！」桃樂絲歡喜地說：「就這麼做，我馬上去拿金帽。」

她把金帽拿到寶座宮，說出咒語，一群有翅膀的猴子就從敞開的窗戶飛進來，站在她面前。

「這是妳第二次召喚我們，妳要我們做什麼？」猴王在小女孩面前鞠躬說。

「我想飛到堪薩斯。」桃樂絲說。

可是猴王搖搖頭。

「沒辦法。」牠說：「我們只屬於這個國家，不能離開這裡。從來沒有一隻有翅膀的猴子去過堪薩斯，我想以後也不會有，因為牠們不屬於那裡。我們很樂意用我們的力量為妳效勞，可是我們不能穿越沙漠。再見。」

猴王又行了個禮，然後張開翅膀，從窗戶飛走，後面跟著整個猴群。

桃樂絲失望得快要哭出來了。

「我白白浪費了金帽的魔力，有翅膀的猴子竟然不能幫助我。」她說。

「這真是太糟糕了！」有著溫柔心腸的樵夫說。

稻草人又開始思考，他的頭脹得好可怕，桃樂絲擔心它會爆開。

「我們叫那個綠鬍鬚的士兵過來，聽聽他的意見。」他說。

士兵就被叫進寶座宮。他看起來很提心吊膽，因為奧茲還在時，他從來沒有獲准跨進那道門。

「這小女孩想要穿越沙漠，該怎麼做才好？」稻草人問士兵。

「我不知道，因為除了奧茲自己之外，從來沒有人越過沙漠。」

「有沒有人可以幫助我？」桃樂絲認真地問。

「格琳達也許可以。」他建議。

「格琳達是誰？」稻草人問。

「南方的女巫。她是所有女巫中法力最強的，統治夸德林人。而且她的城堡就在沙漠旁邊，也許會知道怎麼穿越。」

「我要怎麼去她的城堡？」桃樂絲問。

「那條路直通南方，可是聽說對旅行者很危險。森林裡有野獸，還有一群古怪的人，不喜歡陌生人穿越他們的領

地。這就是為什麼沒有夸德林人來過翡翠城的原因。」

士兵離開後，稻草人說：「雖然很危險，但是看來桃樂絲最好出發去南方找格琳達幫忙。因為桃樂絲繼續留在這裡的話，顯然永遠回不了堪薩斯了。」

「這件事你好好想過了。」錫樵夫說。

「是的。」稻草人說。

「我跟桃樂絲去。」獅子說：「因為你的城市我住膩了，我想念森林和原野。我是隻野獸，你知道的，更何況桃樂絲需要保護。」

「那倒是真的，我的斧頭可以為她效力，所以我也要陪她去南方。」樵夫說。

「我們什麼時候出發？」稻草人問。

「你也要去嗎？」他們驚訝地問。

「當然。多虧了桃樂絲，我才會得到腦子。她把我從玉米田裡的竿子上放下來，帶我來翡翠城。我的好運都是她給的，我絕不會離開她，除非她永遠回到堪薩斯了。」

「謝謝你們。」桃樂絲感激地說：「你們都對我這麼好，可是我想越快出發越好。」

「我們明天早上就走。」稻草人說：「我們現在就去準備吧，因為這段旅程會很漫長。」

第 19 章

戰鬥樹的攻擊

　　隔天早上，桃樂絲跟美麗的綠女孩吻別，所有人都和有綠鬍鬚的士兵握手，士兵一路陪著他們走到城門。守門人再次見到他們時，覺得很奇怪，他們竟然想要離開美麗的城市，出去招引新的麻煩。可是他立刻解開他們的眼鏡，放回綠盒子，祝福他們一路平安。

　　「你現在是我們的統治者了，所以要儘快回來。」他對稻草人說。

　　「當然，只要有這個可能，可是我要先送桃樂絲回家。」稻草人回答。

　　守門人打開外牆的城門，他們就往前走，展開新的旅程。

　　陽光普照，這群夥伴朝著南方前進，每個人都精神奕奕，一起談笑。桃樂絲再度充滿回家的希望，稻草人和錫樵夫很高興能幫忙她；至於獅子，牠愉快地嗅嗅新鮮空氣，尾巴快樂地搖擺，因為又能夠來到原野；而托托則在他們四周跑來跑去，追逐飛蛾和蝴蝶，一直興奮地吠叫。

「都市的生活一點都不適合我，」獅子說著，與大家一起快步走。「自從去到那裡，我就減了許多肌肉，現在我很希望有機會給其他野獸看看我變得多麼勇敢。」

他們回頭看翡翠城最後一眼。見到的是集結在綠牆後面的高樓和尖塔，而聳立在所有建築上方的是奧茲宮殿的尖頂和圓蓋。

「奧茲畢竟不是個壞巫師。」樵夫說著，感覺到他的心在胸膛裡撲撲跳動。

「他知道怎麼給我腦子，而且給的是相當不錯的腦子。」稻草人說。

「如果奧茲也吃了一點他給我的勇氣，早就是個勇敢的人了。」獅子接著說。

桃樂絲沒有吭聲。奧茲給她的承諾並沒有實現，可是他盡力了，所以桃樂絲原諒了他。如他所說的，他是個壞巫師，卻是個好人。

他們在第一天穿過從翡翠城四周延伸的翠綠田野和鮮麗的花叢，當晚就睡在草地上，頭上只有星光籠罩，可是他們睡得很好。

到了早上，他們繼續往前走，來到一座濃密的森林。沒有路可以繞過去，因為左右兩邊似乎只有一望無際的森林，而且他們擔心會迷路，不敢改變行走的方向，只好去尋找最容易穿越森林的地方。

稻草人走在最前面，終於發現一棵大樹長著廣闊的枝

椏，有空間讓這群人穿過去。他走向那棵樹，可是來到第一串樹枝底下時，那些樹枝彎下來纏住他，一下子就把他舉到空中拋出去，讓他一頭栽在同伴的身上。

這並沒有傷到稻草人，但是嚇到了他。桃樂絲扶他起來時，他好像摔得頭暈眼花。

「林子裡有別的空間。」獅子叫著。

「我先來試試，反正被丟出去也不會受傷。」稻草人說著，走向另一棵樹，可是那邊的樹枝立刻抓住他，把他丟回來。

「好奇怪，我們該怎麼辦？」桃樂絲驚叫。

「這些樹好像決定要對付我們，阻止我們往前走。」獅子說。

「我要自己來試試看。」錫樵夫說著，扛起斧頭，大步走向對稻草人很粗暴的第一棵樹。一根粗枝彎下來要抓他時，樵夫用力一砍，樹枝就斷成兩截。那棵樹的所有樹枝都開始抖動，好像很痛苦，錫樵夫就安全地從底下穿過。

「來吧！」他對其他人大叫：「快一點！」

他們都跑過去，平安穿過那棵樹底下，只有托托被一根小樹枝抓住，被甩得哀哀叫。可是樵夫馬上就砍斷了那根樹枝，救出小狗。

其他森林裡的樹都沒有試圖阻撓他們，所以他們認為只有第一排樹可以把枝椏彎下來，那些樹可能是森林的警察，具有將陌生人趕走的魔力。

四名旅伴輕鬆地穿過那些樹，來到森林深處的邊緣，非常驚訝地發現前面有一道高牆，似乎是用白瓷做的。撫摸起來和盤子的表面一樣光滑，比他們的個子還要高。

「我們現在該怎麼辦？」桃樂絲問。

「我來做梯子，我們一定要爬過這道牆。」錫樵夫說。

第 20 章

精美的陶瓷村

　　樵夫用他在森林裡找到的木頭做梯子時，桃樂絲躺下來睡覺，因為走長路讓她累壞了，獅子也蜷臥著睡著了，托托則躺在牠旁邊。

　　稻草人看著錫樵夫工作，對他說：「我想不出為什麼這裡會有牆，也不知道那是用什麼做的。」

　　「不要想了，也不要為牆煩惱，我們爬過去就知道另一邊是什麼了。」錫樵夫回答。

　　過了一會兒，梯子做好了，看起來很粗糙，可是錫樵夫確定它很堅固，可以應付他們的需求。稻草人叫醒桃樂絲、獅子和托托，跟他們說梯子準備好了。稻草人先爬上梯子，可是他很笨拙，桃樂絲必須緊跟在後，以免他摔下去。頭一伸到牆上，稻草人就說：「天啊！」

　　「繼續爬呀。」桃樂絲叫著。

　　稻草人就再往上爬，然後在牆上坐下。桃樂絲把頭探出來時，也大喊：「天啊！」跟稻草人的反應一樣。

　　接著輪到托托，牠立刻叫出聲，可是桃樂絲使牠安靜。

下一個是獅子，錫樵夫殿後。他們倆一從牆上望去，馬上就大叫：「我的天！」他們成一排坐在牆上俯視，看到一幅奇景。

　　眼前是一大片田野，地面像大盤子的底部一樣光滑明亮、白皙。上面散布著許多完全用陶瓷做成的房屋，漆上最鮮艷的顏色。這些房屋相當小，最大的也才到桃樂絲的腰部。另外還有美麗的小穀倉，四周圍著陶瓷柵欄，許多陶瓷做的牛、羊、馬、豬和雞隻成群地站在那裡。

　　擠牛奶的女工與牧羊女穿著顏色鮮艷的緊身上衣，長袍上都是金色的斑點。公主們身上穿的是最華麗的金、銀、紫色連衣裙，牧羊人穿的則是及膝的短褲，上面有粉紅、黃和藍色條紋，鞋子上有金色飾釦。至於王子們頭上有珠寶鑲的王冠，身穿貂皮長袍和綢緞緊身上衣。滑稽的小丑戴著打褶的袍子，臉頰上塗著紅圈圈，戴著高而尖的帽子。而最奇怪的是，這些人都是陶瓷做的，連他們的衣服也是，而且個子很小，最高的也只到桃樂絲的膝蓋。

　　起初都沒有人注意這些旅行者，只有一隻頭超大的紫色小瓷狗跑到牆邊，以纖細的聲音對他們吠叫，然後就跑開了。

　　「我們要怎麼下去？」桃樂絲問。

　　他們覺得梯子太重，拉不上來，稻草人就從牆上跳下去，其他人直接跳到他身上，以免堅硬的地面傷了他們的腳。當然他們都極盡地避免落在他的頭上，才不會被針刺到。所有人都安全落地之後，他們扶起身體已被壓扁的稻草人，拍拍他的稻草，讓他恢復原狀。

「我們一定要穿過這個奇怪的地方，才能去到另一邊。」桃樂絲說：「因為除了往正南方走，走其他的路線都不明智。」

他們開始通過瓷人的土地，他們最先遇到的是正在為一隻瓷牛擠奶的瓷製擠牛奶女工。他們走近那隻牛時，牛突然踢了一下，把凳子、桶子，甚至擠牛奶女工都踢倒了，他們全部摔到瓷製的地面上，發出很大的匡噹聲。

桃樂絲很震驚地看到那隻牛斷了一隻腳，那個桶子也破成碎片掉在地上，而那可憐女工的左手肘也出現了裂痕。

「哎呀！」擠牛奶女工氣得大叫：「看看你們做的好事！我的牛斷了腳，我必須帶牠去修理店，請師傅把腳黏上去。你們幹嘛來這裡嚇我的牛啊？」

對於這場意外，桃樂絲覺得很難過。

「我們在這裡一定要很小心。」好心腸的錫樵夫說：「不然我們會傷到這些美麗的小人兒，使他們無法復原。」

再往前走了一會兒，桃樂絲遇到衣著最光鮮的小公主，她看到這群陌生人時突然停下腳步，然後就跑走了。

桃樂絲想要多看看那個公主，就跟在後面跑，那瓷女孩卻大叫說：「不要追我！不要追我！」

她細小的聲音好像很害怕，桃樂絲就停下來說：「為什麼不行？」

「因為我跑的時候，可能會跌倒而摔傷。」公主停下腳步回答，保持安全的距離。

　　「妳不能修補嗎？」桃樂絲問。

　　「噢，可以，可是妳知道的，修過以後就不會這麼美了。」公主回答。

　　「我想也是。」桃樂絲說。

　　「那是小丑先生，我們的一個小丑。」瓷小姐說：「他總是想要倒立，把自己打破太多次了，所以修補過一百個地方，看起來一點都不漂亮。他走過來了，你們可以好好看看他。」

　　果然有個愉快的小丑往他們這邊走來，桃樂絲看他雖然穿著紅、黃和綠色的美麗衣服，卻全身都是亂七八糟的裂痕，可以明顯看出有許多地方都修補過。

　　小丑把手伸進口袋，先是鼓起臉頰，對他們傲慢地點點頭，然後說：

　　「美麗的小姐，妳為何盯著可憐的老小丑先生？妳是這麼的僵硬呆板，好像吞了一張撲克牌一樣！」

　　「先生，請安靜！」公主說：「你沒看到這裡有一些陌生人，必須尊重他們？」

　　「哦，我希望這就是尊重。」小丑說著，馬上倒立。

　　「不要理會小丑先生。」公主對桃樂絲說：「他的腦袋已經裂得很厲害，因此變笨了。」

　　「噢，我一點都不介意。」桃樂絲繼續說：「可是妳

好美啊，我好喜歡妳。妳肯不肯讓我帶妳回堪薩斯，把妳放在艾姆嬸嬸的壁爐架上？我可以用籃子裝著妳走。」

「那會讓我很不快樂。」瓷公主回答：「妳看，我們在自己的家鄉過著滿足的生活，可以自由走動、說話。可是一被帶走，我們的關節就會馬上變硬，只能筆直地站著，看起來漂亮而已。當然人們希望把我們擺在爐架、櫃子和客廳的桌子上，可是我們在故鄉的生活會愉快許多。」

「我一點都不想讓妳過得不快樂。」桃樂絲叫道：「既然這樣，我就只能跟妳說再見了。」

「再見。」公主回答。

他們謹慎地穿過陶瓷村。小動物和所有人都驚慌地避開他們，生怕這些陌生人把他們摔壞。過了大約一個小時，這群旅行者就來到了這個村落的另一頭，抵達另一道瓷牆。

這種牆沒有第一道那麼高，他們踩在獅子的背上，就可以勉強爬上去。接著獅子併起四隻腳，跳到牆上，尾巴卻在這時將一個瓷教堂翻倒，使它摔得粉碎。

「真糟糕。」桃樂絲說：「可是我們已經很幸運了，除了摔壞一條牛腿和一個教堂，沒有對這些小人兒造成更多傷害。他們實在是太脆弱了！」

「他們真的是。」稻草人說：「我很慶幸自己是稻草做的，不會那麼容易損壞。這世界上竟還有比當稻草人還要糟的事！」

第 21 章

獅子成為獸王

　　他們在矮樹叢中走了一段又長又累的路，來到另一座森林，那裡的樹木比之前見過的還要高大、古老。

　　「這個森林讓人覺得好舒服。」獅子說著，高興地四處張望。「我沒有見過比這裡還要漂亮的地方。」

　　「好像有點陰暗。」稻草人說。

　　「一點也不會。」獅子回答：「我希望這一生都能住在這裡。看看腳下的乾葉子有多麼柔軟，還有附在這些老樹上的苔蘚是多麼青翠厚實。當然這是所有野獸所希望的最美好的住處了。」

　　「也許現在就有野獸在森林裡。」桃樂絲說。

　　「我猜有。」獅子回應說：「可是沒看見任何一隻。」

　　他們穿過森林，直到天黑了，沒辦法再走下去。桃樂絲和托托、獅子躺下睡覺，樵夫和稻草人則照常在旁邊守候。

　　天亮時，他們又出發了。還沒有走多遠，他們就聽到低沉的隆隆聲，好像有許多野生動物在咆哮。托托嗚嗚叫了幾聲，可是其他人都不害怕，繼續沿著前人踩出來的小徑走。來到了樹林中的空曠地帶，那裡聚集著幾百隻各種各樣的野獸。有老虎、大象、熊、狼和狐狸，以及自然歷史中的其他動物。在那一刻桃樂絲覺得好害怕，可是獅子解釋說，那些動物是在開會，從牠們的嘶吼和咆哮可以判斷出，牠們遇到大麻煩了。

獅子說話時，有些野獸留意到牠，龐大的群眾就立刻安靜下來，好像中了魔法似的。體型最大的老虎過來對獅子行禮，開口說：「歡迎你，獸王！你來得正好，可以幫我們對抗敵人，為所有森林的動物帶來和平。」

「你們遇到什麼麻煩了？」獅子平靜地說。

「我們受到了威脅。」老虎回答：「對方是凶惡的敵人，最近才來到這個森林。牠是個無比龐大的怪獸，像隻大蜘蛛，身體有象那麼大，腳和樹幹一樣長。牠有八條長腿，在森林中爬行時，會用一隻腳捕捉動物，把牠送進嘴裡，就像蜘蛛吃蒼蠅那樣。只要這隻凶惡的怪物活著一天，我們一天就不得安寧。你過來時，我們正在開會討論要怎麼保護自己。」

獅子想了一會兒。「森林裡有其他獅子嗎？」牠問。

「沒有，本來有一些，但是怪獸把牠們都吃掉了。而且牠們沒有一隻像你這麼大，這麼勇敢。」

「如果我消滅了你們的敵人，你們會向我低頭，當森林之王一樣順從嗎？」獅子問道。

「我們非常樂意。」老虎回答，其他野獸也都發出同樣響亮的吼聲：「我們願意！」

「現在那隻蜘蛛在哪裡？」獅子問。

「在那邊的橡樹林。」老虎說，用前掌指著。

「請保護好我的朋友們，我現在就去擊敗那怪獸。」獅子說。

牠跟同伴說了聲再見，驕傲地大步走去迎戰敵人。

獅子發現那巨大的蜘蛛時，牠正躺著睡覺，看起來好醜，獅子根本就瞧不起牠。蜘蛛的腳果然像老虎所說的那麼長，牠的身體覆蓋著粗黑的毛髮，還有個大嘴巴，裡面有一排三十公分長的獠牙，可是牠的頭與矮胖的身軀是由細得像蜂腰的脖子連接。這讓獅子想到了攻擊這個怪物的妙方，知道趁牠睡覺時攻擊會比牠醒來時容易，因此牠用力跳起來，直接撲到怪物的背上，然後用帶有利爪的沉重腳掌一揮，把蜘蛛的頭從身體上打掉。獅子跳下來，看著蜘蛛的長腳慢慢停止扭動，確定牠已經死了。

獅子回到空地上，森林的野獸都在那裡等著。牠驕傲地宣布：「你們不必再害怕那個敵人了。」

野獸們都向獅子行禮，稱牠為王，獅子則答應說，等桃樂絲安全回到堪薩斯，就會立刻回來統領牠們。

第 22 章
夸德林村

　　四個旅行者安全地穿過其餘的森林，從陰暗中走出來時，看到眼前是一座陡峭的小山，從山頂到山腳都覆蓋著岩石。

　　「那一定很難爬。」稻草人說：「可是無論如何我們一定要穿過那座山。」

　　他在前面領路，其他人跟在後面。他們快抵達第一塊岩石時，聽到一道粗獷的聲音大叫：「回去！」

　　「你是誰？」稻草人問。有一顆頭從岩石上面探出來，然後同樣的聲音又說了：「這座山是我們的，我們不准任何人經過。」

　　「可是我們一定要經過這裡，因為我們要去夸德林村。」稻草人說。

　　「可是你們不能！」那聲音回答後，有個他們見過的最奇怪的人從岩石後面走出來。

　　他長得矮小又肥碩，有一顆平頂的大頭，由一條滿是皺紋的粗脖子支撐。可是他一條手臂也沒有。看到這一點，稻

122

草人就不害怕了,因為這個人沒有能力阻止他們上山。他說:「我很抱歉不能照你的話做,不論你高不高興,我們都一定要經過你們的山。」他大膽地往前走。

那人的頭快得像閃電一樣射出去,脖子不斷延伸,直到平坦的頭頂擊中稻草人,使他栽下來,一路翻滾到山下。那顆頭和之前同樣迅速地回到身上,一邊發出刺耳的笑聲一邊說:「這可不像你所以為的那麼容易!」

另一邊的岩石傳來喧鬧的齊笑聲,桃樂絲看到幾百個沒有手臂的鎚子頭站在山坡上,每塊岩石後面都有一個。

獅子被這陣由稻草人的災難所引發的笑聲激怒,牠發出怒吼,產生打雷似的回聲,然後往山上衝去。

又有一顆頭迅速射出，大獅子就好像被大砲擊中一樣滾下山坡。

　　桃樂絲跑下山扶稻草人站起來，獅子也跑到她的身邊，覺得渾身痠痛。牠說：「沒辦法對抗這些會射擊的頭，沒有人抵擋得了。」

　　「那我們該怎麼辦？」她問。

　　「召喚有翅膀的猴子吧。」錫樵夫建議：「妳還有一次召喚牠們的權利。」

　　「好。」她答道，戴上那頂金帽，說出神奇的咒語。猴子來得和之前一樣快，不到幾分鐘，就全部站在她前面。

　　「妳有什麼吩咐？」猴王深深鞠躬說。

　　「帶我們翻過這座山到夸德林村。」女孩回答。

　　「遵命！」猴王說著，有翅膀的猴子就把四名旅行者和托托用手臂架起，帶著他們飛起來。經過山上時，鎚子頭都氣憤地大喊大叫，把頭高高地射到空中，卻打不到有翅膀的猴子。猴子們帶著桃樂絲和她的同伴安全地越過山頂，將他們放在美麗的夸德林村。

　　「這是妳最後一次召喚我們。」猴王對桃樂絲說：「所以再見了，祝妳好運。」

　　「再見，非常謝謝你們。」女孩回答。猴群飛到空中，一轉眼就消失蹤影。

　　夸德林似乎是富裕而快樂的地方，有一畦畦成熟的穀物，其中交錯著舖造良好的道路，還有美麗的小溪流，上面橫跨著堅固的橋樑。欄杆和房屋、橋樑都塗著鮮紅色，就像溫基人所塗的黃色和曼其金人的藍色。夸德林人長得矮矮胖胖，看起來圓滾滾的，和藹可親，全都穿著紅衣服，與綠色的草地和黃色的穀子形成強烈的對比。

猴子把這群旅行者放在一座農莊附近，他們四人就走過去敲門。一個農婦出來開門，桃樂絲向她要東西吃，婦人就讓他們吃了頓豐盛的晚餐，附帶三種蛋糕和四種餅乾，還有一碗牛奶給托托。

「這裡離格琳達的城堡有多遠？」女孩問。

「這條路不好。」農婦說：「走去南方的那條路，你們很快就能抵達。」

他們謝謝這個好心的婦人，恢復了精神，就走過田野，穿越精巧的橋，就看到一座美麗的城堡。門前有三個年輕女孩，身穿漂亮的、金色鑲邊的紅色制服。桃樂絲走過去時，其中一個問她：「妳們來這個南方國度做什麼？」

「我們是來見統治這裡的好女巫，妳可以帶我去見她嗎？」桃樂絲回答。

「告訴我妳的名字，我就去問格琳達是否要接見妳。」他們分別報上名，女兵就進到城堡裡面。過了一會兒，她回來說，桃樂絲可以馬上和同伴進去。

第 23 章

好女巫實現桃樂絲的願望

　　他們先被帶到城堡裡的一間房間，桃樂絲在那裡洗洗臉、梳梳頭，獅子抖落鬃毛上的塵土，稻草人把自己拍打成最好看的形狀，錫樵夫則是把他的錫皮磨亮，在關節抹油。

　　他們都整理得體面之後，就跟著女兵進入一個房大間，格琳達女巫就坐在一個紅寶石鑲成的寶座上。

　　在他們眼中，她又漂亮又年輕。她的頭髮是鮮豔的紅色，滑順的捲髮垂到肩上。她的衣服是純白色的，可是眼睛是藍的，親切地望著小女孩。

　　「孩子，我可以為妳做什麼？」她問。

　　桃樂絲把她所有的事情告訴她：龍捲風把她帶到奧茲國、她如何找到同伴，以及他們所遇到的神奇經歷。

　　「我現在最大的願望是回到堪薩斯，因為艾姆嬸嬸一定會以為我發生了不幸，那會讓她很悲傷，而除非今年的收穫比去年好，不然亨利叔叔也會承受不了。」

　　格琳達靠過來親吻這可愛小女孩往上仰的甜美面龐。

　　「祝福妳。」她慈愛地說：「我一定可以告訴妳回堪薩斯的路。」她接著說：「可是，如果我告訴妳，妳一定要給我那頂金帽。」

「我很樂意！」桃樂絲大叫。「事實上，帽子現在對我也沒有用了，妳有了它，就可以對有翅膀的猴子們下令三次。」

「我確實只需要牠們服務三次。」格達琳帶著微笑說。

桃樂絲把金帽拿給她，女巫就對稻草人說：「桃樂絲離開以後，你要做什麼？」

「我要回翡翠城，因為奧茲要我統治那座城，而且那裡的人民喜歡我。我唯一擔心的是要怎麼越過鎚子頭的山。」

「靠著金帽，我可以命令有翅膀的猴子帶你回翡翠城，不然讓那些人失去這麼好的統治者是很可惜。」格琳達說。

「我真的很好嗎？」稻草人問。

「你很特別。」格琳達回答。

她轉向錫樵夫問道：「桃樂絲離開這個國家以後，你會怎麼樣？」

他倚在斧頭上，想了一會兒，然後說：「溫基人對我很好，在壞女巫死掉時，他們希望我來統治他們。我很喜歡溫基人，如果可以回西方，我想做的事就是永遠統領他們。」

「我對有翅膀的猴子下的第二個命令就是帶你安全回到溫基國。」格琳達說：「你的頭腦看起來也許沒有比稻草人大，可是你真的比他機靈，只要你磨得很亮。我相信你可以聰明地把溫基人治理得很好。」

接著女巫轉向毛茸茸的大獅子，問牠說：「等桃樂絲回家以後，你要怎麼辦？」

　　「越過鎚子頭的山，有一座古老的森林，住在那裡的所有野獸們已經認我為牠們的首領。如果我可以回到那座森林，就可以在那裡快樂地過一輩子。」

　　「我對有翅膀的猴子下的第三個命令就是帶你回那座森林。」格琳達說：「而把金帽的魔力用完之後，我會把它還給猴王，牠們從此以後就自由了。」

　　稻草人和錫樵夫、獅子都很誠心地感謝好女巫的仁慈，這時桃樂絲激動地說：「妳的心確實和妳的外表一樣美！可是妳還沒有告訴我要怎麼回堪薩斯啊。」

　　「妳的銀鞋就可以帶妳越過沙漠。」格琳達說：「如果妳知道那雙鞋子的魔力，早在妳來到這個國家的第一天，就可以回去看妳的艾姆嬸嬸了。」

　　「可是那樣子我就得不到神奇的腦子了！」稻草人大叫。「我就有可能一生都待在農夫的田裡了。」

　　「而我就不會得到我可愛的心，可能會站在森林裡生鏽到世界末日。」錫樵夫說。

　　「而我會一輩子都是個膽小鬼。」獅子斷言說：「所有森林的野獸都不會對我說什麼好話。」

　　「這倒是真的。」桃樂絲說：「我很高興能幫到這些好朋友。可是現在他們每個人都得到了最想要的東西，也都很高興有可以治理的地方，我想我要回堪薩斯了。」

「那雙銀鞋有神奇的力量。」好女巫說：「其中最奇妙的是，它只要三步就可以把妳帶到世界上任何地方，而每一步都只需一轉眼的時間。妳唯一要做的是連敲鞋跟三次，命令鞋子帶妳去想去的地方。」

「如果真是這樣，我馬上就要請它帶我回堪薩斯。」小女孩興奮地說。她摟住獅子的脖子，跟牠吻別，然後溫柔地拍拍牠的大頭。接著她親吻了錫樵夫，他正在哭泣，對關節的危害很大。她沒有去親稻草人描了五官的臉，而是將他填塞的柔軟身體抱在懷裡，這時她發現自己也在掉淚，因為要離開可愛的同伴令她感傷。

好心的格琳達從紅寶石寶座走下來，跟小女孩吻別，桃樂絲謝謝她對同伴和自己所表現的仁慈。桃樂絲接著嚴肅地抱起托托，最後一次說再見，然後連敲鞋跟三次，嘴裡說：「帶我回艾姆嬸嬸的家！」

她立刻在空中旋轉，速度快得只能看到或感覺到風在她耳邊呼嘯而過。銀鞋只走了三步，她就突然停下來，在草地上翻滾了許多次，才知道身在何處。她終於站起來，看看四周。「天啊！」她大叫。因為她就坐在堪薩斯廣闊的草原上，前面就是亨利叔叔在龍捲風捲走舊房子以後新蓋的農舍。亨利叔叔正在穀倉擠牛奶，托托已經從桃樂絲的懷裡跳開，高興地跑向穀倉吠叫。

桃樂絲站起來，發現自己只穿著襪子。原來她在空中飛的時候，銀鞋從她腳上鬆脫，永遠遺失在沙漠裡了。

第 24 章

回家

　　艾姆嬸嬸剛從房子裡面出來為捲心菜澆水，她頭一抬，就看到桃樂絲正在跑向她。「我親愛的孩子!」她大聲叫著，把小女孩抱在懷裡，不斷地親吻她的臉。「妳到底是從哪裡冒出來的?」

　　「從奧茲國來的，托托也是。」桃樂絲鄭重地說。「噢，艾姆嬸嬸!我好高興，終於回家了!」

Introduction

Folklore, legends, myths and fairy tales have followed childhood through the ages, for every healthy youngster has a wholesome and instinctive love for stories fantastic, marvelous and manifestly unreal. The winged fairies of Grimm and Andersen have brought more happiness to childish hearts than all other human creations.

Yet the old time fairy tale, having served for generations, may now be classed as "historical" in the children's library; for the time has come for a series of newer "wonder tales" in which the stereotyped genie, dwarf and fairy are eliminated, together with all the horrible and blood-curdling incidents devised by their authors to point a fearsome moral to each tale. Modern education includes morality; therefore the modern child seeks only entertainment in its wonder tales and gladly dispenses with all disagreeable incident.

Having this thought in mind, the story of "The Wonderful Wizard of Oz" was written solely to please children of today. It aspires to being a modernized fairy tale, in which the wonderment and joy are retained and the heartaches and nightmares are left out.

L. Frank Baum

Chicago, April, 1900.

01
The Cyclone

Dorothy lived in the midst of the great Kansas prairies, with Uncle Henry, who was a farmer, and Aunt Em, who was the farmer's wife. Their house was small, for the lumber to build it had to be carried by wagon many miles. There were four walls, a floor and a roof, which made one room; and this room contained a rusty looking cookstove, a cupboard for the dishes, a table, three or four chairs, and the beds. Uncle Henry and Aunt Em had a big bed in one corner, and Dorothy a little bed in another corner. There was no garret at all, but a small hole dug in the ground, called a cyclone cellar, where the family could go in case one of those great whirlwinds arose, mighty enough to crush any building in its path. It was reached by a trap door in the middle of the floor, from which a ladder led down into the small, dark hole.

When Dorothy stood in the doorway and looked around, she could see nothing but the great gray prairie on every side. Not a tree nor a house broke the broad sweep of flat country that reached to the edge of the sky in all directions. The sun had baked the plowed land into a gray mass, with little cracks running through it. Even the grass was not green, for the sun had burned the tops of the long blades until they were the same gray color to be seen everywhere. Once the house had been painted, but the sun blistered the paint and the rains washed it away, and now the house was as dull and gray as everything else.

When Aunt Em came there to live she was a young, pretty wife. The sun and wind had taken the sparkle from her eyes, the red from her cheeks and lips, and left them a sober gray. She was thin and gaunt, and never smiled now. When Dorothy, who was an orphan, first came to her, Aunt Em had been so startled by the child's laughter that she would scream and press her hand upon her heart whenever Dorothy's merry voice reached her ears; and she still looked at the little girl with wonder that she could find anything to laugh at.

Uncle Henry never laughed. He worked hard from morning till night and did not know what joy was. He was gray also, from his long beard to his rough boots, and he looked stern and solemn, and rarely spoke.

It was Toto that made Dorothy laugh, and saved her from growing as gray as her other surroundings. Toto was not gray; he was a little black dog, with long silky hair and small black eyes that twinkled merrily on either side of his funny, wee nose. Toto played all day long, and Dorothy played with

him, and loved him dearly.

Today, however, they were not playing. Uncle Henry sat upon the doorstep and looked anxiously at the sky, which was even grayer than usual. Dorothy stood in the door with Toto in her arms and looked at the sky too. Aunt Em was washing the dishes.

From the far north they heard a low wail of the wind, and Uncle Henry and Dorothy could see where the long grass bowed in waves before the coming storm. There now came a sharp whistling in the air from the south, and they saw ripples in the grass coming from that direction also.

Suddenly Uncle Henry stood up. "There's a cyclone coming, Em," he called to his wife. "I'll go look after the stock." Then he ran toward the sheds where the cows and horses were kept.

Aunt Em dropped her work and came to the door. One glance told her of the danger close at hand. "Quick, Dorothy!" she screamed. "Run for the cellar!"

Toto jumped out of Dorothy's arms and hid under the bed, and the girl started to get him. Aunt Em, badly frightened, threw open the trap door in the floor and climbed down the ladder into the small, dark hole. Dorothy caught Toto at last and started to follow her aunt.

When she was halfway across the room there came a great shriek from the wind, and the house shook so hard that she lost her footing and sat down suddenly upon the floor.

Then a strange thing happened.

The house whirled around two or three times and rose slowly through the air. Dorothy felt as if she were going up in a balloon.

The north and south winds met where the house stood and made it the exact center of the cyclone. In the middle of a cyclone the air is generally still, but the great pressure of the wind on every side of the house raised it up higher and higher, until it was at the very top of the cyclone; and there it remained and was carried miles and miles away as easily as a feather.

It was very dark, and the wind howled horribly around her, but Dorothy found she was riding quite easily. After the first few whirls around, and one other time when the house tipped badly, she felt as if she were being rocked gently, like a baby in a cradle.

Toto did not like it. He ran about the room, now here, now there, barking loudly; but Dorothy sat quite still on the floor and waited to see what would happen.

Once Toto got too near the open trap door and fell in; and at first the little girl thought she had lost him. But soon she saw one of his ears sticking up through the hole, for the strong pressure of the air was keeping him up so that he could not fall. She crept to the hole, caught Toto by the ear, and dragged him into the room again, afterward closing the trap door so that no more accidents could happen.

Hour after hour passed away, and slowly Dorothy got over her fright; but she felt quite lonely, and the wind shrieked so loudly all about her that she nearly became deaf. At first, she had wondered if she would be dashed to pieces when the house fell again; but as the hours passed and nothing terrible happened, she stopped worrying and resolved to wait calmly and see what the future would bring. At last she crawled over the swaying floor to her bed and lay down upon it; and Toto followed and lay down beside her.

In spite of the swaying of the house and the wailing of the wind, Dorothy soon closed her eyes and fell fast asleep.

02

The Council with the Munchkins

She was awakened by a shock, so sudden and severe that if Dorothy had not been lying on the soft bed she might have been hurt. As it was, the jar made her catch her breath and wonder what had happened; and Toto put his cold little nose into her face and whined dismally. Dorothy sat up and noticed that the house was not moving. The bright sunshine came in at the window, flooding the little room. She sprang from her bed and with Toto at her heels ran and opened the door.

The little girl looked about her, and her eyes growing bigger and bigger at the wonderful sights.

The cyclone had set the house down very gently in the midst of a country of marvelous beauty. There were lovely patches of greensward all about, with stately trees bearing rich and luscious fruits. Banks of gorgeous flowers were on every hand, and birds with rare and brilliant plumage sang and fluttered in the trees and bushes. A little way off was a

small brook, rushing and sparkling along between green banks, and murmuring in a very grateful voice.

While she stood looking eagerly at the strange and beautiful sights, she noticed there were three men and one woman coming toward her, and all were oddly dressed. They wore round hats that rose to a small point a foot above their heads, with little bells around the brims that tinkled sweetly as they moved. The hats of the men were blue; the little woman's hat was white, and she wore a white gown that hung in pleats from her shoulders. Over it were sprinkled little stars that glistened in the sun like diamonds. The men were dressed in blue, of the same shade as their hats, and wore well-polished boots with a deep roll of blue at the tops. The little woman was doubtless much older. Her face was covered with wrinkles, and her hair was nearly white.

The little old woman walked up to Dorothy, made a low bow and said, in a sweet voice: "You are welcome, most noble Sorceress, to the land of the Munchkins. We are so grateful to you for having killed the Wicked Witch of the East, and for setting our people free from bondage."

Dorothy listened to this speech with wonder. What could the little woman possibly mean by calling her a sorceress? Dorothy was an innocent, harmless little girl, who had been carried by a cyclone many miles from home; and she had never killed anything in all her life.

But the little woman evidently expected her to answer; so

Dorothy said, with hesitation, "You are very kind, but there must be some mistake. I have not killed anything."

"Your house did," replied the little old woman, with a laugh, "and that is the same thing. See!" she continued, pointing to the corner of the house. "There are her two feet, still sticking out from under a block of wood."

There, indeed, just under the corner of the great beam the house rested on, two feet were sticking out, shod in silver shoes with pointed toes.

"Oh, dear! Oh, dear!" cried Dorothy, clasping her hands together in dismay. "The house must have fallen on her. Whatever shall we do?"

"There is nothing to be done," said the little woman calmly. "She was the Wicked Witch of the East. She has held all the Munchkins in bondage for many years, making them slave for her night and day. Now they are all set free and are grateful to you for the favor."

"Who are the Munchkins?" inquired Dorothy.

"They are the people who live in this land of the East where the Wicked Witch ruled."

"Are you a Munchkin?" asked Dorothy.

"No, but I am their friend, although I live in the land of the North. When they saw the Witch of the East was dead the Munchkins sent a swift messenger to me, and I came at once. I am the Witch of the North."

"Oh, gracious!" cried Dorothy. "Are you a real witch?"

"Yes, indeed," answered the little woman. "But I am a good witch, and the people love me. I am not as powerful as the Wicked Witch was who ruled here, or I should have set the people free myself."

"But I thought all witches were wicked," said the girl, who was half frightened at facing a real witch.

"Oh, no, that is a great mistake. There were only four witches in all the Land of Oz, and two of them, those who live in the North and the South, are good witches. I know this is true, for I am one of them myself, and cannot be mistaken. Those who dwelt in the East and the West were, indeed, wicked witches; but now that you have killed one of them, there is but one Wicked Witch in all the Land of Oz--the one who lives in the West."

"But," said Dorothy, after a moment's thought, "Aunt Em has told me that the witches were all dead--years and years ago."

"Who is Aunt Em?" inquired the little old woman.

"She is my aunt who lives in Kansas, where I came from."

The Witch of the North seemed to think for a time, with her head bowed and her eyes upon the ground. Then she looked up and said, "I do not know where Kansas is, for I have never heard that country mentioned before. But tell me, is it a civilized country?"

"Oh, yes," replied Dorothy.

"Then that accounts for it. In the civilized countries I believe there are no witches left, nor wizards, nor sorceresses, nor magicians. But the Land of Oz has never been civilized, for we are cut off from all the rest of the world. Therefore we still have witches and wizards amongst us."

"Who are the wizards?" asked Dorothy.

"Oz himself is the Great Wizard," answered the Witch, sinking her voice to a whisper. "He is more powerful than all the rest of us together. He lives in the City of Emeralds."

Dorothy was going to ask another question, but just then the Munchkins, who had been standing silently by, gave a loud shout and pointed to the corner of the house where the Wicked Witch had been lying.

"What is it?" asked the little old woman, and looked, and began to laugh. The feet of the dead Witch had disappeared entirely, and nothing was left but the silver shoes.

"She was so old," explained the Witch of the North, "that she dried up quickly in the sun. But the silver shoes are yours, and you shall have them to wear." She reached down and picked up the shoes, and after shaking the dust out of them handed them to Dorothy.

"The Witch of the East was proud of those silver shoes," said one of the Munchkins, "and there is some charm connected with them; but what it is we never knew."

Dorothy carried the shoes into the house and placed them on the table. Then she came out again to the Munchkins

and said:

"I am anxious to get back to my aunt and uncle, for I am sure they will worry about me. Can you help me find my way?"

The Munchkins and the Witch first looked at one another, and then at Dorothy, and then shook their heads.

"At the East, not far from here," said one, "there is a great desert, and none could live to cross it."

"It is the same at the South," said another, "for I have been there and seen it. The South is the country of the Quadlings."

"I am told," said the third man, "that it is the same at the West. And that country, where the Winkies live, is ruled by the Wicked Witch of the West, who would make you her slave if you passed her way."

"The North is my home," said the old lady, "and at its edge is the same great desert that surrounds this Land of Oz. I'm afraid, my dear, you will have to live with us."

Dorothy began to sob at this, for she felt lonely here. The little old woman took off her cap and balanced the point on the end of her nose, while she counted "One, two, three" in a solemn voice. At once the cap changed to a slate, on which was written in big, white chalk marks:

LET DOROTHY GO TO THE CITY OF EMERALDS

The little old woman took the slate, and having read the words on it, asked, "Is your name Dorothy?"

"Yes," answered the child, looking up and drying her tears.

"Then you must go to the City of Emeralds. Perhaps Oz will help you."

"Where is this city?" asked Dorothy.

"It is exactly in the center of the country, and is ruled by Oz, the Great Wizard I told you of."

"Is he a good man?" inquired the girl anxiously.

"He is a good Wizard. Whether he is a man or not I cannot tell, for I have never seen him."

"How can I get there?" asked Dorothy.

"You must walk. It is a long journey, through a country that is sometimes pleasant and sometimes dark and terrible. However, I will use all my magic arts to keep you from harm."

"Won't you go with me?" pleaded the girl.

"No, I cannot do that," she replied, "but I will give you my kiss, and no one will dare injure a person who has been kissed by the Witch of the North."

She kissed Dorothy gently on the forehead. Where her lips touched the girl they left a round, shining mark, as Dorothy found out soon after.

"The road to the City of Emeralds is paved with yellow brick," said the Witch, "so you cannot miss it. When you get to Oz do not be afraid of him, but tell your story and ask him to help you. Good-bye, my dear."

The three Munchkins bowed low to her and wished her a

pleasant journey, after which they walked away through the trees. The Witch gave Dorothy a friendly little nod, whirled around on her left heel three times, and straightway disappeared, much to the surprise of little Toto, who barked after her loudly enough when she had gone, because he had been afraid even to growl while she stood by.

But Dorothy, knowing her to be a witch, had expected her to disappear in just that way, and was not surprised in the least.

03

How Dorothy Saved the Scarecrow

When Dorothy was left alone she began to feel hungry. So, she went to the cupboard and cut herself some bread, which she spread with butter. She gave some to Toto, and taking a pail from the shelf she carried it down to the little brook and filled it with clear, sparkling water. Toto ran over to the trees and began to bark at the birds sitting there. Dorothy went to get him, and saw such delicious fruit hanging from the branches that she gathered some of it, finding it just what she wanted to help out her breakfast.

Then she went back to the house, and helped herself and Toto to a good drink of the cool, clear water, she set about making ready for the journey to the City of Emeralds.

Dorothy had only one other dress, but that happened to be clean and was hanging on a peg beside her bed. It was gingham, with checks of white and blue; and although the blue was somewhat faded with many washings, it was still a

pretty frock. The girl washed herself carefully, dressed herself in the clean gingham, and tied her pink sunbonnet on her head. She took a little basket and filled it with bread from the cupboard, laying a white cloth over the top. Then she looked down at her feet and noticed how old and worn her shoes were.

"They surely will never do for a long journey, Toto," she said. And Toto looked up into her face with his little black eyes and wagged his tail.

At that moment Dorothy saw lying on the table the silver shoes that had belonged to the Witch of the East.

"I wonder if they will fit me," she said to Toto. "They would be just the thing to take a long walk in, for they could not wear out."

She took off her old leather shoes and tried on the silver ones, which fitted her as well as if they had been made for her.

Finally, she picked up her basket. "Come along, Toto," she said. "We will go to the Emerald City and ask the Great Oz how to get back to Kansas again."

And so, with Toto trotting along soberly behind her, she started on her journey.

It did not take long to find the road paved with yellow bricks. Within a short time she was walking briskly toward the Emerald City, her silver shoes tinkling merrily on the hard, yellow road-bed. The sun shone bright and the birds sang sweetly, and Dorothy did not feel nearly so bad as a little girl would who had been suddenly whisked away from her own country and set down in the midst of a strange land.

She was surprised, as she walked along, to see how pretty the country was about her. There were neat fences at the sides of the road, painted a dainty blue color, and beyond them were fields of grain and vegetables in abundance. The houses of the Munchkins were odd-looking dwellings, for each was round, with a big dome for a roof. All were painted blue, for in this country of the East blue was the favorite color.

Toward evening, when Dorothy was tired with her long walk and began to wonder where she should pass the night, she came to a house rather larger than the rest. On the green lawn before it many men and women were dancing. Five little fiddlers played as loudly as possible, and the people were laughing and singing, while a big table near by was loaded with delicious fruits and nuts, pies and cakes, and many other good things to eat.

The people greeted Dorothy kindly, and invited her to supper and to pass the night with them; for this was the home of one of the richest Munchkins in the land, and his friends were gathered with him to celebrate their freedom from the bondage of the Wicked Witch.

Dorothy ate a hearty supper and was waited upon by the rich Munchkin himself, whose name was Boq. When Boq saw her silver shoes he said, "You must be a great sorceress."

"Why?" asked the girl.

"Because you wear silver shoes and have killed the Wicked Witch. Besides, you have white in your frock, and only witches and sorceresses wear white."

"My dress is blue and white checked," said Dorothy, smoothing out the wrinkles in it.

"It is kind of you to wear that," said Boq. "Blue is the color of the Munchkins, and white is the witch color. So we know you are a friendly witch."

Dorothy did not know what to say to this, for all the people seemed to think her a witch, and she knew very well she was only an ordinary little girl who had come by the chance of a cyclone into a strange land.

Boq led Dorothy into the house. There's a bed, of which sheets were made of blue cloth, and Dorothy slept soundly till morning, with Toto curled up on the blue rug beside her.

*   *   *

"How far is it to the Emerald City?" the girl asked.

"I do not know," answered Boq gravely, "for I have never been there. It is better for people to keep away from Oz, unless they have business with him. But it will take you many days to the Emerald City. The country here is rich and pleasant, but you must pass through rough and dangerous places before you reach the end of your journey."

This worried Dorothy a little, but she knew that only the

Great Oz could help her get to Kansas again, so she bravely resolved not to turn back.

She bade her friends good-bye, and again started along the road of yellow brick. When she had gone several miles she stopped to rest, and climbed to the top of the fence beside the road and sat down. There was a great cornfield beyond the fence, and not far away she saw a Scarecrow, placed high on a pole to keep the birds from the ripe corn.

Dorothy leaned her chin upon her hand and gazed thoughtfully at the Scarecrow. Its head was a small sack stuffed with straw, with eyes, nose, and mouth painted on it. An Munchkin's pointed blue hat was perched on his head, and the rest of the figure was a blue suit of clothes, worn and faded, which had also been stuffed with straw. On the feet were some old boots with blue tops, such as every man wore in this country.

While Dorothy was looking earnestly into the queer, painted face of the Scarecrow, she was surprised to see one of the eyes slowly wink at her. She thought she must have been mistaken at first, but presently the figure nodded its head to her in a friendly way. Then she climbed down from the fence and walked up to it, while Toto ran around the pole and barked.

"Good day," said the Scarecrow, in a rather husky voice.

"Did you speak?" asked the girl, in wonder.

"Certainly," answered the Scarecrow. "How do you do?"

"I'm pretty well, thank you," replied Dorothy politely. "How do you do?"

"I'm not feeling well," said the Scarecrow, with a smile, "for it is very tedious being perched up here night and day to scare away crows."

"Can't you get down?" asked Dorothy.

"No, for this pole is stuck up my back. If you will please take away the pole I shall be greatly obliged to you."

Dorothy reached up both arms and lifted the figure off the pole, for, being stuffed with straw, it was quite light.

"Thank you very much," said the Scarecrow, when he had been set down on the ground. "I feel like a new man."

"Who are you?" asked the Scarecrow when he had stretched himself and yawned. "And where are you going?"

"My name is Dorothy," said the girl, "and I am going to the Emerald City, to ask the Great Oz to send me back to Kansas."

"Where is the Emerald City?" he inquired. "Who is Oz?"

"Why, don't you know?" she returned, in surprise.

"No, indeed. I don't know anything. You see, I am stuffed, so I have no brains at all," he answered sadly.

"Oh," said Dorothy, "I'm awfully sorry for you."

"Do you think," he asked, "if I go to the Emerald City with you, that Oz would give me some brains?"

"I cannot tell," she returned, "but you may come with me, if you like. If Oz will not give you any brains you will be

no worse off than you are now."

"That is true," said the Scarecrow. "You see," he continued confidentially, "I don't mind my legs and arms and body being stuffed, because I cannot get hurt. If anyone treads on my toes or sticks a pin into me, it doesn't matter, for I can't feel it. But I do not want people to call me a fool, and if my head stays stuffed with straw instead of with brains, as yours is, how am I ever to know anything?"

"I understand how you feel," said the little girl, who was truly sorry for him. "If you will come with me I'll ask Oz to do all he can for you."

"Thank you," he answered gratefully.

Dorothy helped him over the fence, and they started along the path of yellow brick for the Emerald City.

Toto smelled around the stuffed man as if he suspected there might be a nest of rats in the straw, and he often growled in an unfriendly way at the Scarecrow.

"Don't mind Toto," said Dorothy. "He never bites."

"Oh, I'm not afraid," replied the Scarecrow. "He can't hurt the straw. Do let me carry that basket for you. I shall not mind it, for I can't get tired. I'll tell you a secret," he continued, as he walked along. "There is only one thing in the world I am afraid of."

"What is that?" asked Dorothy; "the Munchkin farmer who made you?"

"No," answered the Scarecrow; "it's a lighted match."

04
The Road Through the Forest

The road began to be rough, and the walking grew so difficult that the Scarecrow often stumbled over the yellow bricks, which were here very uneven. Sometimes, indeed, they were broken or missing altogether, leaving holes that Scarecrow, having no brains, stepped into. And so he fell at full length on the hard bricks. It never hurt him, however, and Dorothy would pick him up, while he joined her in laughing merrily at his own mishap.

At noon they sat down by the roadside, near a little brook, and Dorothy opened her basket and offered a piece of bread to the Scarecrow, but he refused. "It is lucky that I am never hungry, for my mouth is only painted, and if I should cut a hole in it so I could eat, the straw I am stuffed with would come out, and that would spoil the shape of my head."

When Dorothy had finished her dinner, she told all about Kansas, and how gray everything was there, and how the

cyclone had carried her to this queer Land of Oz.

The Scarecrow listened carefully, and said, "I cannot understand why you should wish to leave this beautiful country and go back to the dry, gray place you call Kansas."

"That is because you have no brains," answered the girl. "No matter how dreary and gray our homes are, we people of flesh and blood would rather live there than in any other country, be it ever so beautiful. There is no place like home."

The Scarecrow sighed. "Of course I cannot understand it," he said. "If your heads were stuffed with straw, like mine, you would probably all live in the beautiful places, and then Kansas would have no people at all. It is fortunate for Kansas that you have brains."

"Won't you tell me a story?" asked the child.

The Scarecrow looked at her reproachfully, and answered: "I was only made day before yesterday. What happened in the world before that time is all unknown to me. My feet would not touch the ground, and I was forced to stay on that pole. It was a lonely life to lead, for I had nothing to think of, having been made such a little while before.

"At first, there are many crows and other birds flew into the cornfield, but as soon as they saw me they flew away again, thinking I was a Munchkin; and this made me feel that I was quite an important person. By and by an old crow flew near me, and after looking at me carefully he perched upon my shoulder and said:

"'I wonder if that farmer thought to fool me in this clumsy manner. Any crow of sense could see that you are only stuffed with straw.' Then he hopped down at my feet and ate all the corn he wanted. The other birds, seeing he was not harmed by me, came to eat the corn too, so in a short time there was a great flock of them about me.

"I felt sad at this, for it showed I was not such a good Scarecrow after all; but the old crow comforted me, saying, 'If you only had brains in your head you would be as good a man as any of them, and a better man than some of them. Brains are the only things worth having in this world, no matter whether one is a crow or a man.'

"After the crows had gone I thought this over, and decided I would try hard to get some brains. By good luck you came along and pulled me off the stake, and from what you say I am sure the Great Oz will give me brains as soon as

we get to the Emerald City."

"I hope so," said Dorothy, "since you seem anxious to have them."

"Oh, yes; I am anxious," returned the Scarecrow. "It is such an uncomfortable feeling to know one is a fool."

"Well," said the girl, "let us go." And she handed the basket to the Scarecrow.

There were no fences at all by the roadside now, and the land was rough. Toward evening they came to a great forest, where the trees grew so big and close together that their branches met over the road of yellow brick. It was almost dark under the trees, for the branches shut out the daylight.

"If this road goes in, it must come out," said the Scarecrow, "and as the Emerald City is at the other end of the road, we must go wherever it leads us."

"Anyone would know that," said Dorothy.

"Certainly; that is why I know it," returned the Scarecrow. "If it required brains to figure out, I never should have said it."

The light faded away, and they found themselves stumbling along in the darkness. Dorothy could not see at all, but Toto could, for some dogs see very well in the dark; and the Scarecrow declared he could see as well as by day. So she took hold of his arm

and managed to get along fairly well.

"If you see any house, or any place where we can pass

the night," she said, "you must tell me; for it is very uncomfortable walking in the dark."

Soon after the Scarecrow stopped. "I see a little cottage at the right of us," he said, "built of logs and branches. Shall we go there?"

"Yes, indeed," answered the child. "I am all tired out."

So the Scarecrow led her through the trees until they reached the cottage, and Dorothy entered and found a bed of dried leaves in one corner. She lay down at once, and with Toto beside her soon fell into a sound sleep. The Scarecrow, who was never tired, stood up in another corner and waited patiently until morning came.

05

The Rescue of
the Tin Woodman

When Dorothy awoke the sun was shining through the trees and Toto had long been out chasing birds around him and squirrels. She sat up and looked around. There was the Scarecrow, still standing patiently, waiting for her.

"We must go and search for water," she said to him.

"Why do you want water?" he asked.

"To wash my face clean after the dust of the road, and to drink, so the dry bread will not stick in my throat."

"It must be inconvenient to be made of flesh," said the Scarecrow thoughtfully, "for you must sleep, and eat and drink. However, you have brains, and it is worth a lot of bother to be able to think properly."

They left the cottage and walked through the trees until they saw a little spring of clear water, where Dorothy drank and bathed and ate her breakfast. There was not much bread left in the basket, and the girl was thankful the Scarecrow did not have to eat, for there was scarcely enough for herself and Toto for the day.

When they about to go back to the road of yellow brick, Dorothy heard a deep groan near by. The sound seemed to come from behind them. They turned and walked through the forest a few steps, when Dorothy discovered something shining in a ray of sunshine that fell between the trees. She ran to see and then gave a little cry of surprise.

One of the big trees had been partly chopped through, and standing beside it, with an uplifted axe in his hands, was a man made entirely of tin. His head and arms and legs were jointed upon his body, but he stood perfectly motionless, as if he could not stir at all.

Dorothy looked at him in amazement, and so did the Scarecrow, while Toto barked sharply and made a snap at the tin legs, which hurt his teeth.

"Did you groan?" asked Dorothy.

"Yes," answered the tin man, "I did. I've been groaning for more than a year, and no one has ever heard me before or come to help me."

"What can I do for you?" she inquired softly.

"Get an oil-can and oil my joints," he answered. "They are rusted so badly that I cannot move them at all; if I am well oiled I shall soon be all right again. You will find an oil-can on a shelf in my cottage."

Dorothy at once ran back to the cottage and found the oil-can, and then she returned and asked anxiously, "Where are your joints?"

"Oil my neck, first," replied the Tin Woodman. So she oiled it, and as it was quite badly rusted the Scarecrow took hold of the tin head and moved it gently from side to side until it worked freely, and then the man could turn it himself.

"Now oil the joints in my arms," he said. And Dorothy oiled them and the Scarecrow bent them carefully.

The Tin Woodman gave a sigh of satisfaction and lowered his axe, which he leaned against the tree.

"This is a great comfort," he said. "I have been holding that axe in the air ever since I rusted, and I'm glad to be able to put it down at last. Now, if you will oil the joints of my legs, I shall be all right once more."

So they oiled his legs until he could move them freely; and he thanked them again and again for his release, for he seemed a very polite creature, and very grateful.

"I might have stood there always if you had not come along," he said; "so you have certainly saved my life. How did you happen to be here?"

"We are on our way to the Emerald City to see the Great

Oz," she answered, "and we stopped at your cottage to pass the night."

"Why do you wish to see Oz?" he asked.

"I want him to send me back to Kansas, and the Scarecrow wants him to put a few brains into his head," she replied.

The Tin Woodman appeared to think deeply for a moment. Then he said:

"Do you suppose Oz could give me a heart?"

"Why, I guess so," Dorothy answered. "It would be as easy as to give the Scarecrow brains."

"True," the Tin Woodman returned. "So, if you will allow me to join your party, I will also go to the Emerald City and ask Oz to help me."

"Come along," said the Scarecrow heartily.

The Tin Woodman had asked Dorothy to put the oil-can in her basket. "For," he said, "if I should get caught in the rain, and rust again, I would need the oil-can badly."

It was a bit of good luck to have their new comrade join the party, for soon after they had begun their journey again they came to a place where the trees and branches grew so thick over the road that the travelers could not pass. But the Tin Woodman set to work with his axe and chopped so well that soon he cleared a passage for the entire party.

Dorothy was thinking so earnestly as they walked along that she did not notice when the Scarecrow stumbled into a

hole and rolled over to the side of the road. Indeed he was obliged to call to her to help him up again.

"Why didn't you walk around the hole?" asked the Tin Woodman.

"I don't know enough," replied the Scarecrow cheerfully. "and that is why I am going to Oz to ask him for some brains."

"Oh, I see," said the Tin Woodman. "But, after all, brains are not the best things in the world."

"Have you any?" inquired the Scarecrow.

"No, my head is quite empty," answered the Woodman. "But once I had brains, and a heart also; so, having tried them both, I should much rather have a heart."

"And why is that?" asked the Scarecrow.

While they were walking through the forest, the Tin Woodman told the following story:

"I was born the son of a woodman who chopped down trees in the forest and sold the wood for a living. When I grew up, I too became a wood chopper, and after my father died I took care of my old mother as long as she lived. Then I made up my mind that instead of living alone I would marry, so that I might not become lonely.

"There was one of the Munchkin girls who was so beautiful that I soon grew to love her with all my heart. She, on her part, promised to marry me as soon as I could earn enough money to build a better house for her. But the girl lived with an old woman who was so lazy that she wished the girl to remain with her and do the cooking and the housework. So she went to the Wicked Witch of the East, and promised her two sheep and a cow if she would prevent the marriage. Thereupon the Wicked Witch enchanted my axe, and when I was chopping away, the axe slipped all at once and cut off my left leg.

"This at first seemed a great misfortune, for I knew a one-legged man could not do very well as a wood-chopper. So I went to a tinsmith and had him make me a new leg out of tin. But when I began chopping again, my axe slipped and cut off my right leg. Again I went to the tinsmith, and again he made me a leg out of tin. After this the enchanted axe cut off my arms, one after the other; but, nothing daunted, I had them replaced with tin ones. The axe then cut off my head, and I thought that was the end of me. But the tinsmith happened to come along, and he made me a new head.

"I thought I had beaten the Wicked Witch then, and I worked harder than ever; but I little knew how cruel my enemy could be. She thought of a new way to kill my love for the beautiful Munchkin maiden, and made my axe slip again, so that it cut right through my body, splitting me into two halves. Once more the tinsmith came to my help and made me a body of tin, fastening my tin arms and legs and head to it, by means of joints, so that I could move around as well as ever. But, alas! I had now no heart, so that I lost all my love

for the Munchkin girl, and did not care whether I married her or not. I suppose she is still living with the old woman, waiting for me to come after her.

"And it did not matter now if my axe slipped, for it could not cut me. There was only one danger--that my joints would rust; but I kept an oil-can in my cottage and took care to oil myself whenever I needed it. However, there came a day when I forgot to do this, and, being caught in a rainstorm, before I thought of the danger my joints had rusted, and I was left to stand in the woods until you came. But during the year I stood there to think that the greatest loss I had known was the loss of my heart. While I was in love I was the happiest man on earth; but no one can love who has not a heart, and so I am resolved to ask Oz to give me one."

"All the same," said the Scarecrow, "I shall ask for brains instead of a heart; for a fool would not know what to do with a heart if he had one."

"I shall take the heart," returned the Tin Woodman; "for brains do not make one happy, and happiness is the best thing in the world."

Dorothy was puzzled to know which of them was right. What worried her most was that the bread was nearly gone, and another meal for herself and Toto would empty the basket. She was not made of tin nor straw, and could not live unless she was fed.

06

The Cowardly Lion

The road paved with yellow brick were much covered by dried branches and dead leaves from the trees, and the walking was not at all good.

Now and then there came a deep growl from some wild animal hidden among the trees. These sounds made the little girl's heart beat fast, for she did not know what made them; but Toto knew, and he walked close to Dorothy's side, and did not even bark in return.

"How long will it be," the child asked of the Tin Woodman, "before we are out of the forest?"

"I cannot tell," was the answer, "for I have never been to the Emerald City. But my father went there once, when I was a boy, and he said it was a long journey.

Just as he spoke there came from the forest a terrible roar, and the next moment a great Lion bounded into the road. With one blow of his paw he sent the Scarecrow

spinning over and over to the edge of the road, and then he struck at the Tin Woodman with his sharp claws. But he could make no impression on the tin, although the Woodman fell over in the road and lay still.

Little Toto ran barking toward the Lion, and the great beast had opened his mouth to bite the dog, when Dorothy, fearing Toto would be killed, and heedless of danger, rushed forward and slapped the Lion upon his nose as hard as she could, while she cried out: "Don't you dare to bite Toto! You ought to be ashamed of yourself, a big beast like you, to bite a poor little dog!"

"I didn't bite him," said the Lion, as he rubbed his nose with his paw where Dorothy had hit it.

"But you tried to," she retorted. "You are a coward."

"I know it," said the Lion, hanging his head in shame. "I've always known it. But how can I help it?"

"What makes you a coward?" asked Dorothy, looking at the great beast in wonder, for he was as big as a small horse.

"It's a mystery," replied the Lion. "I suppose I was born that way. All the other animals in the forest naturally expect me to be brave, for the Lion is everywhere thought to be the King of Beasts. If I roared very loudly every living thing was frightened and got out of my way. If the elephants and the tigers and the bears had ever tried to fight me, I should have run myself--I'm such a coward; but just as soon as they hear me roar they all try to get away from me."

"But that isn't right. The King of Beasts shouldn't be a coward," said the Scarecrow.

"I know it," returned the Lion, wiping a tear from his eye with the tip of his tail. "It is my great sorrow and it makes my life very unhappy. But whenever there is danger, my heart begins to beat fast."

"Perhaps you have heart disease," said the Tin Woodman.

"If you have," continued the Tin Woodman, "you ought to be glad, for it proves you have a heart. For my part, I have no heart; so I cannot have heart disease."

"Perhaps," said the Lion thoughtfully, "if I had no heart I

should not be a coward."

"Have you brains?" asked the Scarecrow.

"I suppose so. I've never looked to see," replied the Lion.

"I am going to the Great Oz to ask him to give me some," remarked the Scarecrow, "for my head is stuffed with straw."

"And I am going to ask him to give me a heart," said the Woodman.

"And I am going to ask him to send Toto and me back to Kansas," added Dorothy.

"Do you think Oz could give me courage?" asked the Cowardly Lion.

"Just as easily as he could give me brains," said the Scarecrow.

"Or give me a heart," said the Tin Woodman.

"Or send me back to Kansas," said Dorothy.

"Then, if you don't mind, I'll go with you," said the Lion, "for my life is simply unbearable without a bit of courage."

"You will be very welcome," answered Dorothy, "for you will help to keep away the other wild beasts. It seems to me they must be more cowardly than you are if they allow you to scare them so easily."

"They really are," said the Lion, "but that doesn't make me any braver, and as long as I know myself to be a coward I shall be unhappy."

So the Lion walking with stately strides at Dorothy's side. Toto did not approve of this new comrade at first, for he could not forget how nearly he had been crushed between the Lion's great jaws. But after a time he became more at ease, and presently Toto and the Cowardly Lion had grown to be good friends.

Once, the Tin Woodman stepped upon a beetle that was crawling along the road, and killed the poor little thing. This made the Tin Woodman very unhappy, for he was always careful not to hurt any living creature; and as he walked along he wept several tears. These tears ran slowly down his face and over the hinges of his jaw, and there they rusted. The Tin Woodman then could not open his mouth, for his jaws were tightly rusted together. He became greatly frightened at this and made many motions to Dorothy to relieve him, but she could not understand. The Lion was also puzzled to know what was wrong. But the Scarecrow seized the oil-can from Dorothy's basket and oiled the Woodman's jaws, so that after a few moments he could talk as well as before.

"This will serve me a lesson," said he, "to look where I step. For if I should kill another bug I should surely cry again, and crying rusts my jaws so that I cannot speak."

Thereafter he walked very carefully, with his eyes on the road, and when he saw a tiny ant he would step over it, so as not to harm it. The Tin Woodman took great care never to be cruel or unkind to anything.

"You people with hearts," he said, "have something to guide you, and need never do wrong; but I have no heart, and so I must be very careful. When Oz gives me a heart of course I needn't mind so much."

07
The Journey to the Great Oz

They were obliged to camp out that night under a large tree in the forest, for there were no houses near. The tree made a good, thick covering to protect them from the dew, and the Tin Woodman chopped a great pile of wood with his axe and Dorothy built a splendid fire that warmed her and made her feel less lonely. She and Toto ate the last of their bread, and now she did not know what they would do for breakfast.

"I will go into the forest and kill a deer for you. You can roast it by the fire, since your tastes are so peculiar that you prefer cooked food, and then you will have a very good breakfast." said the Lion.

"Don't! Please don't," begged the Tin Woodman. "I should certainly weep if you killed a poor deer, and then my jaws would rust again."

But the Lion went away into the forest and found his

own supper. And the Scarecrow found a tree full of nuts and filled Dorothy's basket with them, so that she would not be hungry for a long time. She thought this was very kind and thoughtful of the Scarecrow. The Scarecrow did not mind how long it took him to fill the basket, for it enabled him to keep away from the fire, as he feared a spark might get into his straw and burn him up. So he kept a good distance away from the flames, and only came near to cover Dorothy with dry leaves when she lay down to sleep. These kept her very snug and warm, and she slept soundly until morning.

When it was daylight, the girl bathed her face in a little rippling brook, and soon after they all started toward the Emerald City.

This was to be an eventful day. They had hardly been walking an hour when they saw before them a great ditch that crossed the road and divided the forest as far as they could see on either side. It was a very wide ditch, and when they crept up to the edge and looked into it they could see it was also very deep, and there were many big, jagged rocks at the bottom. The sides were so steep that none of them could climb down, and for a moment it seemed that their journey must end.

The Scarecrow said, "We cannot fly, that is certain. Neither can we climb down into this great ditch. Therefore, if we cannot jump over it, we must stop where we are."

"I think I could jump over it," said the Cowardly Lion,

after measuring the distance carefully in his mind.

"Then we are all right," answered the Scarecrow, "for you can carry us all over on your back, one at a time."

"Well, I'll try it," said the Lion. "Who will go first?"

"I will," declared the Scarecrow, "for, if you found that you could not jump over the gulf, Dorothy would be killed, or the Tin Woodman badly dented on the rocks below. But the fall would not hurt me at all."

"I am terribly afraid of falling, myself," said the Cowardly Lion, "but I suppose there is nothing to do but try it. So get on my back and we will make the attempt."

The Scarecrow sat upon the Lion's back, and the big beast walked to the edge of the gulf and crouched down.

"Why don't you run and jump?" asked the Scarecrow.

"Because that isn't the way we Lions do these things," he replied. Then giving a great spring, he shot through the air and landed safely on the other side. They were all greatly pleased to see how easily he did it, and after the Scarecrow had got down from his back the Lion sprang across the ditch again.

Dorothy took Toto in her arms and climbed on the Lion's back, holding tightly to his mane with one hand. The next moment it seemed as if she were flying through the air; and then, before she had time to think about it, she was safe on the other side. The Lion went back a third time and got the Tin Woodman, and then they all sat down for a few moments to give the beast a chance to rest, for his great leaps had made his breath short, and he panted like a big dog that has been running too long.

They found the forest very thick on this side, and it looked dark and gloomy. After the Lion had rested they started along the road of yellow brick. They soon heard strange noises in the depths of the forest, and the Lion whispered to them that it was in this part of the country that the Kalidahs lived.

"What are the Kalidahs?" asked the girl.

"They are monstrous beasts with bodies like bears and heads like tigers," replied the Lion, "and with claws so long and sharp that they could tear me in two as easily as I could kill Toto. I'm terribly afraid of the Kalidahs."

"I'm not surprised that you are," returned Dorothy. "They must be dreadful beasts."

The Lion was about to reply when suddenly they came to another gulf across the road. But this one was so broad and deep that the Lion knew at once he could not leap across it.

So they sat down to consider what they should do, and after serious thought the Scarecrow said: "Here is a great tree, standing close to the ditch. If the Tin Woodman can chop it down, so that it will fall to the other side, we can walk across it easily."

"That is a first-rate idea," said the Lion. "One would almost suspect you had brains in your head, instead of straw."

So sharp was The Woodman's axe that the tree was soon chopped nearly through. Then the Lion put his strong front legs against the tree and pushed with all his might, and slowly the big tree tipped and fell with a crash across the ditch, with its top branches on the other side.

They had just started to cross this queer bridge when a sharp growl made them all look up, and to their horror they saw running toward them two great beasts with bodies like bears and heads like tigers.

"They are the Kalidahs!" said the Cowardly Lion, beginning to tremble.

"Quick!" cried the Scarecrow. "Let us cross over."

So Dorothy went first, holding Toto in her arms, the Tin Woodman followed, and the Scarecrow came next. The Lion, although he was certainly afraid, turned to face the Kalidahs, and then he gave so loud and terrible a roar that Dorothy screamed and the Scarecrow fell over backward, while even the fierce beasts stopped short and looked at him in surprise.

But, seeing they were bigger than the Lion, and remembering that there were two of them and only one of him, the Kalidahs again rushed forward, and the Lion crossed over the tree and turned to see. Without stopping an instant the fierce beasts also began to cross the tree. And the Lion said to Dorothy: "We are lost, for they will surely tear us to pieces with their sharp claws. But stand close behind me, and I will fight them as long as I am alive."

"Wait a minute!" called the Scarecrow. He had been thinking what was best to be done, and now he asked the Woodman to chop away the end of the tree that rested on their side of the ditch. The Tin Woodman began to use his axe at once, and, just as the two Kalidahs were nearly across, the tree fell with a crash into the gulf, carrying the ugly, snarling brutes with it, and both were dashed to pieces on the sharp rocks at the bottom.

"Well," said the Cowardly Lion, drawing a long breath of relief, "I see we are going to live a little while longer, and I am glad of it, for it must be a very uncomfortable thing not to be alive. Those creatures frightened me so badly that my heart is beating yet."

"Ah," said the Tin Woodman sadly, "I wish I had a heart to beat."

This adventure made the travelers more anxious than ever to get out of the forest, and they walked so fast that Dorothy became tired, and had to ride on the Lion's back. To their great joy the trees became thinner the farther they advanced, and in the afternoon they suddenly came upon a broad river, flowing swiftly just before them. On the other side of the water they could see the road of yellow brick running through a beautiful country, with green meadows dotted with bright flowers and all the road bordered with trees hanging full of delicious fruits.

"How shall we cross the river?" asked Dorothy.

"That is easily done," replied the Scarecrow. "The Tin Woodman must build us a raft, so we can float to the other side."

So the Woodman took his axe and began to chop down small trees to make a raft, and while he was busy at this the Scarecrow found on the riverbank a tree full of fine fruit. This pleased Dorothy, who had eaten nothing but nuts all day, and she made a hearty meal of the ripe fruit.

But it takes time to make a raft, even when one is as industrious and untiring as the Tin Woodman, and when night came the work was not done. So they found a cozy place under the trees where they slept well until the morning; and Dorothy dreamed of the Emerald City, and of the good Wizard Oz, who would soon send her back to her own home again.

08

The Deadly Poppy Field

Our little party of travelers awakened the next morning refreshed and full of hope. The raft was nearly done, and after the Tin Woodman had cut a few more logs and fastened them together with wooden pins, they were ready to start. Dorothy sat down in the middle of the raft and held Toto in her arms. When the Cowardly Lion stepped upon the raft it tipped badly, but the Scarecrow and the Tin Woodman stood upon the other end to steady it, and they had long poles in their hands to push the raft through the water.

They got along quite well at first, but when they reached the middle of the river the swift current swept the raft downstream, farther and farther away from the road of yellow brick. And the water grew so deep that the long poles would not touch the bottom.

"This is bad," said the Tin Woodman, "for if we cannot get to the land we shall be carried into the country of the

Wicked Witch of the West, and she will enchant us and make us her slaves."

"And then I should get no brains," said the Scarecrow.

"And I should get no courage," said the Cowardly Lion.

"And I should get no heart," said the Tin Woodman.

"And I should never get back to Kansas," said Dorothy.

Now the Scarecrow pushed so hard on his long pole that it stuck fast in the mud at the bottom of the river. Then, before he could pull it out again--or let go--the raft was swept away, and the poor Scarecrow was left clinging to the pole in the middle of the river.

"Good-bye!" he called after them, and they were very sorry to leave him.

Down the stream the raft floated, and the poor Scarecrow was left far behind. Then the Lion said: "Something must be done to save us. I think I can swim to the shore and pull the raft after me, if you will only hold fast to the tip of my tail."

So he sprang into the water, and the Tin Woodman caught fast hold of his tail. Then the Lion began to swim with all his might toward the shore. It was hard work, although he was so big; but by and by they were drawn out of the current, and then Dorothy took the Tin Woodman's long pole and helped push the raft to the land.

They were all tired when they reached the shore at last.

"What shall we do now?" asked the Tin Woodman, as the Lion lay down on the grass to let the sun dry him.

"We must get back to the road," said Dorothy.

"The best plan will be to walk along the riverbank until we come to the road again," remarked the Lion.

So, when they were rested, they started along the grassy bank to the road. It was a lovely country, with plenty of flowers and fruit trees and sunshine to cheer them, and had they not felt so sorry for the poor Scarecrow, they could have been very happy.

They walked along as fast as they could. And after a time, the Tin Woodman cried out: "Look!"

Then they saw the Scarecrow perched upon his pole in the middle of the water, looking very lonely and sad.

"What can we do to save him?" asked Dorothy.

The Lion and the Woodman both shook their heads, for they did not know. So they sat down upon the bank and gazed wistfully at the Scarecrow until a Stork flew by, who stopped to rest at the water's edge.

"Who are you and where are you going?" asked the Stork.

"I am Dorothy," answered the girl, "and these are my friends, the Tin Woodman and the Cowardly Lion; and we are going to the Emerald City."

"This isn't the road," said the Stork, as she twisted her long neck and looked sharply at the queer party.

"I know it," returned Dorothy, "but we have lost the Scarecrow, and are wondering how we shall get him again."

"Where is he?" asked the Stork.

"Over there in the river," answered the little girl.

"If he wasn't so big and heavy I would get him for you," remarked the Stork.

"He isn't heavy a bit," said Dorothy eagerly, "for he is stuffed with straw; and if you will bring him back to us, we shall thank you ever and ever so much."

"Well, I'll try," said the Stork, "but if I find he is too heavy to carry I shall have to drop him in the river again."

So the big bird flew over the water and she came to where the Scarecrow was perched upon his pole. Then the Stork with her great claws grabbed the Scarecrow by the arm and carried him up into the air and back to the bank.

When the Scarecrow found himself among his friends again, he was so happy that he hugged them all, even the Lion and Toto.

"Thank you," said Dorothy, and then the kind Stork flew into the air and was soon out of sight.

They walked along listening to the singing of the brightly colored birds and looking at the lovely flowers which now became so thick that the ground was carpeted with them. There were yellow and white and blue and purple blossoms, besides great clusters of scarlet poppies, which were so brilliant in color they almost dazzled Dorothy's eyes.

"Aren't they beautiful?" the girl asked, as she breathed in the spicy scent of the bright flowers.

"I always did like flowers," said the Lion. "They seem so helpless and frail. But there are none in the forest so bright as these."

And soon they found themselves in the midst of a great meadow of poppies. When there are many of these flowers together their odor is so powerful that anyone who breathes it falls asleep, and if the sleeper is not carried away from the scent of the flowers, he sleeps on and on forever.

But Dorothy did not know this, so her eyes grew heavy and she felt she must sit down to rest and to sleep.

But the Tin Woodman would not let her do this.

"We must hurry and get back to the road of yellow brick before dark," he said; and the Scarecrow agreed with him. So they kept walking until Dorothy could stand no longer. Her eyes closed and she forgot where she was and fell among the poppies, fast asleep.

"What shall we do?" asked the Tin Woodman.

"If we leave her here she will die," said the Lion. "The smell of the flowers is killing us all. I myself can scarcely keep my eyes open, and the dog is asleep already."

It was true; Toto had fallen down beside his little mistress. But the Scarecrow and the Tin Woodman, not being

made of flesh, were not troubled by the scent of the flowers.

"Run fast," said the Scarecrow to the Lion, "and get out of this deadly flower bed as soon as you can. We will bring the little girl with us."

So the Lion aroused himself and bounded forward as fast as he could go. In a moment he was out of sight.

"Let us make a chair with our hands and carry her," said the Scarecrow. So they picked up Toto and put the dog in Dorothy's lap, and then they carried the sleeping girl through the flowers.

It seemed that the great carpet of deadly flowers that surrounded them would never end. They followed the bend of the river, and at last came upon their friend the Lion, lying fast asleep among the poppies. The huge beast fallen only a short distance from the end of the poppy bed, where the sweet grass spread in beautiful green fields before them.

"We can do nothing for him," said the Tin Woodman, sadly; "for he is much too heavy to lift. Perhaps he will dream that he has found courage at last."

"I'm sorry," said the Scarecrow. "The Lion was a very good comrade for one so cowardly. But let us go on."

They carried the sleeping girl to a pretty spot beside the river, far enough from the poppy field to prevent her breathing any more of the poison of the flowers, and here they laid her gently on the soft grass and waited for the fresh breeze to waken her.

09

The Queen of the Field Mice

The Tin Woodman heard a low growl, and turning his head he saw a strange beast come bounding over the grass toward them. It was, indeed, a great yellow Wildcat, and the Woodman thought it must be chasing something, for its ears were lying close to its head and its mouth was wide open, showing two rows of ugly teeth, while its red eyes glowed like balls of fire. As it came nearer the Tin Woodman saw that running before the beast was a little gray field mouse, and although he had no heart he knew it was wrong for the Wildcat to try to kill such a pretty, harmless creature.

So the Woodman raised his axe, and as the Wildcat ran by he gave it a quick blow.

The field mouse, now that it was freed from its enemy, stopped short; and coming slowly up to

the Woodman it said, in a squeaky little voice: "Oh, thank you! Thank you ever so much for saving my life."

"Don't speak of it, I beg of you," replied the Woodman. "I have no heart, so I am careful to help all those who may need a friend, even if it happens to be only a mouse."

"Only a mouse!" cried the little animal, indignantly. "Why, I am a Queen--the Queen of all the Field Mice!"

"Oh, indeed," said the Woodman, making a bow.

"Therefore you have done a great deed, as well as a brave one, in saving my life," added the Queen.

At that moment several mice were seen running up as fast as their little legs could carry them, and when they saw their Queen they exclaimed: "Oh, your Majesty, we thought you would be killed! How did you manage to escape the great Wildcat?" They all bowed so low to the little Queen that they almost stood upon their heads.

"This funny tin man," she answered, "killed the Wildcat and saved my life. So hereafter you must all serve him and obey his slightest wish."

"We will!" cried all the mice, in a shrill chorus.

One of the biggest mice spoke. "Is there anything we can do," it asked, "to repay you for saving the life of our Queen?"

"Nothing that I know of," answered the Woodman; but the Scarecrow said, quickly, "Oh, yes; you can save our friend, the Cowardly Lion, who is asleep in the poppy bed."

"A Lion!" cried the little Queen. "He would eat us all up."

"Oh, no," declared the Scarecrow; "this Lion is a coward."

"Really?" asked the Mouse.

"He says so himself," answered the Scarecrow, "and he would never hurt anyone who is our friend. If you will help us to save him I promise that he shall treat you all with kindness."

"Very well," said the Queen, "we trust you. But what shall we do?"

"Are there many of these mice which call you Queen and are willing to obey you?"

"Oh, yes; there are thousands," she replied.

"Then send for them all to come here as soon as possible, and let each one bring a long piece of string."

The Queen turned to the mice that attended her and told them to go at once and get all her people. As soon as they heard her orders they ran away in every direction as fast as possible.

"Now," said the Scarecrow to the Tin Woodman, "you must go to those trees by the riverside and make a truck that will carry the Lion."

So the Woodman went at once to the trees and began to work; and he soon made a truck out of the limbs of trees, from which he chopped away all the leaves and branches. He fastened it together with wooden pegs and made the four wheels out of short pieces of a big tree trunk. So fast and so

well did he work that by the time the mice began to arrive the truck was all ready for them.

They came from all directions, and there were thousands of them: big mice and little mice and middle-sized mice; and each one brought a piece of string in his mouth. It was about this time that Dorothy woke from her long sleep and opened her eyes. She was greatly astonished to find herself with thousands of mice standing around and looking at her timidly. But the Scarecrow told her about everything.

The Scarecrow and the Woodman now began to fasten the mice to the truck, using the strings they had brought. One end of a string was tied around the neck of each mouse and the other end to the truck. Of course the truck was a thousand times bigger than any of the mice who were to draw it; but when all the mice had been harnessed, they were able to pull it quite easily. Even the Scarecrow and the Tin Woodman could sit on it, and were drawn swiftly by their queer little horses to the place where the Lion lay asleep.

After a great deal of hard work, for the Lion was heavy, they managed to get him up on the truck. Then the Queen hurriedly gave her people the order to start, for she feared if the mice stayed among the poppies too long they also would fall asleep.

At first the little creatures, many though they were, could hardly stir the heavily loaded truck; but the Woodman and the Scarecrow both pushed from behind, and they got along better. Soon they rolled the Lion out of the poppy bed to the green fields, where he could breathe the sweet, fresh air again.

Dorothy hanked the little mice warmly for saving her companion from death. Then the mice were unharnessed from the truck and scampered away through the grass to their homes. The Queen of the Mice was the last to leave.

"If ever you need us again," she said, "come out into the field and call, and we shall hear you and come to your assistance. Good-bye!"

"Good-bye!" they all answered, and away the Queen ran.

After this they sat down beside the Lion until he should awaken; and the Scarecrow brought Dorothy some fruit from a tree near by, which she ate for her dinner.

10

The Guardian of the Gate

Cowardly Lion opened his eyes. "I ran as fast as I could," he said, "but the flowers were too strong for me. How did you get me out?"

Then they told him of the field mice, and how they had generously saved him from death; and the Cowardly Lion laughed, and said: "I have always thought myself very big and terrible; yet such little things as flowers came near to killing me, and such small animals as mice have saved my life. How strange it all is! But, comrades, what shall we do now?"

"We must journey on until we find the road of yellow brick again," said Dorothy, "and then we can keep on to the Emerald City."

So, the Lion being fully refreshed, and feeling quite himself again, they all started upon the journey, greatly enjoying the walk through the soft, fresh grass; and it was not long before they reached the road of yellow brick and turned again toward the Emerald City.

The road was smooth and well paved, now, and the country about was beautiful, so that the travelers rejoiced in leaving the forest far behind, and with it the many dangers they had met in its gloomy shades. Once more they could see fences built beside the road; but these were painted green. They passed by several of houses that also was painted green during the afternoon, and sometimes people came to the doors and looked at them as if they would like to ask questions; but no one came near them nor spoke to them because of the great Lion, of which they were very much afraid.

"This must be the Land of Oz," said Dorothy, "and we are getting near the Emerald City."

"Yes," answered the Scarecrow. "Everything is green here, while in the country of the Munchkins blue was the favorite color. But the people do not seem to be as friendly as the Munchkins, and I'm afraid we shall be unable to find a place to pass the night."

They came to a good-sized farmhouse, Dorothy walked boldly up to the door and knocked. A woman opened it just far enough to look out, and said, "What do you want, child, and why is that great Lion with you?"

"We wish to pass the night with you," answered Dorothy; "and the Lion is my friend and comrade, and would not hurt you for the world."

"Is he tame?" asked the woman, opening the door wider.

"Oh, yes," said the girl, "and he is a great coward, too. He will be more afraid of you than you are of him."

"Well," said the woman, after thinking it over, "if that is the case you may come in, and I will give you some supper and a place to sleep."

So they all entered the house, where there were, besides the woman, two children and a man. The man asked: "Where are you all going?"

"To the Emerald City," said Dorothy, "to see the Great Oz."

"Oh!" exclaimed the man. "Are you sure that Oz will see you?"

"Why not?" she replied.

"Why, it is said that he never lets anyone come into his presence. I have been to the Emerald City many times, and it is a beautiful and wonderful place; but I have never been permitted to see the Great Oz, nor do I know of any person who has seen him."

"Does he never go out?" asked the Scarecrow.

"Never. He sits day after day in the great Throne Room of his Palace, and even those who wait upon him do not see him face to face."

"What is he like?" asked the girl.

"That is hard to tell," said the man thoughtfully. "You see, Oz is a Great Wizard, and can take on any form he wishes. So that some say he looks like a bird; and some say he looks like an elephant; and some say he looks like a cat. To others he appears as a beautiful fairy, or a brownie, or in any other form. But who the real Oz is, when he is in his own form, no living person can tell."

"That is very strange," said Dorothy, "but we must try, in some way, to see him, or we shall have made our journey for nothing."

"Why do you wish to see the terrible Oz?" asked the man.

"I want him to give me some brains," said the Scarecrow eagerly.

"Oh, Oz could do that easily enough," declared the man. "He has more brains than he needs."

"And I want him to give me a heart," said the Tin Woodman.

"That will not trouble him," continued the man, "for Oz has a large collection of hearts, of all sizes and shapes."

"And I want him to give me courage," said the Cowardly Lion.

"Oz keeps a great pot of courage in his Throne Room," said the man, "which he has covered with a golden plate, to keep it from running over. He will be glad to give you some."

"And I want him to send me back to Kansas," said Dorothy.

"Where is Kansas?" asked the man, with surprise.

"I don't know," replied Dorothy sorrowfully, "but it is my home, and I'm sure it's somewhere."

"Very likely. Well, Oz can do anything; so I suppose he will find Kansas for you. But first you must get to see him, and that will be a hard task; for the Great Wizard does not like to see anyone. But what do YOU want?" he continued, speaking to Toto. Toto only wagged his tail; for, strange to say, he could not speak.

*   *   *

The next morning, as soon as the sun was up, they started on their way, and soon saw a beautiful green glow in the sky just before them.

"That must be the Emerald City," said Dorothy.

As they walked on, the green glow became brighter and brighter, and it seemed that at last they were nearing the end of their travels. Yet it was afternoon before they came to the great wall that surrounded the City. It was high and thick and of a bright green color.

In front of them, and at the end of the road of yellow brick, was a big gate, all studded with emeralds that glittered so in the sun that even the painted eyes of the Scarecrow were dazzled by their brilliancy.

There was a bell beside the gate, and Dorothy pushed the button and heard a silvery tinkle sound within. Then the big gate swung slowly open. Before them stood a little man about the same size as the Munchkins. He was clothed all in green, from his head to his feet, and even his skin was of a greenish tint. At his side was a large green box.

When he saw Dorothy and her companions the man asked, "What do you wish in the Emerald City?"

"We came here to see the Great Oz," said Dorothy.

The man was so surprised at this answer that he sat down to think it over.

"It has been many years since anyone asked to see Oz," he said, shaking his head in perplexity. "If you come on an idle or foolish errand to bother the wise reflections of the Great Wizard, he might be angry and destroy you all in an instant."

"But it is not a foolish errand, nor an idle one," replied the Scarecrow; "it is important. And we have been told that Oz is a good Wizard."

"So he is," said the green man, "and he rules the Emerald City wisely and well. But to those who are not honest, or who approach him from curiosity, he is most terrible. Since you demand to see the Great Oz I must take you to his Palace. But first you must put on the spectacles."

"Why?" asked Dorothy.

"Because if you did not wear spectacles the brightness and glory of the Emerald City would blind you. Even those who live in the City must wear spectacles night and day, for Oz so ordered it when the City was first built, and I have the

only key that will unlock them."

He opened the big box, and Dorothy saw that it was filled with spectacles of every size and shape. All of them had green glasses in them. The Guardian of the Gates found a pair that would just fit Dorothy and put them over her eyes. There were two golden bands fastened to them that passed around the back of her head, where they were locked together by a little key. When they were on, Dorothy could not take them off had she wished, but of course she did not wish to be blinded by the glare of the Emerald City.

Then the green man fitted spectacles for the Scarecrow and the Tin Woodman and the Lion, and even on little Toto; and all were locked fast with the key.

Then the Guardian of the Gates put on his own glasses and told them he was ready to show them to the Palace. Taking a big golden key from a peg on the wall, he opened another gate, and they all followed him through the portal into the streets of the Emerald City.

11

The Wonderful City of Oz

Even with eyes protected by the green spectacles, Dorothy and her friends were at first dazzled by the brilliancy of the wonderful City. The streets were lined with beautiful houses all built of green marble and studded everywhere with sparkling emeralds. They walked over a pavement of the same green marble, and where the blocks were joined together were rows of emeralds, and glittering in the brightness of the sun. Even the sky above the City had a green tint, and the rays of the sun were green.

There were men, women, and children--walking about, and these were all dressed in green clothes and had greenish skins. Many shops stood in the street. Green candy and green pop corn were offered for sale, as well as green shoes, green hats, and green clothes of all sorts. At one place a child was buying green lemonade and paid for it with green pennies.

Everyone seemed happy and contented and prosperous.

The Guardian of the Gates led them through the streets until they came to the Palace of Oz, the Great Wizard. There was a soldier before the door, dressed in a green uniform and wearing a long green beard.

"Here are strangers," said the Guardian of the Gates to him, "and they demand to see the Great Oz."

"Step inside," answered the soldier, "and I will carry your message to him."

So they passed through the Palace Gates and were led into a big room. The soldier made them all wipe their feet upon a green mat before entering this room, and when they were seated he said politely: "Please make yourselves comfortable while I go to the door of the Throne Room and tell Oz you are here."

They had to wait a long time before the soldier returned. When, at last, he came back, Dorothy asked: "Have you seen Oz?"

"Oh, no," returned the soldier; "I have never seen him. But I spoke to him as he sat behind his screen and gave him your message. He said he will grant you an audience, if you so desire; but each one of you must enter his presence alone, and he will admit but one each day. Therefore, as you must remain in the Palace for several days, I will have you shown to rooms where you may rest in comfort after your journey."

"Thank you," replied the girl; "that is very kind of Oz."

The soldier now blew upon a green whistle, and at once a

young girl, dressed in a pretty green silk gown, entered the room. She had lovely green hair and green eyes, and she bowed low before Dorothy as she said, "Follow me and I will show you your room."

So Dorothy taking the dog in her arms followed the green girl to the sweetest little room in the world, with a soft comfortable bed that had sheets of green silk and a green velvet counterpane. There was a tiny fountain in the middle of the room, that shot a spray of green perfume into the air, to fall back into a beautifully carved green marble basin.

In a wardrobe were many green dresses, made of silk and satin and velvet; and all of them fitted Dorothy exactly.

"Make yourself perfectly at home," said the green girl, "and if you wish for anything ring the bell. Oz will send for you tomorrow morning."

Others she also led to rooms. Scarecrow found himself alone in his room he stood stupidly in one spot, just within the doorway, to wait till morning. He remained all night staring at a little spider which was weaving its web in a corner of the room. The Tin Woodman not being able to sleep, he passed the night moving his joints up and down to make sure they kept in good working order. The Lion would have preferred a bed of dried leaves in the forest; but he had too much sense to let this worry him, so he sprang upon the bed and rolled himself up like a cat and purred himself asleep in a minute.

The next morning, after breakfast, the green maiden came to dress Dorothy in one of the prettiest gowns, made of green brocaded satin. Dorothy tied a green ribbon around Toto's neck.

First they came to a great hall in which were many ladies and gentlemen of the court, all dressed in rich costumes. These people always came to wait outside the Throne Room every morning, although they were never permitted to see Oz. As Dorothy entered they looked at her curiously, and one of them whispered: "Are you really going to look upon the face of Oz the Terrible?"

"Of course," answered the girl, "if he will see me."

"Oh, he will see you," said the soldier who had taken her message to the Wizard, " Indeed, at first he was angry and said I should send you back where you came from. Then he asked me what you looked like, and when I mentioned your silver shoes he was very much interested. At last I told him about the mark upon your forehead, and he decided he would admit you to his presence."

Just then a bell rang, and the green girl said to Dorothy, "That is the signal. You must go into the Throne Room alone."

She opened a little door and Dorothy walked boldly through and found herself in a big, round room with a high arched roof. And the walls and ceiling and floor were covered with large emeralds set closely together. In the center of the roof was a great light, as bright as the sun, which made the emeralds sparkle in a wonderful manner.

There's a big throne of green marble that stood in the middle of the room. It was shaped like a chair and sparkled with gems. In the center of the chair was an enormous Head, without a body to support it or any arms or legs whatever. There was no hair upon this head, but it had eyes and a nose and mouth, and was much bigger than the head of the biggest giant.

Then the mouth moved, and Dorothy heard a voice say:

"I am Oz, the Great and Terrible. Who are you, and why do you seek me?"

It was not such an awful voice as she had expected; so she took courage and answered: "I am Dorothy, the Small and Meek. I have come to you for help."

The eyes looked at her thoughtfully for a full minute. Then said the voice: "Where did you get the silver shoes?"

"I got them from the Wicked Witch of the East, when my house fell on her and killed her," she replied.

"Where did you get the mark upon your forehead?" continued the voice.

"That is where the Good Witch of the North kissed me when she bade me good-bye and sent me to you," said the girl.

Again the eyes looked at her sharply, and they saw she was telling the truth. Then Oz asked, "What do you wish me

to do?"

"Send me back to Kansas, where my Aunt Em and Uncle Henry are," she answered earnestly. "I don't like your country, although it is so beautiful. And I am sure Aunt Em will be dreadfully worried over my being away so long."

The eyes winked, and then they turned up to the ceiling and down to the floor and they seemed to see every part of the room. And at last Oz asked: "Why should I do this for you?" asked Oz.

"Because you are strong and I am weak; because you are a Great Wizard and I am only a little girl."

"But you were strong enough to kill the Wicked Witch of the East," said Oz.

"That just happened," returned Dorothy, "I could not help it."

"Well," said the Head, "I will give you my answer. You have no right to expect me to send you back to Kansas unless you do something for me in return. In this country everyone must pay for everything he gets. If you wish me to use my magic power to send you home again you must do something for me first. Help me and I will help you."

"What must I do?" asked the girl.

"Kill the Wicked Witch of the West," answered Oz.

"But I cannot!" exclaimed Dorothy, greatly surprised.

"You killed the Witch of the East and you wear the silver shoes, which bear a powerful charm. There is now but one

Wicked Witch left in all this land, and when you can tell me she is dead I will send you back to Kansas--but not before."

The little girl began to weep, she was so much disappointed; and the eyes winked again and looked upon her anxiously, as if the Great Oz felt that she could help him if she would.

"I never killed anything, willingly," she sobbed. "Even if I wanted to, how could I kill the Wicked Witch? If you, who are Great and Terrible, cannot kill her yourself, how do you expect me to do it?"

"I do not know," said the Head; "but that is my answer, and until the Wicked Witch dies you will not see your uncle and aunt again. The Witch is tremendously Wicked--and ought to be killed. Now go, and do not ask to see me again until you have done your task."

Sorrowfully Dorothy left the Throne Room and went back where the Lion and the Scarecrow and the Tin Woodman were waiting to hear what Oz had said to her.

"There is no hope for me," she said sadly, "for Oz will not send me home until I have killed the Wicked Witch of the West; and that I can never do."

Her friends were sorry, but could do nothing to help her; so Dorothy went to her own room and lay down on the bed and cried herself to sleep.

The next morning the soldier with the green whiskers came to the Scarecrow and said: "Come with me, for Oz has

sent for you."

So the Scarecrow followed him and was admitted into the great Throne Room, where he saw, sitting in the emerald throne, a most lovely Lady. Growing from her shoulders were wings, gorgeous in color and so light that they fluttered if the slightest breath of air reached them.

The Scarecrow had bowed elegantly before this beautiful creature, she looked upon him sweetly, and said: "I am Oz, the Great and Terrible. Who are you, and why do you seek me?"

Now the Scarecrow, who had expected to see the great Head Dorothy had told him of, was much astonished; but he answered her bravely. "I am only a Scarecrow, stuffed with straw. I have no brains, and I come to you praying that you will put brains in my head instead of straw, so that I may become as much a man as any other in your dominions."

"Why should I do this for you?" asked the Lady.

"Because you are wise and powerful, and no one else can help me," answered the Scarecrow.

"I never grant favors without some return," said Oz; "but this much I will promise. If you will kill the Wicked Witch of the West, I will bestow upon you a great many brains, and such good brains that you will be the wisest man in all the Land of Oz."

"I thought you asked Dorothy to kill the Witch," said the Scarecrow, in surprise.

"So I did. I don't care who kills her. But until she is dead I will not grant your wish. Now go, and do not seek me again until you have earned the brains you so greatly desire."

The Scarecrow went sorrowfully back to his friends and told them what Oz had said; and Dorothy was surprised to find that the Great Wizard was not a Head, as she had seen him, but a lovely Lady.

"All the same," said the Scarecrow, "she needs a heart as much as the Tin Woodman."

On the next morning, the Tin Woodman followed the soldier and came to the great Throne Room. He saw neither the Head nor the Lady, for Oz had taken the shape of a most terrible great Beast. It had a head like that of a rhinoceros, only there were five eyes in its face. There were five long arms growing out of its body, and it also had five long, slim legs. Thick, woolly hair covered every part of it, and a more dreadful-looking monster could not be imagined. It was fortunate the Tin Woodman had no heart at that moment, for it would have beat loud and fast from terror.

"I am Oz, the Great and Terrible," spoke the Beast, in a voice that was one great roar. "Who are you, and why do you seek me?"

"I am a Woodman, and made of tin. Therefore I have no heart, and cannot love. I pray you to give me a heart that I may be as other men are."

"Why should I do this?" demanded the Beast.

"Because I ask it, and you alone can grant my request," answered the Woodman.

Oz gave a low growl at this, but said, gruffly: "If you indeed desire a heart, you must earn it."

"How?" asked the Woodman.

"Help Dorothy to kill the Wicked Witch of the West," replied the Beast. "When the Witch is dead, I will give you the biggest and kindest and most loving heart in all the Land of Oz."

So the Tin Woodman was forced to return sorrowfully to his friends and tell them of the terrible Beast he had seen. They all wondered greatly at the many forms the Great Wizard could take upon himself, and the Lion said: "If he is a Beast when I go to see him, I shall roar my loudest, and so frighten him that he will grant all I ask. And if he is the lovely Lady, I shall pretend to spring upon her, and so compel her to do my bidding. And if he is the great Head, I will roll this head until he promises to give us what we desire."

The next morning the soldier with the green whiskers led the Lion to the great Throne Room and bade him enter the presence of Oz.

The Lion at once passed through the door, and glancing around saw, to his surprise, that before the throne was a Ball of Fire, so fierce and glowing he could scarcely bear to gaze upon it. His first thought was that Oz had by accident caught on fire and was burning up; but when he tried to go nearer,

the heat was so intense
that it singed his
whiskers, and he crept
back tremblingly to a
spot nearer the door.
Then a low,
quiet voice came
from the Ball of
Fire, and these were
the words it spoke:
"I am Oz, the Great
and Terrible. Who
are you, and why do
you seek me?"

And the Lion answered,
"I am a Cowardly Lion, afraid of everything. I came to you to
beg that you give me courage, so that in reality I may become
the King of Beasts."

"Why should I give you courage?" demanded Oz.

"Because of all Wizards you are the greatest, and alone
have power to grant my request," answered the Lion.

The Ball of Fire burned fiercely for a time, and the voice
said, "Bring me proof that the Wicked Witch is dead, and
that moment I will give you courage. But as long as the Witch
lives, you must remain a coward."

The Lion was angry at this speech, but could say nothing

in reply. The Ball of Fire became so furiously hot that he turned tail and rushed from the room.

"What shall we do now?" asked Dorothy sadly.

"There is only one thing we can do," returned the Lion, "and that is to go to destroy the Wicked Witch."

Dorothy wanted to cry, but she said: "I suppose we must try it; but I do not want to kill anybody, even to see Aunt Em again."

"I will go; but I'm too much of a coward to kill the Witch," said the Lion.

"I will go too," declared the Scarecrow; "but I shall not be of much help to you, I am such a fool."

"I haven't the heart to harm even a Witch," remarked the Tin Woodman; "but if you go I certainly shall go with you."

Therefore it was decided to start upon their journey the next morning, and the Woodman sharpened his axe on a green grindstone and had all his joints properly oiled. The Scarecrow stuffed himself with fresh straw and Dorothy put new paint on his eyes that he might see better. The green girl, who was very kind to them, filled Dorothy's basket with good things to eat, and fastened a little bell around Toto's neck with a green ribbon.

They went to bed quite early and slept soundly until daylight, when they were awakened by the crowing of a green cock that lived in the back yard of the Palace, and the cackling of a hen that had laid a green egg.

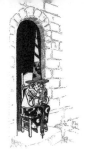

12

The Search for the Wicked Witch

The Guardian of the Gates unlocked their spectacles to put them back in his great box, and then he politely opened the gate for our friends.

"Which road leads to the Wicked Witch of the West?" asked Dorothy.

"There is no road," answered the Guardian of the Gates. "No one ever wishes to go that way."

"How, then, are we to find her?" inquired the girl.

"That will be easy," replied the man, "when she knows you are in the country of the Winkies she will find you, and make you all her slaves."

"Perhaps not," said the Scarecrow, "for we mean to destroy her."

"Oh, that is different," said the Guardian of the Gates. "Keep to the West, where the sun sets, and you cannot fail to find her."

They thanked him and bade him good-bye, and turned toward the West, walking over fields of soft grass dotted here and there with daisies and buttercups. Dorothy still wore the pretty silk dress she had put on in the palace, but now, to her surprise, she found it was no longer green, but pure white. The ribbon around Toto's neck had also lost its green color and was as white as Dorothy's dress.

As they advanced the ground became rougher and hillier, for there were no farms nor houses in this country of the West, and the ground was untilled. In the afternoon the sun shone hot in their faces, so that before night Dorothy and Toto and the Lion were tired, and lay down upon the grass and fell asleep, with the Woodman and the Scarecrow keeping watch.

They were a long distance off, but the Wicked Witch of the West saw them right away, even with only one eye, which is so powerful. So she blew upon a silver whistle that hung around her neck.

At once there came running to her from all directions a pack of great wolves. They had long legs and fierce eyes and sharp teeth.

"Go to those people," said the Witch, "and tear them to pieces."

"Are you not going to make them your slaves?" asked the leader of the wolves.

"No," she answered, "one is of tin, and one of straw; one

is a girl and another a Lion. None of them is fit to work."

So the wolf dashed away at full speed, followed by the others.

It was lucky the Scarecrow and the Woodman were awake and heard the wolves coming.

"This is my fight," said the Woodman, "so get behind me and I will meet them as they come."

He seized his axe, which he had made very sharp, and as the leader of the wolves came on the Tin Woodman swung his arm and chopped the wolf's head from its body, so that it immediately died. As soon as he could raise his axe another wolf came up, and he also fell under the sharp edge of the Tin Woodman's weapon. There were forty wolves, and forty times a wolf was killed, so that at last they all lay dead in a heap before the Woodman.

Then he put down his axe and sat beside the Scarecrow, who said, "It was a good fight, friend."

Dorothy awoke the next morning. The little girl was quite frightened when she saw the great pile of shaggy wolves, but the Tin Woodman told her all. She thanked him for saving them and sat down to breakfast, after which they started again upon their journey.

Now this same morning the Wicked Witch came to the door of her castle and looked out. She saw all her wolves lying dead. This made her angrier than before, and she blew her silver whistle twice.

Straightway a great flock of wild crows came flying toward her, enough to darken the sky. And the Wicked Witch said to the King Crow, "Fly at once to peck out their eyes and tear them to pieces."

The wild crows flew in one great flock toward Dorothy and her companions. The Scarecrow said, "This is my battle, so lie down beside me and you will not be harmed."

So they all lay upon the ground except the Scarecrow, and he stood up and stretched out his arms. And when the crows saw him they were frightened, and did not dare to come any nearer. But the King Crow said: "It is only a stuffed man. I will peck his eyes out."

The King Crow flew at the Scarecrow, who caught it by the head and twisted its neck until it died. And then another crow flew at him, and the Scarecrow twisted its neck also. There were forty crows, and forty times the Scarecrow twisted a neck, until at last all were lying dead beside him.

When the Wicked Witch looked out again and saw all her crows lying in a heap, she got into a terrible rage, and blew three times upon her silver whistle.

Forthwith there was heard a great buzzing in the air, and a swarm of black bees came flying toward her.

"Go to sting them to death!" commanded the Witch, and the bees turned and flew rapidly to where Dorothy and her friends were walking. But the Woodman had seen them coming, and the Scarecrow had decided what to do.

"Take out my straw and scatter it over the little girl and the dog and the Lion," he said to the Woodman, "and the bees cannot sting them." This the Woodman did, and as Dorothy lay close beside the Lion and held Toto in her arms, the straw covered them entirely.

The bees came and found no one but the Woodman to sting, so they flew at him and broke off all their stings against the tin, without hurting the Woodman at all. And as bees cannot live when their stings are broken that was the end of the black bees, and they lay scattered thick about the Woodman, like little heaps of fine coal.

Then Dorothy and the Lion got up, and the girl helped the Tin Woodman put the straw back into the Scarecrow again, until he was as good as ever. So they started upon their journey once more.

The Wicked Witch was so angry that she gnashed her teeth. And then she called a dozen of her slaves, who were

the Winkies, and gave them sharp spears, telling them to go to the strangers and destroy them.

The Winkies were not a brave people, but they had to do as they were told. So they marched away until they came near to Dorothy. Then the Lion gave a great roar and sprang towards them, and the poor Winkies were so frightened that they ran back as fast as they could.

The Wicked Witch could not understand how all her plans to destroy these strangers had failed.

In her cupboard, there was a Golden Cap, with a circle of diamonds and rubies running round it. This Golden Cap had a charm. Whoever owned it could call three times upon the Winged Monkeys, who would obey any order they were given. But no person could command these strange creatures more than three times. Twice already the Wicked Witch had used the charm of the Cap. Once was when she had made the Winkies her slaves. The second time was when she driven the Great Oz out of the land of the West. Only once more could she use this Golden Cap, Now that her fierce wolves and her wild crows and her stinging bees were gone, and her slaves had been scared away by the Cowardly Lion, she saw there was only one way left to destroy Dorothy and her friends.

So the Wicked Witch took the Golden Cap from her cupboard and placed it upon her head. Then she stood upon her left foot and said slowly: "Ep-pe, pep-pe, kak-ke!"

Next she stood upon her right foot and said: "Hil-lo, hol-lo, hel-lo!"

After this she stood upon both feet and cried in a loud voice: "Ziz-zy, zuz-zy, zik!"

Now the charm began to work. The sky was darkened, and a low rumbling sound was heard in the air. There was a rushing of many wings, a great chattering and laughing, and the sun came out of the dark sky to show the Wicked Witch surrounded by a crowd of monkeys, each with a pair of immense and powerful wings on his shoulders.

One, much bigger than the others, seemed to be their leader. He flew close to the Witch and said, "You have called us for the third and last time. What do you command?"

"Go to destroy them all except the Lion," said the Wicked Witch. "Bring that beast to me, for I have a mind to harness him like a horse and make him work."

"Your commands shall be obeyed," said the leader. Then, with a great deal of chattering and noise, the Winged Monkeys flew away to the place where Dorothy and her friends were walking.

Some of the Monkeys seized the Tin Woodman and carried him through the air until they were over a country thickly covered with sharp rocks. Here they dropped the poor Woodman, who fell a great distance to the rocks, where he lay so battered and dented that he could neither move nor groan.

Others of the Monkeys caught the Scarecrow, and with their long fingers pulled all of the straw out. They threw his

hat and boots and clothes into the top branches of a tall tree.

The remaining Monkeys threw pieces of stout rope around the Lion and wound many coils about his body and head and legs, until he was unable to bite or scratch or struggle in any way. Then they lifted him up and flew away with him to the Witch's castle, where he was placed in a small yard with a high iron fence around it.

But Dorothy they did not harm at all. She stood, with Toto in her arms, watching the sad fate of her comrades. The leader of the Winged Monkeys flew up to her, his long, hairy arms stretched out and his ugly face grinning terribly; but he saw the mark of the Good Witch's kiss upon her forehead and stopped short, motioning the others not to touch her.

"We dare not harm this little girl," he said to them, "for she is protected by the Power of Good, and that is greater than the Power of Evil. All we can do is to carry her to the castle of the Wicked Witch."

So, carefully and gently, they lifted Dorothy in their arms and carried her swiftly through the air until they came to the castle, where they set her down upon the front doorstep. Then the leader said to the Witch: "We have obeyed you as far as we were able. The Tin Woodman and the Scarecrow are destroyed, and the Lion is tied up in your yard. The little girl we dare not harm, nor the dog she carries in her arms. Your power over our band is now ended, and you will never see us again."

Then all the Winged Monkeys, with much laughing and chattering and noise, flew into the air and were soon out of sight.

The Wicked Witch was both surprised and worried when she saw the mark on Dorothy's forehead, for she knew well that neither the Winged Monkeys nor she, herself, dare hurt the girl in any way. And then she saw the Silver Shoes, began to tremble with fear, for she knew what a powerful charm belonged to them. At first the Witch was tempted to run away; but she happened to find out that the little girl did not know of the wonderful power the Silver Shoes gave her. So the Wicked Witch laughed to herself, then she said to Dorothy, harshly and severely: "Come with me; and see that you mind everything I tell you, for if you do not I will make an end of you."

Dorothy followed her to the kitchen, where the Witch bade her clean the pots and kettles and sweep the floor and keep the fire fed with wood.

Dorothy went to work meekly.

The Witch thought she would go into the courtyard and harness the Cowardly Lion like a horse. But as she opened the gate the Lion gave a loud roar and bounded at her so fiercely that the Witch was afraid, she ran out and shut the gate again.

"If I cannot harness you," said the Witch to the Lion, speaking through the bars of the gate, "I can starve you. You shall have nothing to eat until you do as I wish."

Now the Wicked Witch had a great longing to have for her own the Silver Shoes which the girl always wore. If she could only get hold of the Silver Shoes, they would give her more power than all the other things she had lost.

She might just steal them. But the child was so proud of her pretty shoes that she never took them off except at night and when she took her bath. The Witch was too much afraid of the water, so she never came near when Dorothy was bathing. Indeed, the old Witch never touched water, nor ever let water touch her in any way.

But the wicked creature was very cunning, and she finally thought of a trick that would give her what she wanted. She placed a bar of iron in the middle of the kitchen floor, and then by her magic arts made the iron invisible to human eyes. So that when Dorothy walked across the floor she stumbled over the bar, not being able to see it, and fell at full length. She was not much hurt, but in her fall one of the Silver Shoes came off; and before she could reach it, the Witch had snatched it away and put it on her own skinny foot.

The wicked woman was greatly pleased, for as long as she had one of the shoes she owned half the power of their charm, and Dorothy could not use it against her, even had she known how to do so.

The little girl grew angry, and said to the Witch, "Give me back my shoe!"

"I will not," retorted the Witch, "for it is now my shoe."

"You are a wicked creature!" cried Dorothy. "You have no right to take my shoe from me."

"I shall keep it, just the same," said the Witch, laughing at her, "and someday I shall get the other one from you, too."

This made Dorothy so very angry that she picked up the bucket of water that stood near and dashed it over the Witch, wetting her from head to foot.

Instantly the wicked woman gave a loud cry of fear, and then, as Dorothy looked at her in wonder, the Witch began to shrink and fall away.

"See what you have done!" she screamed. "In a minute I shall melt away. Didn't you know water would be the end of me?" asked the Witch, in a wailing, despairing voice.

"Of course not," answered Dorothy. "How should I?"

"Well, in a few minutes I shall be all melted, and you will have the castle to yourself. I have been wicked in my day, but

I never thought a little girl like you would ever be able to melt me and end my wicked deeds. Look out--here I go!"

With these words the Witch fell down in a brown, melted, shapeless mass and began to spread over the clean boards of the kitchen floor. Seeing that she had really melted away to nothing, Dorothy drew another bucket of water and threw it over the mess. She then swept it all out the door. After picking out the silver shoe, which was all that was left of the old woman, she cleaned and dried it with a cloth, and put it on her foot again.

Then, being at last free to do as she chose, she ran out to the courtyard to tell the Lion that the Wicked Witch of the West had come to an end, and that they were no longer prisoners in a strange land.

13

The Rescue

The Cowardly Lion was much pleased to hear that the Wicked Witch had been melted by a bucket of water, and Dorothy at once unlocked the gate of his prison and set him free. They went in together to the castle, where Dorothy's first act was to call all the Winkies together and tell them that they were no longer slaves.

There was great rejoicing among the yellow Winkies, for they had been made to work hard during many years for the Wicked Witch, who had always treated them with great cruelty. They kept this day as a holiday, then and ever after, and spent the time in feasting and dancing.

"If our friends, the Scarecrow and the Tin Woodman, were only with us," said the Lion, "I should be quite happy."

"Don't you suppose we could rescue them?" asked the girl anxiously.

"We can try," answered the Lion.

So they called the yellow Winkies and asked them if they

would help to rescue their friends, and the Winkies said that they would be delighted to do all in their power for Dorothy, who had set them free from bondage. So she chose a number of the Winkies who looked as if they knew the most, and they all started away. They traveled that day and part of the next until they came to the rocky plain where the Tin Woodman lay, all battered and bent. His axe was near him, but the blade was rusted and the handle broken off short.

The Winkies lifted him tenderly in their arms, and carried him back to the Yellow Castle again, Dorothy shedding a few tears by the way at the sad plight of her old friend, and the Lion looking sober and sorry. When they reached the castle Dorothy said to the Winkies: "Are any of your people tinsmiths?"

"Oh, yes. Some of us are very good tinsmiths," they told her.

"Then bring them to me," she said. And when the tinsmiths came, bringing with them all their tools in baskets, she inquired, "Can you straighten out those dents in the Tin Woodman, and bend him back into shape again, and solder him together where he is broken?"

The tinsmiths looked the Woodman over carefully and then answered that they thought they could mend him so he would be as good as ever. So they set to work in one of the big yellow rooms of the castle and worked for three days and four nights, hammering and twisting and bending and soldering and polishing and pounding at the legs and body and head of the Tin Woodman, until at last he was straightened out into his old form, and his joints worked as well as ever. To be sure, there were several patches on him, but the tinsmiths did a good job, and as the Woodman was not a vain man he did not mind the patches at all.

Dorothy called the Winkies to help her again, and they walked all that day and part of the next until they came to the tall tree in the branches of which the Winged Monkeys had tossed the Scarecrow's clothes.

It was a very tall tree, and the trunk was so smooth that no one could climb it; but the Woodman said at once, "I'll chop it down, and then we can get the Scarecrow's clothes."

Now while the tinsmiths had been at work mending the Woodman himself, another of the Winkies, who was a goldsmith, had made an axe-handle of solid gold and fitted it to the Woodman's axe, instead of the old broken handle. Others polished the blade until all the rust was removed and it glistened like burnished silver.

As soon as he had spoken, the Tin Woodman began to chop, and in a short time the tree fell over with a crash, whereupon the Scarecrow's clothes fell out of the branches and rolled off on the ground.

Dorothy picked them up and had the Winkies carry them back to the castle, where they were stuffed with nice, clean straw; and behold! here was the Scarecrow, as good as ever,

thanking them over and over again for saving him.

Now that they were reunited, Dorothy and her friends spent a few happy days at the Yellow Castle, where they found everything they needed to make them comfortable. But one day the girl thought of Aunt Em, and said, "We must go back to Oz, and claim his promise."

"Yes," said the Woodman, "at last I shall get my heart."

"And I shall get my brains," added the Scarecrow joyfully.

"And I shall get my courage," said the Lion thoughtfully.

"And I shall get back to Kansas," cried Dorothy, clapping her hands. "Oh, let us start for the Emerald City tomorrow!"

This they decided to do. The next day they called the Winkies together and bade them good-bye. The Winkies were sorry to have them go, and they had grown so fond of the Tin Woodman that they begged him to stay and rule over them and the Yellow Land of the West. Finding they were determined to go, the Winkies gave Toto and the Lion each a golden collar; and to Dorothy they presented a beautiful bracelet studded with diamonds; and to the Scarecrow they gave a gold-headed walking stick, to keep him from stumbling; and to the Tin Woodman they offered a silver oil-can, inlaid with gold and set with precious jewels.

Dorothy went to the Witch's cupboard to fill her basket with food for the journey, and there she saw the Golden Cap. She tried it on her own head and found that it fitted her exactly. She did not know anything about the charm of the Golden Cap, but she saw that it was pretty, so she made up her mind to wear it and carry her sunbonnet in the basket.

Then, being prepared for the journey, they all started for the Emerald City; and the Winkies gave them three cheers and many good wishes to carry with them.

14

The Winged Monkeys

They knew, of course, they must go straight east, toward the rising sun; and they started off in the right way. But at noon, when the sun was over their heads, they did not know which was east and which was west, and that was the reason they were lost in the great fields. They kept on walking, however, and at night the moon came out and shone brightly. So they lay down among the sweet smelling yellow flowers and slept soundly until morning--all but the Scarecrow and the Tin Woodman.

The next morning the sun was behind a cloud, but they started on, as if they were quite sure which way they were going.

"If we walk far enough," said Dorothy, "I am sure we shall sometime come to some place."

But day by day passed away, and they still saw nothing before them but the scarlet fields. The Scarecrow began to grumble a bit.

"We have surely lost our way," he said, "and unless we find it again in time to reach the Emerald City, I shall never get my brains."

"Nor I my heart," declared the Tin Woodman. "It seems to me I can scarcely wait till I get to Oz, and you must admit this is a very long journey."

"You see," said the Cowardly Lion, with a whimper, "I haven't the courage to keep tramping forever, without getting anywhere at all."

"Suppose we call the field mice," Dorothy suggested. "They could probably tell us the way to the Emerald City."

"To be sure they could," cried the Scarecrow. "Why didn't we think of that before?"

Dorothy blew the little whistle she had always carried about her neck since the Queen of the Mice had given it to her. In a few minutes they heard the pattering of tiny feet, and many of the small gray mice came running up to her. Among them was the Queen herself, who asked, in her squeaky little voice: "What can I do for my friends?"

"We have lost our way," said Dorothy. "Can you tell us where the Emerald City is?"

"Certainly," answered the Queen; "but it is a great way off, for you have had it at your backs all this time." Then she noticed Dorothy's Golden Cap, and said, "Why don't you use the charm of the Cap, and call the Winged Monkeys to you? They will carry you to the City of Oz in less than an hour."

"I didn't know there was a charm," answered Dorothy, in surprise.

"It is written inside the Golden Cap," replied the Queen of the Mice. "But if you are going to call the Winged Monkeys we must run away, for they are full of mischief and think it great fun to plague us."

"Won't they hurt me?" asked the girl anxiously.

"Oh, no. They must obey the wearer of the Cap. Good-bye!" And she scampered out of sight, with all the mice hurrying after her.

Dorothy looked inside the Golden Cap and saw some words written upon the lining. These, she thought, must be the charm, so she read the directions carefully and put the Cap upon her head.

"Ep-pe, pep-pe, kak-ke!" she said, standing on her left foot.

"What did you say?" asked the Scarecrow, who did not know what she was doing.

"Hil-lo, hol-lo, hel-lo!" Dorothy went on, standing this time on her right foot.

"Hello!" replied the Tin Woodman calmly.

"Ziz-zy, zuz-zy, zik!" said Dorothy, who was now standing on both feet. This ended the saying of the charm, and they heard a great chattering and flapping of wings, as the band of Winged Monkeys flew up to them.

The King bowed low before Dorothy, and asked, "What

is your command?"

"We wish to go to the Emerald City," said the child, "and we have lost our way."

"We will carry you," replied the King, and no sooner had he spoken than two of the Monkeys caught Dorothy in their arms and flew away with her. Others took the Scarecrow and the Woodman and the Lion, and one little Monkey seized Toto and flew after them, although the dog tried hard to bite him.

The Scarecrow and the Tin Woodman were rather frightened at first, for they remembered how badly the Winged Monkeys had treated them before; but they saw that no harm was intended, so they rode through the air quite cheerfully, and had a fine time looking at the pretty gardens and woods far below them.

Dorothy found herself riding easily between two of the biggest Monkeys, one of them the King himself. They had made a chair of their hands and were careful not to hurt her.

"Why do you have to obey the charm of the Golden Cap?" she asked.

"That is a long story," answered the King, with a winged laugh; "but as we have a long journey before us, I will pass the time by telling you about it, if you wish."

"I shall be glad to hear it," she replied.

"Once," began the leader, "we were a free people, living happily in the great forest, flying from tree to tree, eating nuts

and fruit, and doing just as we pleased without calling anybody master. Perhaps some of us were rather too full of mischief at times, flying down to pull the tails of the animals that had no wings, chasing birds, and throwing nuts at the people who walked in the forest. But we were careless and happy and full of fun, and enjoyed every minute of the day. This was many years ago, long before Oz came out of the clouds to rule over this land.

"There lived here then, away at the North, a beautiful princess, who was also a powerful sorceress. All her magic was used to help the people, and she was never known to hurt anyone who was good. Her name was Gayelette, and she lived in a handsome palace built from great blocks of ruby. Everyone loved her, but her greatest sorrow was that she could find no one to love in return, since all the men were much too stupid and ugly to mate with one so beautiful and wise. At last, however, she found a boy who was handsome and manly and wise beyond his years. Gayelette made up her mind that when he grew to be a man she would make him her husband, so she took him to her ruby palace and used all her magic powers to make him as strong and good and lovely as any woman could wish. When he grew to manhood, Quelala, as he was called, was said to be the best and wisest man in all the land, while his manly beauty was so great that Gayelette loved him dearly, and hastened to make everything ready for the wedding.

"My grandfather was at that time the King of the Winged Monkeys which lived in the forest near Gayelette's palace, and the old fellow loved a joke better than a good dinner. One day, just before the wedding, my grandfather was flying out with his band when he saw Quelala walking beside the river. He was dressed in a rich costume of pink silk and purple velvet, and my grandfather thought he would see what he could do. At his word the band flew down and seized Quelala, carried him in their arms until they were over the middle of the river, and then dropped him into the water.

"'Swim out, my fine fellow,' cried my grandfather, 'and see if the water has spotted your clothes.' Quelala was much too wise not to swim, and he was not in the least spoiled by all his good fortune. He laughed, when he came to the top of the water, and swam in to shore. But when Gayelette came running out to him she found his silks and velvet all ruined by the river.

"The princess was angry, and she knew, of course, who did it. She had all the Winged Monkeys brought before her, and she said at first that their wings should be tied and they should be treated as they had treated Quelala, and dropped in the river. But my grandfather pleaded hard, for he knew the Monkeys would drown in the river with their wings tied, and Quelala said a kind word for them also; so that Gayelette finally spared them, on condition that the Winged Monkeys should ever after do three times the bidding of the owner of

the Golden Cap. This Cap had been made for a wedding present to Quelala, and it is said to have cost the princess half her kingdom. Of course my grandfather and all the other Monkeys at once agreed to the condition, and that is how it happens that we are three times the slaves of the owner of the Golden Cap, whosoever he may be."

"And what became of them?" asked Dorothy, who had been greatly interested in the story.

"Quelala being the first owner of the Golden Cap," replied the Monkey, "he was the first to lay his wishes upon us. As his bride could not bear the sight of us, he called us all to him in the forest after he had married her and ordered us always to keep where she could never again set eyes on a Winged Monkey, which we were glad to do, for we were all afraid of her.

"This was all we ever had to do until the Golden Cap fell into the hands of the Wicked Witch of the West, who made us enslave the Winkies, and afterward drive Oz himself out of the Land of the West. Now the Golden Cap is yours, and three times you have the right to lay your wishes upon us."

As the Monkey King finished his story Dorothy looked down and saw the green, shining walls of the Emerald City before them. She wondered at the rapid flight of the Monkeys, but was glad the journey was over. The strange creatures set the travelers down carefully before the gate of the City, the King bowed low to Dorothy, and then flew swiftly away, followed by all his band.

"That was a good ride," said the little girl.

"Yes, and a quick way out of our troubles," replied the Lion. "How lucky it was you brought away that wonderful Cap!"

15

The Discovery of Oz,
the Terrible

The four travelers walked up to the great gate of Emerald City and rang the bell. After ringing several times, it was opened by the same Guardian of the Gates they had met before.

"What! Are you back again?" he asked, in surprise. "I thought you had gone to visit the Wicked Witch of the West."

"We did visit her," said the Scarecrow.

"And she let you go back here?" asked the man, in wonder.

"She could not help it, for she is melted," explained the Scarecrow.

"Melted! Well, that is good news, indeed," said the man. "Who melted her?"

"It was Dorothy," said the Lion gravely.

"Good gracious!" exclaimed the man, and he bowed very low indeed before her.

Then he led them into his little room and locked the spectacles from the great box on all their eyes, just as he had done before. Afterward they passed on through the gate into the Emerald City. When the people heard from the Guardian of the Gates that Dorothy had melted the Wicked Witch of the West, they all gathered around the travelers and followed them in a great crowd to the Palace of Oz.

The soldier with the green whiskers was still on guard before the door, but he let them in at once, and they were again met by the beautiful green girl, who showed each of them to their old rooms at once, so they might rest until the Great Oz was ready to receive them.

The soldier had the news carried straight to Oz that Dorothy and the other travelers had come back again, after destroying the Wicked Witch; but Oz made no reply. They thought the Great Wizard would send for them at once, but he did not. They had no word from him the next day, nor the next, nor the next. The waiting was tiresome and wearing, and at last they grew vexed that Oz should treat them in so poor a fashion, after sending them to undergo hardships and slavery. So the Scarecrow at last asked the green girl to take another message to Oz, saying if he did not let them in to see him at once they would call the Winged Monkeys to help them, and find out whether he kept his promises or not. When the Wizard was given this message he was so frightened that he sent word for them to come to the Throne Room at four

minutes after nine o'clock the next morning. He had once met the Winged Monkeys in the Land of the West, and he did not wish to meet them again.

The four travelers passed a sleepless night, each thinking of the gift Oz had promised to bestow on him. Dorothy fell asleep only once, and then she dreamed she was in Kansas, where Aunt Em was telling her how glad she was to have her little girl at home again.

Promptly at nine o'clock the next morning the green-whiskered soldier came to them, and four minutes later they all went into the Throne Room of the Great Oz.

Of course each one of them expected to see the Wizard in the shape he had taken before, and all were greatly surprised when they looked about and saw no one at all in the room. They kept close to the door and closer to one another, for the stillness of the empty room was more dreadful than any of the forms they had seen Oz take.

Presently they heard a solemn Voice, that seemed to come from somewhere near the top of the great dome, and it said: "I am Oz, the Great and Terrible. Why do you seek me?"

They looked again in every part of the room, and then, seeing no one, Dorothy asked, "Where are you?"

"I am everywhere," answered the Voice, "but to the eyes of common mortals I am invisible. I will now seat myself upon my throne, that you may converse with me." Indeed, the Voice seemed just then to come straight from the throne itself; so they walked toward it and stood in a row while Dorothy said: "We have come to claim our promise, Oz."

"What promise?" asked Oz.

"You promised to send me back to Kansas when the Wicked Witch was destroyed," said the girl.

"And you promised to give me brains," said the Scarecrow.

"And you promised to give me a heart," said the Tin Woodman.

"And you promised to give me courage," said the Cowardly Lion.

"Is the Wicked Witch really destroyed?" asked the Voice, and Dorothy thought it trembled a little.

"Yes," she answered, "I melted her with a bucket of water."

"Dear me," said the Voice, "how sudden! Well, come to me tomorrow, for I must have time to think it over."

"You've had plenty of time already," said the Tin Woodman angrily.

"We shan't wait a day longer," said the Scarecrow.

"You must keep your promises to us!" exclaimed Dorothy.

The Lion thought it might be as well to frighten the Wizard, so he gave a large, loud roar, which was so fierce and dreadful that Toto jumped away from him in alarm and tipped over the screen that stood in a corner. As it fell with a crash

they looked that way, and the next moment all of them were filled with wonder. For they saw, standing in just the spot the screen had hidden, a little old man, with a bald head and a wrinkled face, who seemed to be as much surprised as they were. The Tin Woodman, raising his axe, rushed toward the little man and cried out, "Who are you?"

"I am Oz, the Great and Terrible," said the little man, in a trembling voice. "But don't strike me--please don't--and I'll do anything you want me to."

Our friends looked at him in surprise and dismay.

"I thought Oz was a great Head," said Dorothy.

"And I thought Oz was a lovely Lady," said the Scarecrow.

"And I thought Oz was a terrible Beast," said the Tin Woodman.

"And I thought Oz was a Ball of Fire," exclaimed the Lion.

"No, you are all wrong," said the little man meekly. "I have been making believe."

"Making believe!" cried Dorothy. "Are you not a Great Wizard?"

"Hush, my dear," he said. "Don't speak so loud, or you will be overheard--and I should be ruined. I'm supposed to be a Great Wizard."

"And aren't you?" she asked.

"Not a bit of it, my dear; I'm just a common man."

"You're more than that," said the Scarecrow, in a grieved tone; "you're a humbug."

"Exactly so!" declared the little man, rubbing his hands together as if it pleased him. "I am a humbug."

"But this is terrible," said the Tin Woodman. "How shall I ever get my heart?"

"Or I my courage?" asked the Lion.

"Or I my brains?" wailed the Scarecrow, wiping the tears from his eyes with his coat sleeve.

"My dear friends," said Oz, "I pray you not to speak of these little things. Think of me, and the terrible trouble I'm in at being found out."

"Doesn't anyone else know you're a humbug?" asked Dorothy.

"No one knows it but you four--and myself," replied Oz.

"I have fooled everyone so long that I thought I should never be found out. It was a great mistake my ever letting you into the Throne Room. Usually I will not see even my subjects, and so they believe I am something terrible."

"But, I don't understand," said Dorothy, in bewilderment. "How was it that you appeared to me as a great Head?"

"That was one of my tricks," answered Oz. "Step this way, please, and I will tell you all about it."

He led the way to a small chamber in the rear of the Throne Room, and they all followed him. He pointed to one corner, in which lay the great Head, made out of many thicknesses of paper, and with a carefully painted face.

"This I hung from the ceiling by a wire," said Oz. "I stood behind the screen and pulled a thread, to make the eyes move and the mouth open."

"But how about the voice?" she inquired.

"Oh, I am a ventriloquist," said the little man. "I can throw the sound of my voice wherever I wish, so that you thought it was coming out of the Head. Here are the other things I used to deceive you." He showed the Scarecrow the dress and the mask he had worn when he seemed to be the lovely Lady. And the Tin Woodman saw that his terrible Beast was nothing but a lot of skins, sewn together, with slats to keep their sides out. As for the Ball of Fire, the false Wizard had hung that also from the ceiling. It was really a ball of cotton, but when oil was poured upon it the ball burned fiercely.

"Really," said the Scarecrow, "you ought to be ashamed of yourself for being such a humbug."

"I am--I certainly am," answered the little man sorrowfully; "but it was the only thing I could do. Sit down, please, there are plenty of chairs; and I will tell you my story."

So they sat down and listened while he told the following tale.

"I was born in Omaha--"

"Why, that isn't very far from Kansas!" cried Dorothy.

"No, but it's farther from here," he said, shaking his head at her sadly. "When I grew up I became a ventriloquist, and at that I was very well trained by a great master. I can imitate any kind of a bird or beast." Here he mewed so like a kitten that Toto pricked up his ears and looked everywhere to see where she was. "After a time," continued Oz, "I tired of that, and became a balloonist."

"What is that?" asked Dorothy.

"A man who goes up in a balloon on circus day, so as to draw a crowd of people together and get them to pay to see the circus," he explained.

"Oh," she said, "I know."

"Well, one day I went up in a balloon and the ropes got twisted, so that I couldn't come down again. It went way up above the clouds, so far that a current of air struck it and carried it many, many miles away. For a day and a night I

traveled through the air, and on the morning of the second day I awoke and found the balloon floating over a strange and beautiful country.

"It came down gradually, and I was not hurt a bit. But I found myself in the midst of a strange people, who, seeing me come from the clouds, thought I was a great Wizard. Of course I let them think so, because they were afraid of me, and promised to do anything I wished them to.

"Just to amuse myself, and keep the good people busy, I ordered them to build this City, and my Palace; and they did it all willingly and well. Then I thought, as the country was so green and beautiful, I would call it the Emerald City; and to make the name fit better I put green spectacles on all the people, so that everything they saw was green."

"But isn't everything here green?" asked Dorothy.

"No more than in any other city," replied Oz; "but when you wear green spectacles, why of course everything you see looks green to you. The Emerald City was built a great many years ago, for I was a young man when the balloon brought me here, and I am a very old man now. But my people have worn green glasses on their eyes so long that most of them think it really is an Emerald City, and it certainly is a beautiful place, abounding in jewels and precious metals, and every good thing that is needed to make one happy. I have been good to the people, and they like me; but ever since this Palace was built, I have shut myself up and would not see any of them.

"One of my greatest fears was the Witches, for while I had no magical powers at all I soon found out that the Witches were really able to do wonderful things. There were four of them in this country, and they ruled the people who live in the North and South and East and West. Fortunately, the Witches of the North and South were good, and I knew they would do me no harm; but the Witches of the East and West were terribly wicked, and had they not thought I was more powerful than they themselves, they would surely have destroyed me. As it was, I lived in deadly fear of them for many years; so you can imagine how pleased I was when I heard your house had fallen on the Wicked Witch of the East. When you came to me, I was willing to promise anything if you would only do away with the other Witch; but, now that you have melted her, I am ashamed to say that I cannot keep my promises."

"I think you are a very bad man," said Dorothy.

"Oh, no, my dear; I'm really a very good man, but I'm a very bad Wizard, I must admit."

"Can't you give me brains?" asked the Scarecrow.

"You don't need them. You are learning something every day. A baby has brains, but it doesn't know much. Experience is the only thing that brings knowledge, and the longer you are on earth the more experience you are sure to get."

"That may all be true," said the Scarecrow, "but I shall be

very unhappy unless you give me brains."

The false Wizard looked at him carefully.

"Well," he said with a sigh, "I'm not much of a magician, as I said; but if you will come to me tomorrow morning, I will stuff your head with brains. I cannot tell you how to use them, however; you must find that out for yourself."

"Oh, thank you--thank you!" cried the Scarecrow. "I'll find a way to use them, never fear!"

"But how about my courage?" asked the Lion anxiously.

"You have plenty of courage, I am sure," answered Oz. "All you need is confidence in yourself. There is no living thing that is not afraid when it faces danger. The True courage is in facing danger when you are afraid, and that kind of courage you have in plenty."

"Perhaps I have, but I'm scared just the same," said the Lion. "I shall really be very unhappy unless you give me the sort of courage that makes one forget he is afraid."

"Very well, I will give you that sort of courage tomorrow," replied Oz.

"How about my heart?" asked the Tin Woodman.

"Why, as for that," answered Oz, "I think you are wrong to want a heart. It makes most people unhappy. If you only knew it, you are in luck not to have a heart."

"That must be a matter of opinion," said the Tin Woodman. "For my part, I will bear all the unhappiness without a murmur, if you will give me the heart."

"Very well," answered Oz meekly. "Come to me tomorrow and you shall have a heart. I have played Wizard for so many years that I may as well continue the part a little longer."

"And now," said Dorothy, "how am I to get back to Kansas?"

"We shall have to think about that," replied the little man. "Give me two or three days to consider the matter and I'll try to find a way to carry you over the desert. In the meantime you shall all be treated as my guests, and while you live in the Palace my people will wait upon you and obey your slightest wish. There is only one thing I ask in return for my help-- such as it is. You must keep my secret and tell no one I am a humbug."

They agreed to say nothing of what they had learned, and went back to their rooms in high spirits. Even Dorothy had hope that "The Great and Terrible Humbug," as she called him, would find a way to send her back to Kansas, and if he did she was willing to forgive him everything.

16
The Magic Art of the Great Humbug

Next morning the Scarecrow said to his friends: "Congratulate me. I am going to Oz to get my brains at last. When I return I shall be as other men are."

"I have always liked you as you were," said Dorothy simply.

"It is kind of you to like a Scarecrow," he replied. "But surely you will think more of me when you hear the splendid thoughts my new brain is going to turn out." Then he said good-bye to them all in a cheerful voice and went to the Throne Room, where he rapped upon the door.

"Come in," said Oz.

The Scarecrow went in and found the little man sitting down by the window, engaged in deep thought.

"I have come for my brains," remarked the Scarecrow, a little uneasily.

"Oh, yes; sit down in that chair, please," replied Oz. "You

must excuse me for taking your head off, but I shall have to do it in order to put your brains in their proper place."

"That's all right," said the Scarecrow. "You are quite welcome to take my head off, as long as it will be a better one when you put it on again."

So the Wizard unfastened his head and emptied out the straw. Then he entered the back room and took up a measure of bran, which he mixed with a great many pins and needles. Having shaken them together thoroughly, he filled the top of the Scarecrow's head with the mixture and stuffed the rest of the space with straw, to hold it in place.

When he had fastened the Scarecrow's head on his body again he said to him, "Hereafter you will be a great man, for I have given you a lot of bran-new brains."

The Scarecrow was both pleased and proud at the fulfillment of his greatest wish, and having thanked Oz warmly he went back to his friends.

Dorothy looked at him curiously. His head was quite bulged out at the top with brains.

"How do you feel?" she asked.

"I feel wise indeed," he answered earnestly. "When I get used to my brains I shall know everything."

"Why are those needles and pins sticking out of your head?" asked the Tin Woodman.

"That is proof that he is sharp," remarked the Lion.

"Well, I must go to Oz and get my heart," said the

Woodman. So he walked to the Throne Room and knocked at the door.

"Come in," called Oz, and the Woodman entered and said, "I have come for my heart."

"Very well," answered the little man. "But I shall have to cut a hole in your breast, so I can put your heart in the right place. I hope it won't hurt you."

"Oh, no," answered the Woodman. "I shall not feel it at all."

So Oz brought a pair of tinsmith's shears and cut a small, square hole in the left side of the Tin Woodman's breast. Then, going to a chest of drawers, he took out a pretty heart, made entirely of silk and stuffed with sawdust.

"Isn't it a beauty?" he asked.

"It is, indeed!" replied the Woodman, who was greatly pleased. "But is it a kind heart?"

"Oh, very!" answered Oz. He put the heart in the Woodman's breast and then replaced the square of tin, soldering it neatly together where it had been cut.

"There," said he; "now you have a heart that any man might be proud of. I'm sorry I had to put a patch on your breast."

"Never mind the patch," exclaimed the happy Woodman. "I am very grateful to you, and shall never forget your kindness."

"Don't speak of it," replied Oz.

Then the Tin Woodman went back to his friends, who wished him every joy on account of his good fortune.

The Lion now walked to the Throne Room and knocked at the door.

"Come in," said Oz.

"I have come for my courage," announced the Lion, entering the room.

"Very well," answered the little man; "I will get it for you."

He went to a cupboard and reaching up to a high shelf took down a square green bottle, the contents of which he poured into a green-gold dish, beautifully carved. Placing this before the Cowardly Lion, who sniffed at it as if he did not like it, the Wizard said: "Drink."

"What is it?" asked the Lion.

"Well," answered Oz, "if it were inside of you, it would be courage. You know, of course, that courage is always inside one; so that this really cannot be called courage until you have swallowed it. Therefore I advise you to drink it as soon as

possible."

The Lion hesitated no longer, but drank till the dish was empty.

"How do you feel now?" asked Oz.

"Full of courage," replied the Lion, who went joyfully back to his friends to tell them of his good fortune.

Oz, left to himself, smiled to think of his success in giving the Scarecrow and the Tin Woodman and the Lion exactly what they thought they wanted. "How can I help being a humbug," he said, "when all these people make me do things that everybody knows can't be done? It was easy to make the Scarecrow and the Lion and the Woodman happy, because they imagined I could do anything. But it will take more than imagination to carry Dorothy back to Kansas, and I'm sure I don't know how it can be done."

17

How the Balloon Was Launched

For three days Dorothy heard nothing from Oz. These
were sad days for the little girl, although her friends were all
quite happy and contented. The Scarecrow told them there
were wonderful thoughts in his head; but he would not say
what they were because he knew no one could understand
them but himself. When the Tin Woodman walked about he
felt his heart rattling around in his breast; and he told
Dorothy he had discovered it to be a kinder and more tender
heart than the one he had owned when he was made of flesh.
The Lion declared he was afraid of nothing on earth, and
would gladly face an army or a dozen of the fierce Kalidahs.

Thus each of the little party was satisfied except Dorothy,
who longed more than ever to get back to Kansas.

On the fourth day, to her great joy, Oz sent for her, and
when she entered the Throne Room he greeted her pleasantly:

"Sit down, my dear; I think I have found the way to get

you out of this country."

"And back to Kansas?" she asked eagerly.

"Well, I'm not sure about Kansas," said Oz, "for I haven't the faintest notion which way it lies. But the first thing to do is to cross the desert, and then it should be easy to find your way home."

"How can I cross the desert?" she inquired.

"Well, I'll tell you what I think," said the little man. "You see, when I came to this country it was in a balloon. You also came through the air, being carried by a cyclone. So I believe the best way to get across the desert will be through the air. Now, it is quite beyond my powers to make a cyclone; but I've been thinking the matter over, and I believe I can make a balloon."

"How?" asked Dorothy.

"A balloon," said Oz, "is made of silk, which is coated with glue to keep the gas in it. I have plenty of silk in the Palace, so it will be no trouble to make the balloon. But in all this country there is no gas to fill the balloon with, to make it float."

"If it won't float," remarked Dorothy, "it will be of no use to us."

"True," answered Oz. "But there is another way to make it float, which is to fill it with hot air. Hot air isn't as good as gas, for if the air should get cold the balloon would come down in the desert, and we should be lost."

"We!" exclaimed the girl. "Are you going with me?"

"Yes, of course," replied Oz. "I am tired of being such a humbug. If I should go out of this Palace my people would soon discover I am not a Wizard, and then they would be vexed with me for having deceived them. So I have to stay shut up in these rooms all day, and it gets tiresome. I'd much rather go back to Kansas with you and be in a circus again."

"I shall be glad to have your company," said Dorothy.

"Thank you," he answered. "Now, if you will help me sew the silk together, we will begin to work on our balloon."

So Dorothy took a needle and thread, and as fast as Oz cut the strips of silk into proper shape the girl sewed them neatly together. First there was a strip of light green silk, then a strip of dark green and then a strip of emerald green; for Oz had a fancy to make the balloon in different shades of the color about them. It took three days to sew all the strips together, but when it was finished they had a big bag of green silk more than twenty feet long.

Then Oz painted it on the inside with a coat of thin glue, to make it airtight, after which he announced that the balloon was ready.

"But we must have a basket to ride in," he said. So he sent the soldier with the green whiskers for a big clothes basket, which he fastened with many ropes to the bottom of the balloon.

When it was all ready, Oz sent word to his people that he

was going to make a visit to a great brother Wizard who lived in the clouds. The news spread rapidly throughout the city and everyone came to see the wonderful sight.

Oz ordered the balloon carried out in front of the Palace, and the people gazed upon it with much curiosity. The Tin Woodman had chopped a big pile of wood, and now he made a fire of it, and Oz held the bottom of the balloon over the fire so that the hot air that arose from it would be caught in the silken bag. Gradually the balloon swelled out and rose into the air, until finally the basket just touched the ground.

Then Oz got into the basket and said to all the people in a loud voice:

"I am now going away to make a visit. While I am gone the Scarecrow will rule over you. I command you to obey him as you would me."

The balloon was by this time tugging hard at the rope that held it to the ground, for the air within it was hot, and this made it so much lighter in weight than the air without that it pulled hard to rise into the sky.

"Come, Dorothy!" cried the Wizard. "Hurry up, or the balloon will fly away."

"I can't find Toto anywhere," replied Dorothy, who did not wish to leave her little dog behind. Toto had run into the crowd to bark at a kitten, and Dorothy at last found him. She picked him up and ran towards the balloon.

She was within a few steps of it, and Oz was holding out

his hands to help her into the basket, when, crack! went the ropes, and the balloon rose into the air without her.

"Come back!" she screamed. "I want to go, too!"

"I can't, my dear," called Oz. "Good-bye!"

"Good-bye!" shouted everyone, and all eyes were turned upward to where the Wizard was riding in the basket, rising every moment farther and farther into the sky.

And that was the last any of them ever saw of Oz, the Wonderful Wizard, though he may have reached Omaha safely, and be there now, for all we know. But the people remembered him lovingly, and said to one another:

"Oz was always our friend. When he was here he built for us this beautiful Emerald City, and now he is gone he has left the Wise Scarecrow to rule over us."

Still, for many days they grieved over the loss of the Wonderful Wizard, and would not be comforted.

18

Away to the South

Dorothy wept bitterly at the passing of her hope to get home to Kansas again; but when she thought it all over she was glad she had not gone up in a balloon. And she also felt sorry at losing Oz, and so did her companions.

The Scarecrow was now the ruler of the Emerald City, and although he was not a Wizard the people were proud of him. "For," they said, "there is not another city in all the world that is ruled by a stuffed man." And, so far as they knew, they were quite right.

The morning after the balloon had gone up with Oz, the four travelers met in the Throne Room and talked matters over. The Scarecrow sat in the big throne and the others stood respectfully before him.

"We are not so unlucky," said the new ruler, "for this Palace and the Emerald City belong to us, and we can do just as we please. When I remember that a short time ago I was up on a pole in a farmer's cornfield, and that now I am the ruler of this beautiful City, I am quite satisfied with my lot."

"I also," said the Tin Woodman, "am well-pleased with my new heart; and, really, that was the only thing I wished in all the world."

"For my part, I am content in knowing I am as brave as any beast that ever lived, if not braver," said the Lion modestly.

"If Dorothy would only be contented to live in the Emerald City," continued the Scarecrow, "we might all be happy together."

"But I don't want to live here," cried Dorothy. "I want to go to Kansas and live with Aunt Em and Uncle Henry."

"Well, then, what can be done?" inquired the Woodman.

The Scarecrow decided to think, and he thought so hard that the pins and needles began to stick out of his brains. Finally, he said:

"Why not call the Winged Monkeys, and ask them to carry you over the desert?"

"I never thought of that!" said Dorothy joyfully. "It's just the thing. I'll go at once for the Golden Cap."

When she brought it into the Throne Room she spoke the magic words, and soon the band of Winged Monkeys flew in through the open window and stood beside her.

"This is the second time you have called us," said the Monkey King, bowing before the little girl. "What do you wish?"

"I want you to fly with me to Kansas," said Dorothy.

But the Monkey King shook his head.

"That cannot be done," he said. "We belong to this country alone and cannot leave it. There has never been a Winged Monkey in Kansas yet, and I suppose there never will be, for they don't belong there. We shall be glad to serve you in any way in our power, but we cannot cross the desert. Good-bye."

And with another bow, the Monkey King spread his wings and flew away through the window, followed by all his band.

Dorothy was ready to cry with disappointment. "I have wasted the charm of the Golden Cap to no purpose," she said, "for the Winged Monkeys cannot help me."

"It is certainly too bad!" said the tender-hearted Woodman.

The Scarecrow was thinking again, and his head bulged out so horribly that Dorothy feared it would burst.

"Let us call in the soldier with the green whiskers," he said, "and ask his advice."

So, the soldier was summoned and entered the Throne Room timidly, for while Oz was alive he never was allowed to come farther than the door.

"This little girl," said the Scarecrow to the soldier, "wishes to cross the desert. How can she do so?"

"I cannot tell," answered the soldier, "for nobody has

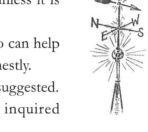

ever crossed the desert, unless it is Oz himself."

"Is there no one who can help me?" asked Dorothy earnestly.

"Glinda might," he suggested.

"Who is Glinda?" inquired the Scarecrow.

"The Witch of the South. She is the most powerful of all the Witches, and rules over the Quadlings. Besides, her castle stands on the edge of the desert, so she may know a way to cross it."

"How can I get to her castle?" asked Dorothy.

"The road is straight to the South," he answered, "but it is said to be full of dangers to travelers. There are wild beasts in the woods, and a race of queer men who do not like strangers to cross their country. For this reason, none of the Quadlings ever come to the Emerald City."

The soldier then left them and the Scarecrow said:

"It seems, in spite of dangers, that the best thing Dorothy can do is to travel to the Land of the South and ask Glinda to help her. For, of course, if Dorothy stays here she will never get back to Kansas."

"You must have been thinking again," remarked the Tin Woodman.

"I have," said the Scarecrow.

"I shall go with Dorothy," declared the Lion, "for I am tired of your city and long for the woods and the country again. I am really a wild beast, you know. Besides, Dorothy will need someone to protect her."

"That is true," agreed the Woodman. "My axe may be of service to her; so I also will go with her to the Land of the South."

"When shall we start?" asked the Scarecrow.

"Are you going?" they asked, in surprise.

"Certainly. If it wasn't for Dorothy I should never have had brains. She lifted me from the pole in the cornfield and brought me to the Emerald City. So, my good luck is all due to her, and I shall never leave her until she starts back to Kansas for good and all."

"Thank you," said Dorothy gratefully. "You are all very kind to me. But I should like to start as soon as possible."

"We shall go tomorrow morning," returned the Scarecrow. "So now let us all get ready, for it will be a long journey."

19

Attacked by the Fighting Trees

The next morning Dorothy kissed the pretty green girl good-bye, and they all shook hands with the soldier with the green whiskers, who had walked with them as far as the gate. When the Guardian of the Gate saw them again he wondered greatly that they could leave the beautiful City to get into new trouble. But he at once unlocked their spectacles, which he put back into the green box, and gave them many good wishes to carry with them.

"You are now our ruler," he said to the Scarecrow; "so you must come back to us as soon as possible."

"I certainly shall if I am able," the Scarecrow replied; "but I must help Dorothy to get home, first."

Guardian then opened the gate of the outer wall, and they walked forth and started upon their journey.

The sun shone brightly as our friends turned their faces toward the Land of the South. They were all in the best of

spirits and laughed and chatted together. Dorothy was once more filled with the hope of getting home, and the Scarecrow and the Tin Woodman were glad to be of use to her. As for the Lion, he sniffed the fresh air with delight and whisked his tail from side to side in pure joy at being in the country again, while Toto ran around them and chased the moths and butterflies, barking merrily all the time.

"City life does not agree with me at all," remarked the Lion, as they walked along at a brisk pace. "I have lost much flesh since I lived there, and now I am anxious for a chance to show the other beasts how courageous I have grown."

They now turned and took a last look at the Emerald City. All they could see was a mass of towers and steeples behind the green walls, and high up above everything the spires and dome of the Palace of Oz.

"Oz was not such a bad Wizard, after all," said the Tin Woodman, as he felt his heart rattling around in his breast.

"He knew how to give me brains, and very good brains, too," said the Scarecrow.

"If Oz had taken a dose of the same courage he gave me," added the Lion, "he would have been a brave man."

Dorothy said nothing. Oz had not kept the promise he made her, but he had done his best, so she forgave him. As he said, he was a good man, even if he was a bad Wizard.

The first day's journey was through the green fields and bright flowers that stretched about the Emerald City on every side. They slept that night on the grass, with nothing but the stars over them; and they rested very well indeed.

In the morning they traveled on until they came to a thick wood. There was no way of going around it, for it seemed to extend to the right and left as far as they could see; and, besides, they did not dare change the direction of their journey for fear of getting lost. So, they looked for the place where it would be easiest to get into the forest.

The Scarecrow, who was in the lead, finally discovered a big tree with such wide-spreading branches that there was room for the party to pass underneath. So, he walked forward to the tree, but just as he came under the first branches they bent down and twined around him, and the next minute he was raised from the ground and flung headlong among his fellow travelers.

This did not hurt the Scarecrow, but it surprised him, and he looked rather dizzy when Dorothy picked him up.

"Here is another space between the trees," called the Lion.

"Let me try it first," said the Scarecrow, "for it doesn't hurt me to get thrown about." He walked up to another tree, as he spoke, but its branches immediately seized him and tossed him back again.

"This is strange," exclaimed Dorothy. "What shall we do?"

"The trees seem to have made up their minds to fight us,

and stop our journey," remarked the Lion.

"I believe I will try it myself," said the Woodman, and shouldering his axe, he marched up to the first tree that had handled the Scarecrow so roughly. When a big branch bent down to seize him the Woodman chopped at it so fiercely that he cut it in two. At once the tree began shaking all its branches as if in pain, and the Tin Woodman passed safely under it.

"Come on!" he shouted to the others. "Be quick!" They all ran forward and passed under the tree without injury, except Toto, who was caught by a small branch and shaken until he howled. But the Woodman promptly chopped off the branch and set the little dog free.

The other trees of the forest did nothing to keep them back, so they made up their minds that only the first row of trees could bend down their branches, and that probably these were the policemen of the forest, and given this wonderful power in order to keep strangers out of it.

The four travelers walked with ease through the trees until they came to the farther edge of the wood. Then, to their surprise, they found before them a high wall which seemed to be made of white china. It was smooth, like the surface of a dish, and higher than their heads.

"What shall we do now?" asked Dorothy.

"I will make a ladder," said the Tin Woodman, "for we certainly must climb over the wall."

20

The Dainty China Country

While the Woodman was making a ladder from wood which he found in the forest Dorothy lay down and slept, for she was tired by the long walk. The Lion also curled himself up to sleep and Toto lay beside him.

The Scarecrow watched the Woodman while he worked, and said to him:

"I cannot think why this wall is here, nor what it is made of."

"Rest your brains and do not worry about the wall," replied the Woodman. "When we have climbed over it, we shall know what is on the other side."

After a time the ladder was finished. It looked clumsy, but the Tin Woodman was sure it was strong and would answer their purpose. The Scarecrow waked Dorothy and the Lion, and Toto, and told them that the ladder was ready. The Scarecrow climbed up the ladder first, but he was so awkward that Dorothy had to follow close behind and keep him from

falling off. When he got his head over the top of the wall the Scarecrow said, "Oh, my!"

"Go on," exclaimed Dorothy.

So, the Scarecrow climbed farther up and sat down on the top of the wall, and Dorothy put her head over and cried, "Oh, my!" just as the Scarecrow had done.

Then Toto came up, and immediately began to bark, but Dorothy made him be still.

The Lion climbed the ladder next, and the Tin Woodman came last; but both of them cried, "Oh, my!" as soon as they looked over the wall. When they were all sitting in a row on the top of the wall, they looked down and saw a strange sight.

Before them was a great stretch of country having a floor as smooth and shining and white as the bottom of a big platter. Scattered around were many houses made entirely of china and painted in the brightest colors. These houses were quite small, the biggest of them reaching only as high as Dorothy's waist. There were also pretty little barns, with china fences around them; and many cows and sheep and horses and pigs and chickens, all made of china, were standing about in groups.

But the strangest of all were the people who lived in this queer country. There were milkmaids and shepherdesses, with brightly colored bodices and golden spots all over their gowns; and princesses with most gorgeous frocks of silver and gold and purple; and shepherds dressed in knee breeches with pink and yellow and blue stripes down them, and golden buckles on their shoes; and princes with jeweled crowns upon their heads, wearing ermine robes and satin doublets; and funny clowns in ruffled gowns, with round red spots upon their cheeks and tall, pointed caps. And, strangest of all, these people were all made of china, even to their clothes, and were so small that the tallest of them was no higher than Dorothy's knee.

No one did so much as look at the travelers at first, except one little purple china dog with an extra-large head, which came to the wall and barked at them in a tiny voice, afterwards running away again.

"How shall we get down?" asked Dorothy.

They found the ladder so heavy they could not pull it up, so the Scarecrow fell off the wall and the others jumped down upon him so that the hard floor would not hurt their feet. Of course they took pains not to light on his head and get the pins in their feet. When all were safely down they picked up the Scarecrow, whose body was quite flattened out, and patted his straw into shape again.

"We must cross this strange place in order to get to the other side," said Dorothy, "for it would be unwise for us to go any other way except due South."

They began walking through the country of the china people, and the first thing they came to was a china milkmaid milking a china cow. As they drew near, the cow suddenly

gave a kick and kicked over the stool, the pail, and even the milkmaid herself, and all fell with a great clatter.

Dorothy was shocked to see that the cow had broken her leg off, and that the pail was lying in several small pieces, while the poor milkmaid had a nick in her left elbow.

"There!" cried the milkmaid angrily. "See what you have done! My cow has broken her leg, and I must take her to the mender's shop and have it glued on again. What do you mean by coming here and frightening my cow?"

Dorothy was quite grieved at this mishap.

"We must be very careful here," said the kind-hearted Woodman, "or we may hurt these pretty little people so they will never get over it."

A little farther on Dorothy met a most beautifully dressed young Princess, who stopped short as she saw the strangers and started to run away.

Dorothy wanted to see more of the Princess, so she ran after her. But the china girl cried out:

"Don't chase me! Don't chase me!"

She had such a frightened little voice that Dorothy stopped and said, "Why not?"

"Because," answered the Princess, also stopping, a safe distance away, "if I run I may fall down and break myself."

"But could you not be mended?" asked the girl.

"Oh, yes; but one is never so pretty after being mended, you know," replied the Princess.

"I suppose not," said Dorothy.

"Now there is Mr. Joker, one of our clowns," continued the china lady, "who is always trying to stand upon his head. He has broken himself so often that he is mended in a hundred places, and doesn't look at all pretty. Here he comes now, so you can see for yourself."

Indeed, a jolly little clown came walking toward them, and Dorothy could see that in spite of his pretty clothes of red and yellow and green he was completely covered with cracks, running every which way and showing plainly that he had been mended in many places.

The Clown put his hands in his pockets, and after puffing out his cheeks and nodding his head at them saucily, he said:

"My lady fair, why do you stare at poor old Mr. Joker? You're quite as stiff and prim as if you'd eaten up a poker!"

"Be quiet, sir!" said the Princess. "Can't you see these are strangers, and should be treated with respect?"

"Well, that's respect, I expect," declared the Clown, and immediately stood upon his head.

"Don't mind Mr. Joker," said the Princess. "He is considerably cracked in his head, and that makes him foolish."

"Oh, I don't mind him a bit," said Dorothy. "But you are so beautiful," she continued, "that I am sure I could love you dearly. Won't you let me carry you back to Kansas, and stand you on Aunt Em's mantel? I could carry you in my basket."

"That would make me very unhappy," answered the china

Princess. "You see, here in our country we live contentedly, and can talk and move around as we please. But whenever any of us are taken away our joints at once stiffen, and we can only stand straight and look pretty. Of course that is all that is expected of us when we are on mantels and cabinets and drawing-room tables, but our lives are much pleasanter here in our own country."

"I would not make you unhappy for all the world!" exclaimed Dorothy. "So I'll just say good-bye."

"Good-bye," replied the Princess.

They walked carefully through the china country. The little animals and all the people scampered out of their way, fearing the strangers would break them, and after an hour or so the travelers reached the other side of the country and came to another china wall.

It was not so high as the first, however, and by standing upon the Lion's back they all managed to scramble to the top. Then the Lion gathered his legs under him and jumped on the wall; but just as he jumped, he upset a china church with his tail and smashed it all to pieces.

"That was too bad," said Dorothy, "but really I think we were lucky in not doing these little people more harm than breaking a cow's leg and a church. They are all so brittle!"

"They are, indeed," said the Scarecrow, "and I am thankful I am made of straw and cannot be easily damaged. There are worse things in the world than being a Scarecrow."

21

The Lion Becomes the King of Beasts

After a long and tiresome walk through the underbrush they entered another forest, where the trees were bigger and older than any they had ever seen.

"This forest is perfectly delightful," declared the Lion, looking around him with joy. "Never have I seen a more beautiful place."

"It seems gloomy," said the Scarecrow.

"Not a bit of it," answered the Lion. "I should like to live here all my life. See how soft the dried leaves are under your feet and how rich and green the moss is that clings to these old trees. Surely no wild beast could wish a pleasanter home."

"Perhaps there are wild beasts in the forest now," said Dorothy.

"I suppose there are," returned the Lion, "but I do not

see any of them about."

They walked through the forest until it became too dark to go any farther. Dorothy and Toto and the Lion lay down to sleep, while the Woodman and the Scarecrow kept watch over them as usual.

When morning came, they started again. Before they had gone far they heard a low rumble, as of the growling of many wild animals. Toto whimpered a little, but none of the others was frightened, and they kept along the well-trodden path until they came to an opening in the wood, in which were gathered hundreds of beasts of every variety. There were tigers and elephants and bears and wolves and foxes and all the others in the natural history, and for a moment Dorothy was afraid. But the Lion explained that the animals were holding a meeting, and he judged by their snarling and growling that they were in great trouble.

As he spoke several of the beasts caught sight of him, and at once the great assemblage hushed as if by magic. The biggest of the tigers came up to the Lion and bowed, saying:

"Welcome, O King of Beasts! You have come in good time to fight our enemy and bring peace to all the animals of the forest once more."

"What is your trouble?" asked the Lion quietly.

"We are all threatened," answered the tiger, "by a fierce enemy which has lately come into this forest. It is a most tremendous monster, like a great spider, with a body as big as an elephant and legs as long as a tree trunk. It has eight of these long legs, and as the monster crawls through the forest he seizes an animal with a leg and drags it to his mouth, where he eats it as a spider does a fly. Not one of us is safe while this fierce creature is alive, and we had called a meeting to decide how to take care of ourselves when you came among us."

The Lion thought for a moment.

"Are there any other lions in this forest?" he asked.

"No; there were some, but the monster has eaten them all. And, besides, they were none of them nearly so large and brave as you."

"If I put an end to your enemy, will you bow down to me and obey me as King of the Forest?" inquired the Lion.

"We will do that gladly," returned the tiger; and all the other beasts roared with a mighty roar: "We will!"

"Where is this great spider of yours now?" asked the Lion.

"Yonder, among the oak trees," said the tiger, pointing with his forefoot.

"Take good care of these friends of mine," said the Lion, "and I will go

at once to fight the monster."

He bade his comrades good-bye and marched proudly away to do battle with the enemy.

The great spider was lying asleep when the Lion found him, and it looked so ugly that its foe turned up his nose in disgust. Its legs were quite as long as the tiger had said, and its body covered with coarse black hair. It had a great mouth, with a row of sharp teeth a foot long; but its head was joined to the pudgy body by a neck as slender as a wasp's waist. This gave the Lion a hint of the best way to attack the creature, and as he knew it was easier to fight it asleep than awake, he gave a great spring and landed directly upon the monster's back. Then, with one blow of his heavy paw, all armed with sharp claws, he knocked the spider's head from its body. Jumping down, he watched it until the long legs stopped wiggling, when he knew it was quite dead.

The Lion went back to the opening where the beasts of the forest were waiting for him and said proudly:

"You need fear your enemy no longer."

Then the beasts bowed down to the Lion as their King, and he promised to come back and rule over them as soon as Dorothy was safely on her way to Kansas.

22

The Country
of the Quadlings

The four travelers passed through the rest of the forest in safety, and when they came out from its gloom saw before them a steep hill, covered from top to bottom with great pieces of rock.

"That will be a hard climb," said the Scarecrow, "but we must get over the hill, nevertheless."

So, he led the way and the others followed. They had nearly reached the first rock when they heard a rough voice cry out, "Keep back!"

"Who are you?" asked the Scarecrow.

Then a head showed itself over the rock and the same voice said, "This hill belongs to us, and we don't allow anyone to cross it."

"But we must cross it," said the Scarecrow. "We're going to the country of the Quadlings."

"But you shall not!" replied the voice, and there stepped from behind the rock the strangest man the travelers had ever seen.

He was quite short and stout and had a big head, which was flat at the top and supported by a thick neck full of wrinkles. But he had no arms at all, and, seeing this, the Scarecrow did not fear that so helpless a creature could prevent them from climbing the hill. So, he said, "I'm sorry not to do as you wish, but we must pass over your hill whether you like it or not," and he walked boldly forward.

As quick as lightning the man's head shot forward and his neck stretched out until the top of the head, where it was flat, struck the Scarecrow in the middle and sent him tumbling, over and over, down the hill. Almost as quickly as it came the head went back to the body, and the man laughed harshly as he said, "It isn't as easy as you think!"

A chorus of boisterous laughter came from the other rocks, and Dorothy saw hundreds of the armless Hammer-Heads upon the hillside, one behind every rock.

The Lion became quite angry at the laughter caused by the Scarecrow's mishap, and giving a loud roar that echoed like thunder, he dashed up the hill.

Again a head shot swiftly out, and the great Lion went rolling down the hill as if he had been struck by a cannon ball.

Dorothy ran down and helped the Scarecrow to his feet,

and the Lion came up to her, feeling rather bruised and sore, and said, "It is useless to fight people with shooting heads; no one can withstand them."

"What can we do, then?" she asked.

"Call the Winged Monkeys," suggested the Tin Woodman. "You have still the right to command them once more."

"Very well," she answered, and putting on the Golden Cap she uttered the magic words. The Monkeys were as prompt as ever, and in a few moments the entire band stood before her.

"What are your commands?" inquired the King of the Monkeys, bowing low.

"Carry us over the hill to the country of the Quadlings," answered the girl.

"It shall be done," said the King, and at once the Winged Monkeys caught the four travelers and Toto up in their arms and flew away with them. As they passed over the hill the Hammer-Heads yelled with vexation, and shot their heads high in the air, but they could not reach the Winged Monkeys, which carried Dorothy and her comrades safely over the hill and set them down in the beautiful country of the Quadlings.

"This is the last time you can summon us," said the leader to Dorothy; "so good-bye and good luck to you."

"Good-bye, and thank you very much," returned the girl; and the Monkeys rose into the air and were out of sight in a

twinkling.

The country of the Quadlings seemed rich and happy. There was field upon field of ripening grain, with well-paved roads running between, and pretty rippling brooks with strong bridges across them. The fences and houses and bridges were all painted bright red, just as they had been painted yellow in the country of the Winkies and blue in the country of the Munchkins. The Quadlings themselves, who were short and fat and looked chubby and good-natured, were dressed all in red, which showed bright against the green grass and the yellowing grain.

The Monkeys had set them down near a farmhouse, and the four travelers walked up to it and knocked at the door. It was opened by the farmer's wife, and when Dorothy asked for something to eat the woman gave them all a good dinner, with three kinds of cake and four kinds of cookies, and a bowl of milk for Toto.

"How far is it to the Castle of Glinda?" asked the child.

"It is not a great way," answered the farmer's wife. "Take the road to the South and you will soon reach it."

Thanking the good woman, they started afresh and walked by the fields and across the pretty bridges until they saw before them a very beautiful Castle. Before the gates were three young girls, dressed in handsome red uniforms trimmed with gold braid; and as Dorothy approached, one of them said to her:

"Why have you come to the South Country?"

"To see the Good Witch who rules here," she answered. "Will you take me to her?"

"Let me have your name, and I will ask Glinda if she will receive you." They told who they were, and the girl soldier went into the Castle. After a few moments she came back to say that Dorothy and the others were to be admitted at once.

23
Glinda The Good Witch
Grants Dorothy's Wish

Before they went to see Glinda, however, they were taken to a room of the Castle, where Dorothy washed her face and combed her hair, and the Lion shook the dust out of his mane, and the Scarecrow patted himself into his best shape, and the Woodman polished his tin and oiled his joints.

When they were all quite presentable they followed the soldier girl into a big room where the Witch Glinda sat upon a throne of rubies.

She was both beautiful and young to their eyes. Her hair was a rich red in color and fell in flowing ringlets over her shoulders. Her dress was pure white but her eyes were blue, and they looked kindly upon the little girl.

"What can I do for you, my child?" she asked.

Dorothy told the Witch all her story: how the cyclone

had brought her to the Land of Oz, how she had found her companions, and of the wonderful adventures they had met with.

"My greatest wish now," she added, "is to get back to Kansas, for Aunt Em will surely think something dreadful has happened to me, and that will make her put on mourning; and unless the crops are better this year than they were last, I am sure Uncle Henry cannot afford it."

Glinda leaned forward and kissed the sweet, upturned face of the loving little girl.

"Bless your dear heart," she said, "I am sure I can tell you of a way to get back to Kansas." Then she added, "But, if I do, you must give me the Golden Cap."

"Willingly!" exclaimed Dorothy; "indeed, it is of no use to me now, and when you have it you can command the Winged Monkeys three times."

"And I think I shall need their service just those three times," answered Glinda, smiling.

Dorothy then gave her the Golden Cap, and the Witch said to the Scarecrow, "What will you do when Dorothy has left us?"

"I will return to the Emerald City," he replied, "for Oz has made me its ruler and the people like me. The only thing that worries me is how to cross the hill of the Hammer-Heads."

"By means of the Golden Cap I shall command the

Winged Monkeys to carry you to the gates of the Emerald City," said Glinda, "for it would be a shame to deprive the people of so wonderful a ruler."

"Am I really wonderful?" asked the Scarecrow.

"You are unusual," replied Glinda.

Turning to the Tin Woodman, she asked, "What will become of you when Dorothy leaves this country?"

He leaned on his axe and thought a moment. Then he said, "The Winkies were very kind to me, and wanted me to rule over them after the Wicked Witch died. I am fond of the Winkies, and if I could get back again to the Country of the West, I should like nothing better than to rule over them forever."

"My second command to the Winged Monkeys," said Glinda "will be that they carry you safely to the land of the Winkies. Your brain may not be so large to look at as those of the Scarecrow, but you are really brighter than he is--when you are well polished--and I am sure you will rule the Winkies wisely and well."

Then the Witch looked at the big, shaggy Lion and asked, "When Dorothy has returned to her own home, what will become of you?"

"Over the hill of the Hammer-Heads," he answered, "lies a grand old forest, and all the beasts that live there have made me their King. If I could only get back to this forest, I would pass my life very happily there."

"My third command to the Winged Monkeys," said Glinda, "shall be to carry you to your forest. Then, having used up the powers of the Golden Cap, I shall give it to the King of the Monkeys, that he and his band may thereafter be free for evermore."

The Scarecrow and the Tin Woodman and the Lion now thanked the Good Witch earnestly for her kindness; and Dorothy exclaimed:

"You are certainly as good as you are beautiful! But you have not yet told me how to get back to Kansas."

"Your Silver Shoes will carry you over the desert," replied Glinda. "If you had known their power you could have gone back to your Aunt Em the very first day you came to this country."

"But then I should not have had my wonderful brains!" cried the Scarecrow. "I might have passed my whole life in the farmer's cornfield."

"And I should not have had my lovely heart," said the Tin Woodman. "I might have stood and rusted in the forest till the end of the world."

"And I should have lived a coward forever," declared the Lion, "and no beast in all the forest would have had a good word to say to me."

"This is all true," said Dorothy, "and I am glad I was of use to these good friends. But now that each of them has had what he most desired, and each is happy in having a kingdom

to rule besides, I think I should like to go back to Kansas."

"The Silver Shoes," said the Good Witch, "have wonderful powers. And one of the most curious things about them is that they can carry you to any place in the world in three steps, and each step will be made in the wink of an eye. All you have to do is to knock the heels together three times and command the shoes to carry you wherever you wish to go."

"If that is so," said the child joyfully, "I will ask them to carry me back to Kansas at once."

She threw her arms around the Lion's neck and kissed him, patting his big head tenderly. Then she kissed the Tin Woodman, who was weeping in a way most dangerous to his joints. But she hugged the soft, stuffed body of the Scarecrow in her arms instead of kissing his painted face, and found she was crying herself at this sorrowful parting from her loving comrades.

Glinda the Good stepped down from her ruby throne to give the little girl a good-bye kiss, and Dorothy thanked her for all the kindness she had shown to her friends and herself.

Dorothy now took Toto up solemnly in her arms, and having said one last good-bye she clapped the heels of her shoes together three times, saying:

"Take me home to Aunt Em!"

Instantly she was whirling through the air, so swiftly that all she could see or feel was the wind whistling past her ears.

The Silver Shoes took but three steps, and then she stopped so suddenly that she rolled over upon the grass several times before she knew where she was.

At length, however, she sat up and looked about her.

"Good gracious!" she cried.

For she was sitting on the broad Kansas prairie, and just before her was the new farmhouse Uncle Henry built after the cyclone had carried away the old one. Uncle Henry was milking the cows in the barnyard, and Toto had jumped out of her arms and was running toward the barn, barking furiously.

Dorothy stood up and found she was in her stocking-feet. For the Silver Shoes had fallen off in her flight through the air and were lost forever in the desert.

24

Home Again

Aunt Em had just come out of the house to water the cabbages when she looked up and saw Dorothy running toward her.

"My darling child!" she cried, folding the little girl in her arms and covering her face with kisses. "Where in the world did you come from?"

"From the Land of Oz," said Dorothy gravely. "And here is Toto, too. And oh, Aunt Em! I'm so glad to be at home again!"

國家圖書館出版品預行編目資料

綠野仙蹤 / 李曼·法蘭克·包姆（L. Frank Baum）作；
威廉·丹斯洛（W. W. Denslow）繪；李毓昭譯. -- 臺
中市：晨星，2019.07
　　面；　公分. --（愛藏本；97）
中英雙語典藏版
譯自：The Wonderful Wizard of Oz
ISBN 978-986-443-893-8（精裝）

874.59   108009172

愛藏本：97

綠野仙蹤（中英雙語典藏版）
The Wonderful Wizard of Oz

作者｜李曼·法蘭克·包姆（L. Frank Baum）
繪者｜威廉·丹斯洛（W. W. Denslow）
譯者｜李毓昭

填寫線上回函，立刻享有
晨星網路書店50元購書金

責任編輯｜呂曉婕
封面設計｜鐘文君
美術設計｜黃偵瑜
文字校潤｜謝宜真、呂曉婕

創辦人｜陳銘民
發行所｜晨星出版有限公司
　　　　台中市 407 工業 30 路 1 號
　　　　TEL：04-23595820　FAX：04-23550581
　　　　http://star.morningstar.com.tw
　　　　行政院新聞局局版台業字第 2500 號
法律顧問｜陳思成律師
出版日期｜2019 年 7 月 1 日
初版二刷｜2024 年 1 月 15 日

讀者服務專線｜TEL：（02）23672044／（04）23595819#212
　　　　　　　FAX：（02）23635741／（04）23595493
　　　　　　　E-mail：service@morningstar.com.tw
晨星網路書店｜www.morningstar.com.tw
郵政劃撥｜15060393　知己圖書股份有限公司
印刷｜上好印刷股份有限公司

定價｜新台幣 260 元
ISBN 978-986-443-893-8